Sandy Wishes

Judith Keim

BOOKS BY JUDITH KEIM

THE HARTWELL WOMEN SERIES:

The Talking Tree – 1
Sweet Talk – 2
Straight Talk – 3
Baby Talk – 4
The Hartwell Women – Boxed Set

THE BEACH HOUSE HOTEL SERIES:

Breakfast at The Beach House Hotel – 1
Lunch at The Beach House Hotel – 2
Dinner at The Beach House Hotel – 3
Christmas at The Beach House Hotel – 4
Margaritas at The Beach House Hotel – 5
Dessert at The Beach House Hotel – 6
Coffee at The Beach House Hotel – 7 (2023)
High Tea at The Beach House hotel – 8 (2024)

THE FAT FRIDAYS GROUP:

Fat Fridays – 1
Sassy Saturdays – 2
Secret Sundays – 3

THE SALTY KEY INN SERIES:

Finding Me – 1
Finding My Way – 2
Finding Love – 3
Finding Family – 4
The Salty Key Inn Series . Boxed Set

THE CHANDLER HILL INN SERIES:

Going Home – 1
Coming Home – 2
Home at Last – 3
The Chandler Hill Inn Series – Boxed Set

SEASHELL COTTAGE BOOKS:

A Christmas Star
Change of Heart
A Summer of Surprises
A Road Trip to Remember
The Beach Babes

THE DESERT SAGE INN SERIES:

The Desert Flowers – Rose – 1
The Desert Flowers – Lily – 2
The Desert Flowers – Willow – 3
The Desert Flowers – Mistletoe and Holly – 4

SOUL SISTERS AT CEDAR MOUNTAIN LODGE:

Christmas Sisters – Anthology
Christmas Kisses
Christmas Castles
Christmas Stories – Soul Sisters Anthology
Christmas Joy

THE SANDERLING COVE INN SERIES:

Waves of Hope – 1
Sandy Wishes – 2 (2023)
Salty Kisses – 3 (2023)

THE LILAC LAKE INN SERIES

Love by Design – (2023)
Love Between the Lines – (2023)
Love Under the Stars – (2024)

OTHER BOOKS:

The ABC's of Living With a Dachshund
Once Upon a Friendship – Anthology
Winning BIG – a little love story for all ages

Holiday Hopes
The Winning Tickets (2023)

For more information: **www.judithkeim.com**

PRAISE FOR JUDITH KEIM'S NOVELS

THE BEACH HOUSE HOTEL SERIES

"Love the characters in this series. This series was my first introduction to Judith Keim. She is now one of my favorites. Looking forward to reading more of her books."

BREAKFAST AT THE BEACH HOUSE HOTEL is an easy, delightful read that offers romance, family relationships, and strong women learning to be stronger. Real life situations filter through the pages. Enjoy!"

LUNCH AT THE BEACH HOUSE HOTEL – "This series is such a joy to read. You feel you are actually living with them. Can't wait to read the latest one."

DINNER AT THE BEACH HOUSE HOTEL – "A Terrific Read! As usual, Judith Keim did it again. Enjoyed immensely. Continue writing such pleasantly reading books for all of us readers."

CHRISTMAS AT THE BEACH HOUSE HOTEL – "Not Just Another Christmas Novel. This is book number four in the series and my introduction to Judith Keim's writing. I wasn't disappointed. The characters are dimensional and engaging. The plot is well crafted and advances at a pleasing pace. The Florida location is interesting and warming. It was a delight to read a romance novel with mature female protagonists. Ann and Rhoda have life experiences that enrich the story. It's a clever book about friends and extended family. Buy copies for your book group pals and enjoy this seasonal read."

MARGARITAS AT THE BEACH HOUSE HOTEL – "What a wonderful series. I absolutely loved this book and can't wait for the next book to come out. There was even suspense in it. Thanks Judith for the great stories."

"Overall, Margaritas at the Beach House Hotel is another wonderful addition to the series. Judith Keim takes the reader on a journey told through the voices of these amazing characters we have all come to love through the years! I truly cannot stress enough how good this book is, and I hope you enjoy it as much as I have!"

THE HARTWELL WOMEN SERIES:

"This was an EXCELLENT series. When I discovered Judith Keim, I read all of her books back to back. I thoroughly enjoyed the women Keim has written about. They are believable and you want to just jump into their lives and be their friends! I can't wait for any upcoming books!"

"I fell into Judith Keim's Hartwell Women series and have read & enjoyed all of her books in every series. Each centers around a strong & interesting woman character and their family interaction. Good reads that leave you wanting more."

THE FAT FRIDAYS GROUP :

"Excellent story line for each character, and an insightful representation of situations which deal with some of the contemporary issues women are faced with today."

"I love this author's books. Her characters and their lives are realistic. The power of women's friendships is a common and beautiful theme that is threaded throughout this story."

THE SALTY KEY INN SERIES

FINDING ME – "I thoroughly enjoyed the first book in this series and cannot wait for the others! The characters are endearing with the same struggles we all encounter. The setting makes me feel like I am a guest at The Salty Key

Inn...relaxed, happy & light-hearted! The men are yummy and the women strong. You can't get better than that! Happy Reading!"

FINDING MY WAY- *"Loved the family dynamics as well as uncertain emotions of dating and falling in love. Appreciated the morals and strength of parenting throughout. Just couldn't put this book down."*

FINDING LOVE – *"I waited for this book because the first two was such good reads. This one didn't disappoint.... Judith Keim always puts substance into her books. This book was no different, I learned about PTSD, accepting oneself, there is always going to be problems but stick it out and make it work. Just the way life is. In some ways a lot like my life. Judith is right, it needs another book and I will definitely be reading it. Hope you choose to read this series, you will get so much out of it."*

FINDING FAMILY – *"Completing this series is like eating the last chip. Love Judith's writing, and her female characters are always smart, strong, vulnerable to life and love experiences."*

"This was a refreshing book. Bringing the heart and soul of the family to us."

THE CHANDLER HILL INN SERIES

GOING HOME – *"I absolutely could not put this book down. Started at night and read late into the middle of the night. As a child of the '60s, the Vietnam war was front and center so this resonated with me. All the characters in the book were so well developed that the reader felt like they were friends of the family."*

"I was completely immersed in this book, with the beautiful descriptive writing, and the authors' way of

bringing her characters to life. I felt like I was right inside her story."

COMING HOME – "Coming Home is a winner. The characters are well-developed, nuanced and likable. Enjoyed the vineyard setting, learning about wine growing and seeing the challenges Cami faces in running and growing a business. I look forward to the next book in this series!"

"Coming Home was such a wonderful story. The author has a gift for getting the reader right to the heart of things."

HOME AT LAST – "In this wonderful conclusion, to a heartfelt and emotional trilogy set in Oregon's stunning wine country, Judith Keim has tied up the Chandler Hill series with the perfect bow."

"Overall, this is truly a wonderful addition to the Chandler Hill Inn series. Judith Keim definitely knows how to perfectly weave together a beautiful and heartfelt story."

"The storyline has some beautiful scenes along with family drama. Judith Keim has created characters with interactions that are believable and some of the subjects the story deals with are poignant."

SEASHELL COTTAGE BOOKS

A CHRISTMAS STAR – *"Love, laughter, sadness, great food, and hope for the future, all in one book. It doesn't get any better than this stunning read."*

"A Christmas Star is a heartwarming Christmas story featuring endearing characters. So many Christmas books are set in snowbound places...it was a nice change to read a Christmas story that takes place on a warm sandy beach!" Susan Peterson

CHANGE OF HEART – *"CHANGE OF HEART is the summer read we've all been waiting for. Judith Keim is a master at creating fascinating characters that are simply irresistible. Her stories leave you with a big smile on your face and a heart bursting with love."*

Kellie Coates Gilbert, author of the popular Sun Valley Series

A SUMMER OF SURPRISES – *"The story is filled with a roller coaster of emotions and self-discovery. Finding love again and rebuilding family relationships."*

"Ms. Keim uses this book as an amazing platform to show that with hard emotional work, belief in yourself and love, the scars of abuse can be conquered. It in no way preaches, it's a lovely story with a happy ending."

"The character development was excellent. I felt I knew these people my whole life. The story development was very well thought out I was drawn [in] from the beginning."

THE DESERT SAGE INN SERIES:

THE DESERT FLOWERS – ROSE – *"The Desert Flowers - Rose, is the first book in the new series by Judith Keim. I always look forward to new books by Judith Keim, and this one is definitely a wonderful way to begin The Desert Sage Inn Series!"*

"In this first of a series, we see each woman come into her own and view new beginnings even as they must take this tearful journey as they slowly lose a dear friend. This is a very well written book with well-developed and likable main characters. It was interesting and enlightening as the first portion of this saga unfolded. I very much enjoyed this book and I do recommend it"

"Judith Keim is one of those authors that you can always depend on to give you a great story with fantastic characters. I'm excited to know that she is writing a new series and after reading book 1 in the series, I can't wait to read the rest of the books."!

THE DESERT FLOWERS – LILY – "The second book in the Desert Flowers series is just as wonderful as the first. Judith Keim is a brilliant storyteller. Her characters are truly lovely and people that you want to be friends with as soon as you start reading. Judith Keim is not afraid to weave real life conflict and loss into her stories. I loved reading Lily's story and can't wait for Willow's!

"The Desert Flowers-Lily is the second book in The Desert Sage Inn Series by author Judith Keim. When I read the first book in the series, The Desert Flowers-Rose, I knew this series would exceed all of my expectations and then some. Judith Keim is an amazing author, and this series is a testament to her writing skills and her ability to completely draw a reader into the world of her characters."

THE DESERT FLOWERS – WILLOW – "The feelings of love, joy, happiness, friendship, family and the pain of loss are deeply felt by Willow Sanchez and her two cohorts Rose and Lily. The Desert Flowers met because of their deep feelings for Alec Thurston, a man who touched their lives in different ways.

Once again, Judith Keim has written the story of a strong, competent, confident and independent woman. Willow, like Rose and Lily can handle tough situations. All the characters are written so that the reader gets to know them but not all the characters will give the reader warm and fuzzy feelings.

The story is well written and from the start you will be pulled in. There is enough backstory that a reader can start here but I assure you, you'll want to learn more. There is an ocean of emotions that will make you smile, cringe, tear up or outright cry. I loved this book as I loved books one and two. I am thrilled that the Desert Flowers story will continue. I highly recommend this book to anyone who enjoys books with strong women."

Sandy Wishes

A Sanderling Cove Inn Book - 2

Judith Keim

Wild Quail Publishing

wildquail.pub@gmail.com
www.judithkeim.com

Published in the United States of America by:
Wild Quail Publishing
PO Box 171332
Boise, ID 83717-1332

ISBN# 978-1-954325-43-2

Dedication

This book is dedicated to those people who discover the joy of art in all its many forms and share it with others.

The Five Families of Sanderling Cove

Gran – **Eleanor "Ellie" Weatherby** – dating John Rizzo – husband deceased – 3 daughters:

Vanessa m. Walter Van Pelt, JoAnn single, Leigh m. Jake Winters

Granddaughter – ***Charlotte "Charlie" Bradford*** (Vanessa's daughter)

Granddaughter – ***Brooke Weatherby*** (Jo's daughter)

Granddaughter – ***Olivia "Livy" Winters*** (Leigh's daughter)

Granny Liz – **Elizabeth "Liz" Ensley** – husband Sam - 2 sons:

Henry, m. Diana, divorced, then m. Shannon, and 1 son never married

Grandson – ***Shane Ensley***– lawyer in Miami

Grandson – ***Austin Ensley***– IT guru who sold business and is looking for next opportunity

Mimi**- Karen Atkins** – husband deceased – 1 son, Arthur Atkins, and 1 daughter:

KK. m. Gordon Hendrix,

Grandson -***Dylan Hendrix*** – artist

Granddaughter -***Grace Hendrix*** m. Belinda – owns restaurant called Gills in Clearwater

Arthur m. Elizabeth Brownley

Grandson – ***Adam Atkins*** m. Summer, divorced has daughter Skye

Grandson – ***Brendan Atkins*** – in construction business with Adam

G-Ma – **Sarah Simon** – husband Joel deceased - 1 son:

Benjamin:

Grandson – ***Eric Simon***- plastic surgeon in Tampa, specializes in cleft palates

Granddaughter – ***Shelby Simon*** m. Douglas Sheehan baby due

Grandma – **Pat Dunlap** – husband Ed – 1 daughter:

Katherine m. William Worthington

Grandson – ***Kyle Worthington*** - talent agent in Hollywood

Granddaughter – ***Melissa Worthington***– engaged to Texas oilman

Granddaughter – ***Morgan Worthington***– spoiled baby of family

PROLOGUE

Eleanor "Ellie" Weatherby, now Ellie Rizzo, sat on the patio of the small inn in Provence, France, thinking about her latest message from her friend and co-conspirator, Liz Ensley. Liz and the other three women who lived in Sanderling Cove on the Gulf Coast of Florida, grandmothers all, had decided to make it a special summer for their beloved grandbabies by bringing them all together. With only three great-grands in the bunch, it was time for action, and who better for their grandchildren to marry than other cove kids?

They were trying to be discreet about their matchmaking, of course, but the grandmothers all had reasons to ask their grandchildren to spend time at the cove. For Ellie, it was truly important. She'd married her long-time business partner and lover after years of living and working together, so that each could provide guidance on health decisions going forward. In her seventies, Ellie had decided it was time to choose between selling the Sanderling Cove Inn or finding someone in the family willing to keep it going.

Her granddaughters—Charlotte, Brooke, and Olivia—were a marvelous trio of smart, capable young women. Her hope was that somehow one or the three of them together would be willing to keep the Inn in the family. After spending the summer managing the Inn while she and John enjoyed a long-awaited auto trip and honeymoon through Europe, the three young women should be able to give her an answer.

As for the other business at hand, Charlie had already found the love of her life in Liz's grandson, Shane. She wished them all the loving luck in the world. Brooke and Livy? More time would tell if they'd be as lucky.

CHAPTER ONE

BROOKE

Brooke Weatherby sat on the beach in the early morning light in a complete funk. She was tired of being the dependable one, the boring one out of everyone at Sanderling Cove. She'd agreed to come to the cove unaware her two cousins, Charlotte "Charlie" Bradford and Olivia "Livy" Winters, would be there. All three had been invited to help Gran and John with The Sanderling Cove Inn over the summer while Gran and John went on a long road trip in Europe. She loved her cousins and was happy to have the summer with them. But being with them sometimes made her own failings all too apparent.

She wiggled her toes in the sand, wishing she was different, that she'd find the freedom she needed to be herself. She was filled with determination. They might seem like only sandy wishes to others, but she was going to make them come true.

Gran had especially wanted Brooke to be able to spend the time away from her mother. Though sweet, her mother, Jo Weatherby, suffered from fibromyalgia and depression and depended on Brooke to be her caretaker at times and her friend at other times. It was an exhausting situation that had cost Brooke a relationship in the past. She didn't want that to happen again.

"Time to kick up your heels and have fun," Gran had told her. "You deserve it." She'd gone on to say that the co-dependent relationship with her mother wasn't healthy for either of them.

Later, leaving their small town in upstate New York and arriving in Florida had felt to Brooke as if she'd been given wings. But it would take more than a stay on the Gulf Coast of Florida to change things permanently. Brooke had to decide just who she wanted to become away from the past. She wanted to add some much-needed freedom to her life.

Brooke studied the waves washing into shore for a quick kiss before pulling away again. The ageless pattern was soothing to her. Sandpipers and sanderlings hurried past on tiny feet, leaving their marks behind in the sand. That was one thing she wanted for herself—to leave her mark behind. Something stronger than that of caring for a sick mother.

She looked up as Livy joined her and sat on the sand beside her. "What are you doing up this early?" Livy asked. "You're not on duty today."

On the short side with curly, strawberry-blond hair and blue eyes full of mischief, Livy was everyone's favorite. The fact that she was a fabulous baker was another reason some of the men in the cove gravitated toward her. That, and the fact that Livy was always up for a fun-filled adventure. But she was a hard worker too. She handled the kitchen duties for breakfast, along with Billy Bob, an ex-con who'd worked alongside John for years.

"I was restless and needed some time by the water to collect my thoughts," said Brooke.

Livy frowned, concern etching her brow. "Is everything all right?"

"I guess." Brooke shrugged. "I'm contemplating the future and trying to decide what I want out of life. A lot of deep thinking for sure." She brightened. "On a different, edgier note, I'm thinking of getting a tattoo. Something to prove I'm not still caught in a rut."

"A tattoo?" A smile spread across Livy's face. "You know what? You, Charlie, and I should each get one. Something always to remember this summer. What design would you choose?"

"I'm not sure. What about you? A cupcake? Or cookies?"

Lily laughed. "I like the idea of a small cupcake. You could choose something like a seashell because you and Skye spend so much time looking for them."

Brooke cheered up. She and Adam Atkins' four-year-old daughter Skye had become shell-seeking buddies. Adam was a wonderful single father who intrigued her, but they were simply friends. If Skye wasn't adorable and hadn't attached herself to her, Brooke might not spend much time with them. But when Skye ran to her for a hug, Brooke would never turn her away.

Livy checked her watch and rose. "I'd better get to the kitchen. It's a slow morning, but I can't let Billy Bob think I'm not serious about my job." With Gran and John gone for the summer, Livy's task was to oversee the kitchen staff for the breakfasts for which the Inn was well known.

Billy Bob was a giant of a man, an ex-con who was frightening until you got to know him. The scowls on his face softened only slightly around other people. Tic Tacs seemed to be the only things that made him happy enough to smile. That, or one of Livy's chocolate chip cookies.

After a while, Brooke decided to go to the Inn herself. She wanted to work on the upgrade to the guest registration program Austin Ensley had set up for them. All information from there flowed to their financial reports. She'd been observing the process for a while, and she wanted to make some changes to the new system. Having worked for years in an accounting office, Brooke's role was to help with the financials for the Inn alongside Jake McDonnell, the Inn's accountant and financial advisor.

She and Jake had hit it off from the beginning. A self-made man who'd been raised by a friend of Gran's after his mother died of an overdose, Jake was a kind, ambitious, handsome man who'd never forgotten his roots. Brooke admired him for more than his looks.

When she entered the Inn, she saw Charlotte was in the dining room chatting with a couple who'd risen early and were getting their own coffee from the sideboard before breakfast was served. Tall and slim, with auburn hair tied back in a low ponytail, Charlotte was a striking young woman. She, like Livy and Brooke, was in her late twenties. Recently, Charlotte had become engaged to Shane Ensley. Their relationship had bloomed early and grown quickly into a deep love. Everyone in the cove thought they were perfect together.

Charlotte greeted her with a wave and walked over to her. "What's this about tattoos? Livy says we're all getting one together, and mine has to be of a mermaid."

"Mermaid? That's perfect for you," said Brooke. "Yes, let's do it. I'll do some research and set something up."

Charlotte grinned. "Okay, but mine is going to be small. Nothing that could show in a wedding dress."

"That's cool. Mine will be small too, but I don't care. It's something different. I'm in such a rut." She emitted a long sigh.

Charlotte's expression grew serious. "Are you all right?"

Brooke nodded. "Just full of wishes, I guess."

"Anything I can help you with?" Charlie asked.

"No, but thanks. It's something I have to decide for myself." Feeling better, Brooke headed to the office with a cup of coffee. There, numbers were easy to work with. They were either right or wrong.

Brooke was still working on numbers sometime later when her cell rang. She checked caller ID. *Jo Weatherby.*

"Hi, Mom," said Brooke. She hadn't talked to her mother in days, and though they'd agreed to limit their conversations this summer, Brooke was uncertain about her mother's response, hoping she wouldn't be sent on a guilt trip.

"Hi, Brooke. It's been so long since we've talked that I had to call. How are things going with the Inn? Are you bored to tears?"

"Bored? Anything but," she quickly replied. "Gran and John have done an amazing job of managing the Inn. Charlie, Livy, and I are all busy trying to do the same plus make some improvements."

"I keep thinking of you in that hot, humid summer climate," said Jo.

Brooke knew what her mother was doing—making it sound as if she was concerned for Brooke when actually it was a lead-in to asking her when she was coming home.

Sure enough, Jo said, "I can't wait for you to come home. The house is empty without you."

"Mom, you know I'm committed for the summer and, perhaps, beyond. Nothing is going to make me change my mind." Brooke took a deep breath. "How are you feeling?"

"I've been better, but nothing for you to worry about," her mother said. "If it gets any worse, I'll call the nursing service and have them send someone to stay with me."

Guilt, like a prickly porcupine, poked Brooke in all her sensitive places. She shook her head. She couldn't go back to past behavior, rush home to help. "I'm sure they have capable people on their staff. We've used that nursing service once before. Remember?"

"Yes. They were good. Not as great as having you here, but acceptable."

"That's how we'll leave it, then. Sorry but I'm in the middle of working on financials here, and I'd better go. Jake is due to arrive soon, and I want my work done before he gets here."

"Okay. Love you, sweetie. Talk to you later." Her mother clicked off the call, and Brooke let out a huge sigh. She and her mother had always been a twosome which made her fight for independence more difficult. Her father had died before Brooke was born, leaving Jo to fend for herself. Rather than move closer to her family, Jo had opted to stay in the house in New York she and her fiancé had purchased together.

Brooke went back to her work, but her emotions were still churning. When Jake arrived, she was happy to see him. She had a few ideas she wanted to share.

After agreeing to the changes Brooke wanted to make to the registration process, Jake left the Inn. Brooke paced the office, her mind going over the conversation she'd had with her mother. She desperately wanted to do something to prove her independence. The tattoos would have to wait. She needed to do something now.

She drove to a hair salon nearby. She was tired of being the same person day after day, the one everyone depended on, the one who couldn't seem to relax and just enjoy life.

She entered the salon, and when the owner offered a few surprising suggestions, Brooke smiled. This was more like it.

Later, purple streaks accented her brown highlighted hair. Brooke studied her image with surprise, staring at the way the purple in her hair made her hazel eyes change hues to something browner. She knew that for some people, doing something like this was no big deal. But for her, it was a daring move. She'd been programmed always to do the right, the ladylike thing.

She left for Gran's house proud of her new bold statement.

In her bedroom, she studied her reflection in the mirror still surprised by what she'd done. She was of medium height, and her features were a cross between Livy's and Charlie's, both cute and classic.

Lily peered into Brooke's room. "Wow, a new 'do. I love it! Wait until Charlie sees it. She'll be as surprised as I am," said Livy. "Are we meeting downstairs like always?"

"Yes." Brooke held up the papers she'd prepared for the meeting. "I've got a few new ideas for the registration of guests. That, and a quick review of where we stand on our budget."

"Great," said Livy. "I want to talk about something too."

Brooke liked that her cousins were as sincere as she about doing an outstanding job for Gran and John. She, probably more than they, enjoyed managing the Inn enough to consider doing it in the future. It was a fascinating business.

She and Livy went downstairs to the kitchen.

When Charlotte entered the room for their meeting, she took one look at Brooke and squealed. "What did you do to your hair? Turn around. Let me get a better look."

Brooke twirled in a circle.

"I love it," said Charlotte. "With my auburn hair, it wouldn't work. But on you, it looks great."

Letting out the breath she didn't realize she'd been holding, Brooke felt more confident. Charlotte was more reserved than Livy, and if she liked Brooke's attempt to be different, it was an important sign.

Livy took fresh lemonade from the refrigerator and poured them each a glass before she took a seat at the kitchen table.

"What new things do we have to discuss?" asked Brooke. As the financial manager for the Inn for the summer, she'd been designated to oversee the renovation budget.

"I've done some mockups of brochures I need to show you and Livy for approval," said Charlotte.

"I'd like to get a new grill for the kitchen," said Livy.

"Okay, let's take a look at the budget," said Brooke. "We've completed almost everything on the list of updates. The PR budget is still pretty open. The funds for the kitchen are mostly spent. Livy, how much would the grill cost? And why do we need it?"

Sitting back, listening to Livy, Brooke liked being in charge. She knew she was a capable accountant, but at her job in New York, her work had never been given the respect it deserved. She'd hoped for a partnership one day, but now the thought was unappealing. Another reason not to go back to her old job, her old life.

Charlotte agreed that Livy could have some of her PR funds for the new grill. And when she showed them the new brochures and pamphlets she wanted to have printed, Brooke and Livy eagerly gave their approval for Charlotte to take them to a printer to be produced.

Satisfied things were running smoothly, Brooke ended the meeting.

Charlotte and Livy each had plans for the evening, so Brooke decided to take a walk on the beach. The salt air, the rhythmic sound of the waves rushing to shore and retreating, and the antics of shorebirds skittering along the sand always lifted her spirits.

As she crossed the lawn and entered the sandy beach a small figure raced toward her crying, "Brooke! Brooke!"

Brooke's lips curved. She held out her arms, and Skye rushed into them. An adorable four-year-old with blond curly hair and blue eyes that missed nothing, Adam's daughter and Brooke shared a special relationship.

Skye's arms loosened around Brooke's neck. She stared at

Brooke, and then a huge smile spread across her face. "You've got purple in your hair. How did you do that? I want purple too." She patted Brooke's head gingerly, her face alight with excitement.

Brooke laughed. "I love your hair just the way it is. Like Livy's."

"But I want ..."

Before a real whining session could occur, Brooke said, "Did you find any new shells today with Mimi?"

Skye wiggled to get down and ran over to a bucket nearby, picked it up, and carried it back to her. "We found a scallop shell this morning."

Impressed, Brooke said, "You're learning the names of the shells. That's good."

"Mimi is showing me. She has a book," said Skye proudly.

Skye's great-grandmother, Mimi, walked over to them. She glanced at Brooke's hair and grinned. "Time for something new, huh?"

Brooke returned her smile. Mimi was a lovely woman, upbeat, social, easy to talk to. "Yes. I thought it was time I did something totally different for me."

"Well, I like it," said Mimi. "How are things going with your mother? Is she getting used to having you gone?"

"It's a work in progress. I talked to her earlier. She has her ups and downs."

"Ellie was especially anxious for you to spend the summer here, hoping it would change the situation for you both. I know you're working hard at the Inn, but have fun too, hear."

Brooke grinned. "That's exactly what I intend to do."

Dylan Hendrix, Adam's cousin, walked toward them. "Hey, what's up?" He stopped when he noticed Brooke's hair. "Purple?"

She grinned. "Yes."

"I like it. A shade of amethyst."

She laughed. Only Dylan, who was a well-known artist, would use that word.

"I'm thinking of going out tonight. Want to join me for dinner?" When Dylan smiled as he was doing now, his blue eyes lit.

"That would be great." She studied him. His brown hair was tied back in a man-bun, which accented the features of his face and matched his well-toned body. Dylan was a few years older than she, and his bold paintings had caught the eye of a number of famous people, sending their popularity and their prices into the stratosphere. Yet he was as humble a man as she'd ever met. She liked that about him.

Maybe like her hair, her future was about to change color, become brighter. She wished it would all come true.

CHAPTER TWO

CHARLOTTE

The next morning, with a day off and after delivering the brochures and pamphlets to a printing service in St. Petersburg, Charlotte headed south on I-275 toward its intersection with I-75 and the drive to Miami. She'd promised Shane to accompany him to visit his mother's house on Star Island to help Sophia, his mother's companion, sort through everything inside. With his mother's unexpected death and all the emotions that occasion had brought to the surface for everyone in the family, Charlotte understood how important it was for her to be there with him.

His mother, Diana Ensley Perez, had been a troubled woman who was cruel at times to her two sons, Shane and Austin. Charlotte had met her just once. That one visit for lunch was enough to make her understand how his mother had affected Shane's life in an unhealthy way.

As she drove, Charlotte thought about Shane. He was everything she'd ever wanted in a man—strong but sensitive, kind, smart, and very loving. She'd felt so alone growing up, and his family's easy acceptance of her was a true blessing.

She smiled at the memory of Gran's elated email to her upon hearing of her engagement to Shane. Her connection to Shane was something Gran and her friend Liz had longed for. Having that kind of support was important to her. Even her mother had been pleased to hear of her engagement, although Shane didn't meet her mother's usual standards of a wealthy, successful, socially elite male in New York. Charlotte knew her stepfather, Walter Van Pelt, would get along well with Shane. They were both smart, interesting men.

When she pulled into the garage at Shane's condo, she sighed with pleasure. This place was beginning to feel like home. Sitting in Coconut Grove nearby the CocoWalk development, it had a perfect location. The condo itself was comfortable and easily accommodated her presence. Shane had rearranged closet space for her, so she now left a selection of clothes and dressier items there, things she didn't really need at Sanderling Cove.

After she got settled inside, she called Shane to let him know she'd arrived.

"I'll be there as soon as I can. Want me to bring something for a late lunch?" he asked.

"That's a great idea," she said. He knew she wasn't a cook.

When he arrived, they both forgot about lunch as Shane set down his briefcase and package and swept Charlotte into his arms.

Charlotte nestled against his solid chest thinking he, not the condo, was her true home. She lifted her face.

His lips came down on hers, sending desire swirling through her. He always had that effect on her.

When they pulled apart, Shane grinned. "Wish we could stay here for a while, but as soon as we have lunch, we have to be on our way. I promised Sophie we'd get there as soon as possible." The regret in his voice told her how much he wanted to linger.

"Not a problem. I understand. Are you okay doing this? At one time, you said you never wanted to go to Star Island and your mother's home again."

"I'm doing this for Sophie. She wants to clear the house out and be on her way. With the money she's inherited from my mother, she's going to move to California to be closer to family. We'll sell the house without the furnishings."

Charlotte understood. Diana's home would sell for multiple millions of dollars, and those new owners would want to decorate with items of their own choosing.

They ate their salads quickly. Shane's brother, Austin, had already been through the property, selecting items he wanted for himself. Like Shane, his memories of living there were not good. Shane had once announced he wanted nothing from the house, but Sophie had reminded him that the house contained many valuable items. As Diana's social secretary and companion, Sophie knew more than anyone about the contents, and Shane finally agreed it would be foolish to let everything go to strangers.

They left the condo. As they drove onto Star Island, Charlotte was reminded how exclusive it was. Large homes lined the waterfront, beautiful places that celebrities often purchased. Diana's home was as beautiful as the others.

Charlotte had been too nervous to notice some of the details on her earlier visit, but now as they drove up to it, she studied the front entrance—the tiled entry, the huge pots holding plants and flowers, and the antique lantern hanging from the high ceiling of the *porte cochere*.

Smiling, Sophia Morales emerged from the house and opened her arms to greet Shane as he climbed out of his car.

Shane stooped to accept Sophia's embrace with ease. Short, and with a comfortably round body, Sophia was as warm as Shane's mother had been cold.

Sophia stepped away from Shane and hurried over to her. "Charlie, I'm glad you decided to come here with Shane. There might be a few things you'd like to choose for yourself now that you and Shane are engaged." She took hold of Charlotte's hand. "I see how happy you make Shane. For that, I thank you. He's a very special person."

"He is, indeed," Charlotte said, touched by her words.

"Sure," said Shane. "Help yourself to whatever you want, Charlie. I'll do the same."

"Only things you want, Shane," Charlotte said firmly. Beautiful things might be nice, but not if they held unhappy memories.

"I agree. Okay, Sophia, lead the way," he said.

Sophia led them inside. "An estate buyer will handle anything you and Austin don't want," she said to Shane. "What she can't resell, she will give to charity. Her services are expensive but well worth the trouble. Especially in a big place like this with so much to sort through."

"I hope Austin took a lot," said Shane.

"There's still plenty left," said Sophia. "Let's walk through the rooms first, then you can concentrate on specific areas like the kitchen and the den," Sophia suggested. "The artwork in many of the rooms is valuable. What you don't want, an art appraiser will look at and sell for you. Diana might not have had excellent taste in art, but Ricardo was quite a collector."

After studying the artwork, Charlotte realized that after she and Shane were married, they'd need a bigger place to live in order to properly display the paintings Shane had selected with her approval. She was pleased he'd found things that would give him pleasure. Austin had chosen a number of paintings too.

After they'd toured the rooms, Sophia said, "I have a jeweler lined up to buy any jewelry you and Austin don't choose to keep. There are some lovely pieces that you, Charlie, might like. I know your visit with Diana wasn't pleasant, but I think you should have some of them."

"How about my helping you select some pieces?" said Shane, placing an arm around her. "I can think of a few things I'd love to see on you."

Overcome by the unexpected thoughtfulness, Charlotte said, "If you think it's appropriate, your help would make it much easier for me to choose."

"I'll open the safe and bring the jewelry to you," said Sophia. "And another thing, with the two of you getting married, I'm asking you to please look through things like silver and other items in the dining room, along with the kitchenware. You can come back another day to do that if you wish. But I think it's important to keep as much in the family as possible. I believe Diana would want that. She was proud of all she owned."

"Oh, yes," said Shane. "I know that very well. When I broke one of her special dishes, she got very angry with me."

"I don't want things that we can't enjoy for fear of breaking them," said Charlotte. Now was not the time to mention that she wanted at least three children. And if they were like Shane and her, most likely they'd break a dish or two just by being active like most kids.

Shane led her to the dining room. "Check out a few things here. Austin told me he specifically left the silverware for us. A sort of engagement gift."

While they were looking at things in a sideboard, Sophia arrived with velvet-lined shallow boxes and placed them on top of the dining room table.

The glittering jewels inside the boxes caught Charlotte's attention. She was a person who liked lovely things, but she didn't need a lot of jewelry. Yet, if it pleased Shane, she'd select a few items.

"Austin took your mother's engagement ring," Sophie said quietly. "That, and a couple of necklaces."

Shane lifted a pair of emerald and diamond earrings. “These would look great on you with your auburn hair, Charlie. These and the simple diamond ones.”

She looked at them, stunned that something so beautiful would simply be handed to her.

Shane chose a couple of necklaces, two bracelets, a ring, and a pin. “I remember the night Ricardo gave my mother this pin. It was their anniversary, and he was very excited about giving it to her.”

Charlotte studied the platinum and gold crescent pin brooch in the Tiffany & Co. velvet box and knew its value lay as much in the giving as in the gift. Ricardo had been a good stepfather to the boys and a generous, kind man to their mother.

“Thank you,” said Charlotte. “I love it.” She placed a hand on Shane’s arm. “But that’s enough. I’m feeling a bit overwhelmed.”

He grinned. “I like overwhelming you,” he teased.

She laughed. She knew he wasn’t talking about the jewelry.

By the time Charlotte and Shane left the house with the promise to arrange for someone to help them load up the things they wanted, Charlotte was numb with exhaustion. Her fatigue was as much emotional as it was physical. Shane had a little story behind the things he’d chosen, and from them she got an even better picture of a child raised by a mother who was too self-absorbed to care about the damage she inflicted on her children.

Inside his car, Shane placed a hand on her knee. “Thanks for coming. It means a lot. It’s good for me to face the memories and lay them to rest. It’s helpful to remember that.”

“What are we going to do about the condo?” Charlotte

asked. "Will we store the things you chose until we have more space?"

"That's something I've been thinking about. Will you be willing to move away from Sanderling Cove? I'd like to buy a house in the Miami area for us. It will work best that way. You can set up your own business like you talked about and still do work for the Inn."

"Yes, I've thought of it too. Because, while I don't want to have kids right away, I want them. Not one, not two, but at least three."

He turned to her with a grin. "I like that. We'd better start practicing now."

She laughed, but life wasn't that simple. She knew they had some challenges ahead. Things were happening fast, and now they had all this stuff. Gorgeous or not, it came as a mixed blessing.

Charlotte sighed, wishing she knew how the future would play out.

CHAPTER THREE

LIVY

Livy took a break from working in the kitchen. She had some time between the first wave of guests at breakfast and those who would come later. As she usually did, she ended up sitting in the gazebo where she could survey the area. Early shell seekers were walking along the sand, Eric's sailboat bobbed gently in the water offshore, and some members of the cove families were sitting on their porches with cups of coffee or tea.

She'd grown accustomed to this lifestyle away from the urgency of preparing baked goods to be sold for the business she'd shared with someone less dedicated than she. The fact that everything she did benefited Gran in some way made it that much sweeter here in Sanderling Cove.

A figure strolled toward her. *Austin.*

Livy filled with anxiety. Of all the cove kids, she and Austin seemed to get along the least, and it bothered her. Maybe because she'd had a crush on him as a teenager and a bit of that attraction still lingered. Oh, he did the usual teasing thing about the cookies she baked for everyone, but beyond that, he seldom sought her out or asked to spend time with her. It stung. She wanted to be friends with all the kids here.

"Morning, Livy. Having a break from the kitchen?" he said, standing outside the gazebo.

"Yes, but it's time I got back. We've got a lot of people 'in house' this morning. What are you doing up this early?"

"I have a business meeting in Tampa this morning. Not sure what I'm going to do next," he said. Having just sold his IT business for a lot of money, Austin was trying to decide where and how he'd live.

"Living in Florida would be nice," Livy said. "I'm loving it here."

"Really? I took you for more of a Southern Belle type, like your mother," he said.

"No, I'm not at all like that," Livy said, wishing her southern accent wasn't as pronounced.

"Oh," he said. "Well, then, that's interesting."

Feeling awkward, she stood. "Like I said, I'd better go back to the kitchen. See you later."

As she walked by him, she got a tantalizing whiff of lemony aftershave. No doubt one of the many women who were pursuing him would appreciate the sexy aroma.

Back in the kitchen, Billy Bob looked at her and glanced at the clock in an obvious way. Livy pressed her lips together. She was his boss, not the other way around. But then, Billy Bob had worked with John in the kitchen for years and was still getting used to the new regimen.

She went to work mixing up more biscuits. The Sanderling Cove Inn was well-known for delicious breakfasts. As she kneaded the dough, she wished she could decide what she was going to do with the rest of her life.

CHAPTER FOUR

BROOKE

Brooke took a last look in the mirror, still startled to see her purple-streaked hair. She was pleased Dylan liked it. He was an interesting guy, and she was excited to learn more about him. He'd gone out with Charlotte and Livy, but this would be her first date with him.

As promised, he was waiting for her outside Gran's house at seven. "Thought we'd go to the Pink Pelican," he said, smiling when she joined him.

"That's fine with me. They have great food, and the music is really cool."

He grinned. "Okay. Let's go."

He helped her into his red truck, and they took off.

Dylan drove down Gulf Drive and pulled into the crowded parking lot, easily finding a space. She liked that he handled himself and the truck with confidence.

As they walked toward the restaurant, he turned to her. "I'm glad we have this chance to get to know one another better. Of all of you cousins, you're the quietest."

"So I've been told," she admitted, wondering if by saying 'quietest' he meant 'boring.' Deciding not to play old mental games, she returned his smile. Tonight, the new, daring Brooke was going to emerge.

Inside, the restaurant and bar were crowded, but they found a high-top table for two out on the deck. Soft music flowed through outdoor speakers now, but later, a local band would take over and it would be loud both inside and outside.

A waitress came with menus and glasses of water. "What can I get you to drink?" she asked, her gaze lingering on Dylan.

He faced Brooke. "What would you like?"

"A Texas margarita," she answered. It was one of Livy's favorite drinks, one that she liked to sip slowly.

Dylan ordered a lager for himself, and after the waitress left, he said, "How are things going at the Inn? I helped with the rearrangement of the artwork and the photographs and think those changes make a positive difference."

"I think so too. Livy and I approved the new brochures Charlie put together. Even the new roadside sign makes a difference, don't you think?"

He nodded and sat back as their drinks were delivered. "It's great the three of you are working together to help your grandparents. What happens after they come back?"

"That's a question we all have. I'm becoming fascinated with the hospitality business, but I don't know if that's something I want to continue. Time will tell."

"No boyfriends back home?" he asked.

"No." Brooke's cheeks heated. She'd had only a couple of boyfriends, and nothing seemed to work out.

"Well, then, you're free to make some new choices. That has to be a good feeling,"

Brooke frowned and looked out at the waves washing up to the shore. "Except I have to keep an eye on my mother."

He studied her. "Yeah, I heard all about that. The grandmothers think it's time for you to make some changes. Are you going to do it?"

A new wave of determination washed through her. "Yes," she said with fresh resolve. "Gran says it's time for both of us to be apart. It's another reason I'm thinking of staying in Florida after Gran and John get back from their trip."

"I like an independent woman," he said, giving her an encouraging smile.

His words filled her with pleasure. It was a sign she was doing the right thing.

The waitress came to their table to check if they were ready.

Dylan ordered a second round of drinks, a deluxe burger for himself, and a chicken Caesar salad for her.

They chatted comfortably about different people at the cove, and then Brooke said, "I'm really fascinated by your paintings. Charlie said you're going to give one of them to the Inn. That's very generous of you."

He laughed. "I owe it to everyone at the cove after spending so much time there as a kid painting on a few walls I shouldn't have."

"I know you like big bold colors on large canvases. Did you always do that?"

"I've had formal training using several media in different ways, but large abstract paintings are what I love doing best. There's something freeing about it."

"I'd love to be able to do something like that."

He held up a finger. "You can. Come over to Mimi's garage. I've set up a studio of sorts there. We'll set a time and date, and I'll give you free rein."

"Really? That would be wonderful as long as you don't grade my artistic ability. My background is in accounting, remember?"

"Didn't you draw as a kid? Color in Cinderella-type coloring books?"

Brooke couldn't hold back a giggle. "I loved Princess everything when I was Skye's age and older. So, yes, I colored and cut out things."

"Well, then, we'll get your left brain introduced to your right and see what happens," Dylan said cheerfully.

"Thanks," said Brooke, meaning it more than Dylan might ever suspect. She was so used to being programmed for a certain type of life that she'd pushed other possibilities aside. This would be a great beginning for the new her.

Their food came and they ate watching the crowd around them or turning to the sandy beach beyond them. Though Brooke hadn't wanted to admit it to herself, she'd been nervous at the idea of going out with Dylan. Now, she was grateful she had. He was easy-going and kind.

When the band started playing, he gave her a questioning look.

She stood and took his hand. They danced to the thump-thump of the rock music, and once again, Brooke gave herself permission simply to enjoy.

By the time the band began a slow number she was ready for it.

Dylan easily held her in his arms and moved to the music with sure steps.

Sighing with happiness, Brooke leaned her head against his chest, more relaxed than she could ever remember on a date. But then, they were just cove kids getting together.

When they left the building, Dylan took hold of her hand and led her to his truck in an unselfconscious way. But the tingle in Brooke's fingers made her all too aware.

At home, Dylan drew up to Gran's house and turned to her. "I had a nice time. I hope we can do this again."

"Me, too," said Brooke. She paused, wondering if he was going to kiss her.

But even though they faced one another, he didn't attempt anything like that.

"Thanks again," she said, climbing out of the truck.

He pulled away, and she was left hoping this wouldn't be their only date. She'd enjoyed spending time with him.

Brooke awoke slowly not wishing to leave a dream of herself with Dylan and some other members of the cove. She cuddled her pillow, trying to remember details of it, still feeling a sense of happiness. Whatever it was, she decided being with Dylan was a positive thing. It was opening up feelings she'd hidden inside for a long time—feelings of new possibilities instead of expectations.

Later, when Brooke went into the office, Jake was already there. "Ready to go over the budget for next month?" he asked, waving her to a chair beside him.

"Sure. Let me finish my sweet roll, and I'll be there." Ordinarily, she would've set down her breakfast and moved toward him without delay. Not today.

He looked at her. "Everything all right?"

"Just taking it easy for a moment. How have you been? Doing anything interesting lately?"

Surprise showed in his expression. "Actually, I was on a date at the Pink Pelican last night. You didn't see me, but I saw you with Dylan Hendrix."

"He's just another one of us cove kids, but we had an enjoyable time. The band is terrific," she replied, unwilling to say more.

"Yes, I thought so too. Next time you go there, we should meet up." His lips curved. "By the way, the purple in your hair is cool. Who knew?"

Brooke lifted a hand to her head and fingered her hair, feeling like a completely different person from the woman who'd first moved into Gran's for the summer. Both of her cousins had changed. There was no reason she shouldn't change too.

After going over the budget, agreeing on figures and projections, Brooke rose from the chair next to Jake's. "When

Charlie gets back, I'll have a better idea of printing costs. But I think the cost for mailing brochures is pretty accurate. We're going to begin a mailing campaign using a list of previous guests, as well as an email campaign."

"It's satisfying to see reservation numbers growing," said Jake. "They'll be even better after your campaign. Ellie and John are hard workers, but they've needed a break for some time. It's wonderful they can have one while you and your cousins manage the Inn. Any idea if you'll continue to stay and help them after they return?"

Brooke shook her head, worried about a possible sale of the place. She, Livy, and Charlotte were growing to love the Inn and, like Gran, would hate to see it go to anyone outside the family.

"It's almost lunch time. Want to go with me to Gracie's?" Jake said.

"That sounds delightful. I never get tired of going there," Brooke said. "Not that I've been that often."

"Okay, then, my treat," said Jake. "No awkward splitting of the bill."

Brooke laughed. "That sounds unlike you. Every number counts with you."

He grinned. "That's me, the accountant. Not me, the friend. There's a difference you know."

"I like that." She'd had a crush on Jake from the beginning. Now, knowing they could be friends who go out for a meal together was a pleasant twist in the new reality she was creating for herself.

Gracie's, the breakfast and lunch operation at the Salty Key Inn, had become an institution along the Gulf Coast of Florida. The food was delicious, and the service from the mostly older servers was excellent. Any wait for a seat was worth it.

While they stood outside the restaurant in line, Jake struck up a conversation with an older couple in front of them. Listening to them chat, Brooke studied Jake. He was a tall, well-built man with light-brown hair. Behind horn-rimmed glasses, his brown eyes sparkled. Though she was attracted to him, she had no desire to act on it because at this point in her life, she needed to know that if she decided to stay working at the Inn, there would be no personal issues that could hinder their professional relationship. He hadn't mentioned a girlfriend, but she couldn't imagine he didn't have one.

When they were called inside, Brooke was delighted to be seated at a corner table where she had an excellent view of people coming and going. Gracie's was the type of place that attracted a variety of diners. Even the stories behind the people serving them was interesting. The uncle of the three women owning the Salty Key Inn had taken in friends and acquaintances who needed help, given them jobs, and provided them with a place to live and work. Gratefulness for their job made these restaurant workers the best ever.

Mary, a gray-haired woman with quite a bit of bulk, approached their table. "And what may I bring you on this fine, summer day?" She handed them menus.

Brooke ordered a glass of iced tea, and the tropical chicken salad plate. Jake ordered a Coke and a steak sandwich, a more typical "guy" meal.

"I couldn't help overhearing your conversation with the people in front of us," she said to Jake. "From the sound of it, you might be getting a new client."

Jake grinned. "I pick up a lot of clients not only by word of mouth but by simply talking to people and handing them my business card."

Brooke thought of the new business cards they were having printed up for The Sanderling Cove Inn. Maybe attaching them to brochures would be a way for others to spread the news.

Brooke and Jake talked about the new brochures as they waited for their meals. Brooke liked being able to bounce ideas off Jake. He took his time to answer, but his responses were always insightful.

Their meals came, and Brooke dug into her chicken salad with eagerness. Pineapple chunks, pistachios, and a slight flavor of curry in the sauce were tasty additions to the chunks of tender chicken. She glanced across the table at Jake. He was enjoying his meal too.

"Hello, Jake," said a blonde woman approaching them. "I thought you were going to call me." She smiled sweetly at him, but her voice held disappointment.

Jake stood. "Sorry, Allie. I've been super busy. Meet my client, Brooke Weatherby."

Brooke gave her a polite nod, then waited while Jake walked Allie out of the restaurant where they could talk privately.

He returned a few minutes later and apologized.

"No problem," said Brooke, pleased with her earlier decision to keep things on a professional level. Otherwise, she might end up like the blonde. Disappointed.

He gave her a grateful look. And for the rest of the meal, they kept conversation to the workings at the Inn.

CHAPTER FIVE

CHARLOTTE

Charlotte left Shane's condo and drove back to the Gulf Coast eager to see the brochures she'd left with the printers. If they were going to show a significant change in the Inn, they had to build their reservations. In addition to email, a direct mailing campaign would help, especially because it was going to people who already liked the Inn or to businesses that could direct guests to them.

Having selected items for a home she'd share with Shane, Charlotte was torn about plans for the future. The condo was one thing. A big house was another. One symbolized more freedom than the other. And having nice things was ... well ... nice, but a responsibility also.

She loved Shane with all her heart and always would, but she thought they'd have more "play time" before settling down. Being with her cousins at the Inn was the perfect place for her right now. Things had happened fast between her and Shane, but no big plans would be made for a while.

Before reaching the cove, she stopped in St. Petersburg to pick up the brochures. The clerk inside the store beamed at her as he placed two cardboard boxes on the counter and pulled out a brochure to show her.

"They're beautiful," he said. "The colors, shapes, design, everything. You mentioned you might open your own PR consulting business. If you do, I can bring a lot of business to you."

Charlotte thanked him, wondering why everything sounded so easy when she knew life wasn't that way.

CHAPTER SIX

LIVY

Livy sat in the office with Brooke and Charlotte as excited as they were about the new brochures. "Dylan and you did a fabulous job of getting photos of the Inn both inside and out. They show up very well, and with just the few changes we made, the rooms look different."

"Almost like new," said Brooke. "I can't wait to see what additional reservations they bring. Then the reservations system Austin installed for us will be put to a test."

Livy studied Charlotte. "What's wrong, Charlie? You don't seem to be as excited as we are."

Charlotte shrugged. "I'm feeling a little overwhelmed. Nothing important, really, except things between Shane and me seem to be on fast-forward."

"You're not thinking of backing out of your relationship with him, are you?" said Brooke, looking aghast.

Charlotte shook her head and placed a hand on Brooke's arm. "No, no. Nothing like that. I *love* him. But things seem to be moving at lightspeed, and I don't know what I want in the future. How about you?"

Brooke let out a long sigh. "Like you, I don't know what I want. But, Charlie, you're lucky you know who you'll be sharing your future with. Livy and I don't have that figured out. Right, Livy?"

Livy nodded. "But then, I don't want to think about that right now. It's all about rediscovering who I am, helping with the Inn, and having fun this summer. Isn't that what we're all supposed to be doing? Working hard and having fun?" Charlie and Brooke might want to have a man in their lives, but she didn't. She'd felt trapped in her relationship with Wayne. He was a horrible control freak who'd taken a lot of self-confidence away from her. She needed this time to be entanglement free and to regain her self-esteem.

CHAPTER SEVEN

BROOKE

The next morning after doing some work in the office, Brooke decided to walk over to check on Dylan. He'd mentioned having her stop by anytime, and she was anxious to see him at work.

At his grandmother's house, she debated whether to knock at the door or head right for the garage. She decided to catch Dylan at his work and went to the side door of the garage and opened it.

Inside, she was almost blinded by the bright lights Dylan had placed around the perimeter of the garage. Dylan stood in the middle of the room in front of a large canvas positioned on the floor.

He turned to her with a grin. "You made it."

She stepped forward. "What are you working on?"

"A new piece for sale in a New York gallery. What do you think? I'm almost finished."

She studied the various swipes and curls of various colors including orange, purple, and red. "I like it."

"I'm calling it 'Sunrise on the Gulf.' I know it needs something else but not sure what," he said, closing his eyes to a slit and studying it.

"How about more blue color at the bottom and a swipe of gray at the top?" she said, and then wished she hadn't when Dylan turned to her with a frown.

"Hmmm...where did that come from?" he asked.

Brooke shrugged. "I don't know."

His lips curved. "Let's try it. If I don't like it, I'll do something else."

After mixing some colors, he picked up what looked like a regular painter's brush and swiped those colors across the canvas—blue at the bottom and gray at the top below orange colors. He stood back and studied it. Then he turned to her with a smile. "Brooke, you're a genius."

She laughed. She was no genius, and they both knew it. Still, his compliment meant a lot to her.

Dylan's brown gaze settled on her. "Would you like to try painting? I've got a couple of smaller canvases prepped."

Her eyes rounded in surprise. "Really?"

"Why not? It's a wonderful release to be able to express yourself like this. Every once in a while, I do a painting class for extra money. We have a great time."

"Okay, show me what to do."

Dylan set up an easel for her, handing her paintbrushes in different sizes, and showed her the containers of paint. "For today, use these colors, okay?"

She selected a medium-size brush, feeling as excited as she had been in the past when she'd faced an uncolored page in one of her favorite coloring books.

Boldly, she dabbed the brush in red paint and painted a circle. Seeing its color against the stark white background, Brooke giggled.

Dylan looked over at her and grinned. "Feels good, huh?"

"Yes," Brooke said, unable to hide her delight. She dipped her brush into the red paint once more and swiped a broad stroke over the circle. Then without adding paint to the brush, she made another bold stroke away from the circle. She looked over at Dylan for his approval but he was ignoring her.

When she'd added all the color she wanted to the canvas,

she waved Dylan over. "I want to add different colors."

"We'll let these dry and then you can do that," said Dylan. He looked at her painting. "Very interesting. Do you know what you'll call this?"

She shook her head. "Not yet. Not until I see some yellows and greens."

"So, you have a picture in your head?" he asked.

"Yes. I don't know what it is exactly, but I know what I want it to look like," she said, wondering if she sounded like a moron.

"Interesting, Brooke. I believe behind all those numbers of yours, there might be an artist."

Unexpected tears stung Brooke's eyes. His discovering a hidden talent beneath the surface she presented was a gift.

"Hey, are you alright?" he asked, thumbing the tears that had escaped off her cheek.

She could only nod. The fact that he cared meant even more to her.

"That's all we can do today. I'll show you how to clean your brushes, and then how about grabbing a sandwich with me? I make a mean ham and cheese."

"That would be great," she said. "I'm working the social hour this evening at the Inn, but I have time for lunch before I have to help with the stuffing and mailing of brochures."

Brooke learned that Dylan was very careful with his brushes and diligently cleaned them and the space around his paintings. He'd even gone to the expense of having the concrete floor of the garage painted with an epoxy coating that kept dust to a minimum.

When they went inside to the kitchen, Skye rushed over to her. "Brooke! Brooke! Come play with me."

Brooke gave Skye a hug and knelt beside her. "Sweetie, I'm going to have lunch and then go help Charlie and Livy at the

Inn. But another time, I promise I will."

Skye's lower lip came out.

Brooke stood and lifted Skye into her arms. "No pouting. Tomorrow we'll set up a special time to be together."

Dylan's grandmother walked into the kitchen. "Now Skye, leave Brooke alone. She and Dylan are having lunch."

Skye grew serious and then looked up at Brooke. "Can I sit next to you at lunch?"

"Sure," said Brooke, smiling at her.

"Ham and Swiss on rye bread okay?" Dylan asked her.

"That sounds delicious, and light on the mustard," said Brooke. "Thanks."

"Don't forget chips and pickles," said Mimi. "They're available too." Mimi was an excellent cook and had hosted many kids' lunches in the past.

"What can I do to help?" Brooke asked Dylan.

"Nothing," he said. "I'll have these sandwiches ready in a jiffy. I'm hungry."

"Me, too, said Brooke. "I didn't realize painting could work up an appetite."

"It's more than painting. It's creating, expressing yourself, reaching deep inside for emotion," said Dylan as if talking to a class.

She was both amused and impressed.

They sat down together at the kitchen table. Skye wiggled into a chair next to Brooke but was soon bored and left.

Alone again, Dylan said, "Guess you like kids, huh?"

"Oh, yes. I grew up as an only child, so I want a family with two children at least."

"But not for a long while, I guess," said Dylan.

Brooke gave him a quizzical look. "Why would you say that?"

He gazed out the window. "My ex-girlfriend told me no

woman in today's world wants to be burdened with kids right away, maybe never."

Brooke frowned and shook her head. "That's not true. I know many women my age who want a family. Maybe not right after getting married but sooner rather than later."

He turned and rested his gaze on her. "Happy to hear that. Grace and I grew up with parents who loved having kids. Mom wanted many more, but we two were all she could have."

"Both of your cousins, Adam and his brother Brendan, have kids. Their parents must have been the same way."

He acknowledged that with a smile. "Both of our families are warm and loving. Knowing Mimi, you can understand why. My mom is a lot like her."

"It's interesting how much our grandmothers have played a part in our lives. Even now, it's sweet of them to bring us all together as much as possible this summer."

"Yeah, I think so too. Even after the summer is over, I might stay here for part of the year, maybe the winter months. I love Santa Fe and the mountains there, but the winters can be very cold."

"It's impressive that you can do your artwork in both places," said Brooke. "I know I don't want to return to New York. I'm not going to get back in that rut."

"How about your mother? Would she move too?"

"I don't know," Brooke said as she considered the possibilities. "For the first time in my life, I'm not going to make any decision based on what she wants. I'll always be there for her, of course. But I'm trying to be independent. It's what Gran wants for me and what I want for myself."

"That's good to know." He chuckled when Skye came into the kitchen and flung herself into his lap. He hugged her close.

"Mimi says it's time to lie down with books." Skye gave Brooke a longing look. "Just one story, Brooke?"

Brooke glanced at Dylan and grinned. "Guess I have no choice."

"A real pushover." He winked. "But I like it."

Later, as she was working in the office with Livy and Charlotte stuffing envelopes with brochures, Brooke's thoughts kept straying to Dylan. Beneath his off-beat appearance, he was still the same sweet person he'd been as a boy.

"You seem happy this afternoon," said Livy, nudging her. "What's up?"

"Believe it or not, I'm starting a painting project with Dylan," Brooke said. "He said I might have talent."

"You mean painting as in being an artist?" Charlotte said.

"Yes. I've already begun painting something I hope to hang here in the Inn."

"How exciting. I remember you used to be talented at drawing and stuff," Charlotte said.

"That's before I felt I had to have a way to earn a steady income. Nothing like working with numbers, boring as they are, to have a consistent job."

"Brooke, I'm happy for you that you're making changes. Speaking of that, when are the three of us going to get our tattoos?" said Livy.

Brooke raised her hand. "How about tomorrow afternoon? I'll call and make an appointment if you're game."

"Sounds like a plan," said Livy. "Are you in, Charlie?"

"Why not? A tiny mermaid will be a sweet reminder of how lucky I was to save Shane."

Brooke clapped her on the back. "We're very glad you did." A shell would be the perfect thing for her. It would remind her of Skye.

CHAPTER EIGHT

ELLIE

Ellie sat in a corner of the living room in a charming inn in the castle town of Crupet, Belgium, focusing on the latest email from Liz. As much as she and John were enjoying their trip, Ellie waited eagerly for these emails telling her about the latest happenings at Sanderling Cove. The thought of Charlotte and Shane being engaged brought a rush of pleasure to her. She wished Livy and Brooke would find equally good men to settle down with. One reason she and John would remain on their European trip for the entire summer was to give all the cove grandchildren time to really get to know one another, and hopefully, fall in love.

She focused on the screen and read:

> **"Karen has encouraged Adam to return to the cove sooner rather than later. While Skye is happy with her Mimi, she misses her daddy. More importantly, Karen is hoping that Adam will finally see Brooke as the perfect woman to become his wife and Skye's mother. She's going to do everything she can to make it happen.**
>
> **"Brooke recently put purple in her hair, a pure act of rebellion in my mind. We all say bravo to that.**
>
> **"Livy is still having fun, going out, enjoying herself after working at the Inn. All three of your granddaughters are working hard there. Though I'll**

give nothing away, I think you'll be pleased.

"Now that Shane is settled, I'm trying to keep an eye on Austin. Surely, one of the young ladies at the cove is suitable for him.

"Enough matchmaking. We all miss you and John.

"Happy Travels. Liz"

Ellie closed the lid to her computer and stood up. She missed Sanderling Cove but was delighted by all she and John had seen and done on their trip enjoying tasty food, excellent wine, and new vistas. Each day she asked herself if she wanted to sell the Sanderling Cove Inn, but she simply couldn't decide. The end of summer and their return to the cove, discovering what her granddaughters had done in her absence, would provide her with an answer.

CHAPTER NINE

BROOKE

Brooke sat with her cousins in a coffee shop in St. Petersburg chatting and trying not to feel the sting from the tattoo above her left ankle. All three had helped design the small picture on her body, and they all agreed each one was tasteful. Even so, their mothers would, no doubt, be unhappy about them. As free-spirited as Gran was, her daughters tended to stick to rules and what they considered ladylike behavior.

Brooke liked the simplicity of the pink seashell design she'd chosen. As she'd hoped, she was sure it would be a reminder of this summer, which was turning out to be much better than she'd dared to hope.

She brushed a crumb off the bright pink T-shirt she'd borrowed from Gran. It read: "*Wine gets better with age. I get better with wine.*" When Charlotte and Livy had seen it on her, they'd laughed.

"You're rebelling too?" Charlotte said. Since becoming engaged to Shane she'd not worn any more of Gran's T-shirts.

Brooke let out a laugh. "I'm feeling really good about things, not quite so programmed. The saying on this shirt reminds me to keep it going."

"I get it," said Livy. "It's great you're having such a fabulous summer. My summer has been great for me, too, though I'm still not sure what I'm going to do when Gran and John return. I just know I won't be going back to Virginia."

"And I'm not returning to New York," said Brooke with a new firmness.

"You know I'm staying in Florida, but Shane and I haven't decided where it's going to be in the Miami area," said Charlotte. "Even though we have the ability to choose, we can't decide. It's driving me crazy."

Brooke reached over and clasped Charlotte's hand. "You don't have to rush, do you?"

Charlotte let out a long sigh and shook her head. "You're right. We don't have to make that decision right now. I don't know why I'm worried about it."

"No matter where you move, you can still do PR work for the Inn. Right?" said Livy.

"Yes," said Charlotte. "A fiancé, a new life, a new business. Maybe I don't need to worry after all. It's more settled than I thought."

"I'm not thinking of the future. I just want to enjoy each day," said Brooke. "Guess what? I'm going to sign up for an online art course from a school in St. Petersburg in the fall. After painting with Dylan, I've discovered it's something I really enjoy, and I want to learn more about it. Cool, huh?"

"Very cool," Livy agreed. "Dylan's a great guy."

"Yes," said Brooke. "We have fun together."

"I hear Adam is coming back soon," said Charlotte. "Do you think he'll be more sociable this time?"

Brooke shrugged. "Mimi Karen asked me to help him settle in. She thinks it's important to Skye."

"What did you say to her?" Livy asked.

"I said I'd try to help, that if it's important to Skye, I'd do it. I love that little girl."

"I know you do," said Charlotte. "But don't get burned by Adam because you're trying to help. Shane doesn't think Adam's ever going to trust a woman again."

"I'm not planning to get involved with Adam, I just said I would help," Brooke said more snappishly than she wished.

"I think it's sweet that you've agreed to it," said Livy. "But you're just starting to find new freedom. You don't want to get tied down to anyone now, do you?"

Brooke sat back and thought a moment. "No, you're right. I don't."

"That's smart," said Charlotte. "I just don't want you to get hurt."

Brooke smiled at her. "Thanks. I know that and appreciate your concern."

They left the coffee shop, and Livy drove them back to the cove to get ready for socializing with the guests. Brooke wondered what it would be like if she continued at the Inn—working 24/7. She wasn't sure how she felt about that.

Later, after the social hour, Brooke headed to Gran's house, content to sit out on the porch and relax. She couldn't wait to tell Dylan about the course she intended to sign up for. Tomorrow, she'd continue to put a few touches on the painting she'd started with him.

She heard her name being called and looked up to see Dylan crossing the lawn toward her. Smiling, she lifted her hand and waved.

He came right up to the porch. "Want some company?"

"Actually, I do," she said smiling at him. "I want to tell you about the painting course I want to take online at one of the art schools in St. Petersburg."

He came onto the porch and took a seat in a chair beside her. "You're really interested in art now, huh?"

"Yes. I can't believe how happy it makes me to open up this creative side of me. It's making such a difference. Everything seems much brighter, more intense now that I see those colors and how they complement each other more clearly." She beamed at him. "I can't thank you enough, Dylan."

"That's superb, Brooke. I like that you get why I've chosen it as my career. I can't imagine doing anything else. But it's a business too. I'm sure you understand that."

"For you, yes. For me, it'll be a hobby. I still have to consider making a living."

Dylan leaned forward. "If you're interested, I could use your help setting up some financial files. I need to decide whether to move to a larger studio space in Santa Fe or remain where I am, sharing a studio with a couple of other artists and a metal worker."

"I'd be more than glad to help you work up some comparative pricing, that sort of thing. Let me know when you're ready," she said, pleased by the suggestion.

"Do you think you'll have any time off tomorrow? I'm thinking of visiting the Sarasota Art Museum. As long as I'm here for the summer as I promised Mimi, I want to see a few of the museums in the area. I took Charlie to the Dali Museum, and she loved it."

"I'd be delighted to go with you. I'll have time after breakfast and before prepping appetizers," Brooke said. "Maybe we can visit several places in the coming weeks."

"Yes, but Mimi told me you're going to be busy helping Adam and Skye get better acquainted with the area. I think she's hoping that he'll move to Florida."

Brooke hid her dismay. She wanted to help Adam and Skye, but she didn't like Mimi's assumption she'd spend all her free time with them.

"How I spend my free time is my decision," she said. "Seeing museums, visiting local gardens, and things like that are all activities I want to do. It's as if the world is exploding with color, and I want to see it all."

Dylan laughed and stood. "I'd better go. I promised Skye I'd tuck her in bed. With Adam away, it's become a ritual."

"What a great guy you are," she said.

He shrugged. "I've always liked kids. Being with them gives you the opportunity to see the world through their eyes. Like colors are to you."

She stood and faced him. "Thanks for the invitation. I can't wait to see the museum."

He studied her. "I'll pick you up at eleven o'clock unless you change your mind."

"I won't change my mind," Brooke said.

She watched him cross the lawn thinking this friendship might be the best thing to happen to her in a long time.

The next morning, Brooke was ready to leave with Dylan when he called. "Sorry, Brooke, but I can't make it. I have to pick up Adam at the airport. This is a last-minute thing. There was a problem with Skye, and Mimi has to stay here with her. Sorry, but we'll make it another time."

"Okay, I understand," said Brooke, disappointed. "I'll wait to go there until you're ready. In the meantime, I'd like to come back to the studio and work on my painting. I know where the paints and brushes are. Do you mind?"

"Go ahead and get started. I should be back in an hour or two depending on when his flight arrives," he said. "As soon as I return, I'll meet you at the studio."

Brooke ended the call worried that having Adam in the cove would cut into her time with Dylan. But she'd made a promise to Mimi, and though she wanted to make some changes in her life, she'd always remain true to her word.

She checked in with Charlotte and Livy, then made her way

to Mimi's garage and slipped inside through the side door.

She turned on the lights and stood a moment to study the space and the stacks of paintings leaning against the wall. Looking at his work, Brooke realized how talented Dylan was. The four or five completed paintings were quite different from those at the Santa Fe gallery she'd looked up online. Those paintings reflected the mountains around Santa Fe and the muted colors there. These newer paintings had blues, greens, and various shades of pink in tiny bits and pieces on the canvases. Nothing too obvious.

Brooke decided to approach Dylan with an idea, and after doing a little checking online, she was satisfied it could work for him.

She pulled out her small canvas and looked at it from all angles, even turning it upside down. She wanted to get a better sense of how the colors affected the shapes. It surprised her how easily she could identify their reactions. She knew she didn't have Dylan's talent, but it made her want to learn more.

Her cell phone rang. *Her mother*.

She clicked on the call. "Hi, Mom, how are you?"

"Not well, but not to worry. A nurse is coming in to help me for the next week or so. I'm tired and listless, and every bone in my body aches. It's just a flare-up, I know, but when the agency called to check up on me, I agreed it might be time for someone to stay with me for a bit."

"I made arrangements with the nursing agency before I left. Any expenses will be taken care of," Brooke said.

"Yes, I know. I just wanted to let you know. Anything new happening there?"

Brooke hesitated and then decided not to tell her mother about her newfound love of art. Her mother had struggled to raise her on her own and tended to see things as either practical or frivolous. "The Inn is coming along nicely. We're starting a publicity campaign and have drawn in some new guests. It's pretty exciting when that happens."

"Yes, but what's going to happen to the place if Gran decides to sell. You'll have done all that work for nothing."

"No, all the operating statistics will have been improved along with the profitability and therefore the value of the property, which will bring in more money," Brooke said patiently. Her mother had never been a financial numbers person even though she was a computer nerd.

"Well, it'll be a relief when the summer is over. I've kept your room exactly as you left it."

"I haven't made any permanent decisions yet, but I may stay in Florida." Brooke realized she'd better present the idea right away so her mother could become used to it.

"Oh, but ..." her mother began.

"Let's not talk about it now," said Brooke. "Have you been reading some books lately?" Her mother loved to read, had found it a source of pleasure on difficult days.

"Actually, I've been listening to some books on tape. That works best on my bad days. It's a pleasant diversion."

"I'm glad," said Brooke, pleased her mother had found something new on her own. "I'd better go. I'm on a schedule. That's one thing about helping to manage the Inn. There's always a schedule."

"Okay, sweetie. Have a good day. Miss you."

"Miss you too," said Brooke automatically. She loved her mother but wasn't ready to return to their co-dependent relationship.

Later, she'd just finished putting away the paint and was washing the brushes outside the garage when Dylan pulled into the driveway. He and Adam climbed out of the truck and faced her.

Brooke's breath caught. She'd forgotten how handsome

Adam was. He had just enough time to study her before his attention was caught by Skye running toward him on sturdy little legs.

"Daddy! Daddy! You're here."

He laughed and swept her up in his arms.

Watching Adam's face as he hugged Skye, Brooke's eyes stung. He obviously adored his daughter. She hoped someday to have a family with a man who was as loving.

Mimi approached, embraced Adam, and stood back, admiring him. "Welcome to your Florida home. We're happy to have you here."

"Thanks. Brendan and I have been talking about maybe turning our entire business over to him. We set it up when we were just brothers out of college. It's doing well, but I may be ready to go out on my own. Maybe do something here. We'll see."

Mimi clapped her hands together. "How wonderful. That would be a dream come true for me. With your grandfather gone, it can get pretty lonely."

Adam shook his head. "Even with all the other ladies of the cove?" he said, teasing her.

She laughed. "Well, they're delightful best friends, but I want to see more of you and my great-grandbaby."

"We'll see," he said, and turned to Dylan. "Thanks for the ride, Cuz."

"No problem," said Dylan. "See you later. Gotta get back to my work."

"I'll go with you," said Brooke. "First, I have to finish cleaning my brushes."

Adam frowned. "You're an artist, too?"

She shook her head and laughed. "Hardly. But I'm discovering I like it as a hobby."

"You couldn't have a better teacher," said Adam before he,

Mimi, and Skye headed indoors, and Brooke went back to her work cleaning brushes.

After she'd finished, she stepped inside the garage.

Dylan had taken off his clean shirt and was pulling on one covered with splotches of paint. She couldn't help admiring the breadth of his shoulders and his abs, but when he turned to her, she quickly looked away.

"Hey, Dylan. Can we talk? I have an idea for you."

He grinned. "You do, do you?"

Her lips curved. "Yes. I've looked up your work online and know you have the gallery in Santa Fe. After looking at the paintings you've recently completed during your visit here, I think you need to show these particular pieces in Florida. It's subtle, but the colors are better suited for here. Most of them are beach scenes, sort of, in a very contemporary way."

"I've been thinking along those lines, but it's the old business problem. I'd need someone to handle the paintings in this area."

She paused, feeling the rush of blood to her cheeks. When she spoke, her voice was high with tension. "I could do that for you. I'm thinking of staying in Florida and could handle the business end for you. If you trusted me, that is."

He approached her and steadied his gaze on her. "I'd trust you with my life, Brooke. You're such an honorable person."

Brook blinked rapidly with surprise. *Honorable? Is that what she wanted him to say?*

Flustered, she tried to focus on the issue. "You're a prolific artist with work in demand. Rather than storing any paintings, you could be building your reputation and income by displaying them in both areas. That's all I'm trying to say."

"And you would run the business end of it for me?"

"Yes, that's what I'm proposing to do. I love your work. We could even get Charlie to work on PR things for you."

His grin sent light to those blue eyes of his, softening his face with pleasure. “I like it. Let me think it over. First, though, let’s work on the gallery and studio issues in Santa Fe. What do you charge per hour?”

“Oh,” she said, surprised she hadn’t worked that out in her mind. “Let’s see what you’re talking about and we’ll go from there.”

“Okay, deal. I’ll get in touch with my accountant and gallery manager and get back to you with the information you’ll need. Thanks, Brooke, for thinking of me.”

“Sure. I figure we can help each other.”

“All right, then. Tomorrow–lunch and a museum. Sound okay?”

“Yes,” said Brooke, wondering why she felt as if she was standing on a precipice about to take a flying leap.

CHAPTER TEN

CHARLOTTE

Charlotte waited at the Tampa International airport with Shane. They were to meet his father, Henry, and his wife, Shannon, in the baggage claim area. They'd flown down to Florida from Atlanta to give Shane and his brother support by attending their mother's memorial service. Long divorced, Shane's parents had endured a horrible marriage, marred by Diana's mental illness and manipulative ways.

Charlotte could feel the energy level rise in Shane when his father and stepmother appeared. She was as happy to see them as he. They were a kind, loving couple who'd easily accepted her and made her feel like a part of their family.

She chatted with Shannon while Shane and his father walked over to the luggage carousel.

"I'll be relieved when this service is over and the family can put this all behind them," said Shannon. "I talked to Austin the other day and he's been stressed by the idea of speaking at the service. Shane told Henry that he wouldn't make any remarks. Henry told him it was his decision. Diana was a horrible mother to Shane, especially."

"It makes me mad every time he tells me a little more about it. The see-sawing back and forth between being nice or nasty would have been difficult for anyone. Even now, I understand his hesitation to trust people."

"How did the selection of things from the house go? Shane

was adamant about not keeping anything from there. I'm pleased for him that he changed his mind," said Shannon.

"Me, too, but to be totally honest, it's a burden to have things in storage before we can put them to use. We need to find a new place to live, something bigger than his condo. I wasn't quite ready for that."

Shannon gave her a little squeeze. "It's all happened fast between you and Shane, but there's no reason to be in a big hurry. The important thing is you know how you feel about one another and know you want to spend your lives together. From here on in, you can slow down. Everything will fall into place. You'll see."

Charlotte smiled at her. "Thanks. I needed to hear that. My mother is all about planning a big, fancy wedding in New York, and I'm not sure it's something I want."

"Relax, honey," said Shannon. "There's no rush."

They turned as the men approached with luggage.

"Ready to go?" Shane asked her.

"Sure," Charlotte answered, knowing the next couple of days would be difficult.

CHAPTER ELEVEN

LIVY

When Granny Liz called and asked Livy for a favor, she didn't hesitate to say yes. Livy loved Liz almost as much as Gran. Best friends, the two of them—Gran and Liz—had always supported Livy for whatever she wanted to do. Becoming a professional baker hadn't been on her mother's wish list for her. But Livy had succeeded in spite of that.

"Austin needs a ride to the airport. He has an unexpected business meeting in California. A business deal."

"Aren't Shane and Charlotte at the airport now?" Livy said, wondering why they hadn't taken Austin with them.

"Yes, but Austin wasn't ready to go. He's cleaning out his room now so Henry and Shannon can comfortably move in."

"How long is he going to be gone?" Livy asked, surprising herself with unexpected disappointment.

"Just overnight. He has to be back for Diana's service," said Granny Liz. "Can you do it? The rest of the family is busy."

"Of course. Give me a few minutes and I'll be there."

She grabbed her keys and went to her car intent on picking him up. But just as she got to her SUV, he appeared carrying a briefcase.

"Thanks, Livy. I appreciate this. Something unexpected came up, and I have to make this meeting. It could be important."

"No problem. I'm happy to do this for Granny Liz," she said

climbing behind the wheel.

He slid into the passenger seat beside her. "Granny Liz? Not me?"

She laughed. "I didn't mean that the way it sounded. Sure, I'm delighted to do this for you. It gets me away from the Inn for a while. This day-to-day schedule is a bit wearing."

"I thought you were used to it, having owned your own bakery," Austin said.

"I was, but now that I'm away from it, I'm thinking of doing something that doesn't require me to be up very early every morning. I could maybe bake a few things for restaurants for dinner crowds."

"That might be a lot easier," he said. "You deserve some time off. How's it going with Billy Bob?"

"He's a tough old guy who's really a softie, but he works hard not to show it," said Livy. "We basically get along."

"He's an interesting guy. I've had a chance to talk to him about fishing. He's a big fisherman on his days off."

"I didn't know that," said Livy. "I'll have to ask him about it. So far, we haven't discussed much about our personal lives."

"Yours seems pretty active around here. Do you have something going on with Eric? You're doing a lot of sailing with him."

"Eric? We're just friends. I'm interested in getting reacquainted with the cove kids and doing things with them. What about you? I haven't seen you hanging out here too much."

"I've been spending time in Miami with some old friends. It's a comfortable group."

"But you'll be staying at the cove when you're not there?"

"That's the plan," said Austin. "I promised Granny Liz I would. My parents are here now. As soon as I return tomorrow, I'll spend time with them. Then we have my mother's service to get through. Are you planning on being there?"

"Yes," said Livy quietly. "I want to support you and Shane. I know it's been tough."

"My mother was something else. I'm working on what I should talk about at the service. It won't be easy."

"I've heard that it's easiest if you pick someone out in the crowd and speak to them alone. If you want, I can be that person for you. I don't remember much about your mother, so I'll seem pretty neutral."

He turned and grinned at her. "Really? You'd do that for me?"

"Sure. Why not?" Livy said, keeping her eyes on the road.

"Thanks. I'll find some way to repay you. When I get back, let's go out sometime. Unless you're too busy?"

"I'll manage to find the time," Livy said, chuckling softly. Austin hadn't mentioned her cookies once.

CHAPTER TWELVE

BROOKE

On this June morning, Brooke slid into a pew beside Livy, who'd insisted they sit up front and in the center of the row, allowing Austin to keep his eye on her as he paid tribute to his mother. It was a sweet idea on Livy's part, Brooke thought, knowing how nervous she herself would be in Austin's role. Shane still hadn't made up his mind about speaking.

She was as surprised as everyone else when more and more people joined the congregation.

"People from the charity organizations Diana and Ricardo supported," Henry said softly to his wife, sitting behind Brooke where she could hear him.

Music played softly in the background as she sat in the Miami chapel Diana had requested for her service. Brooke thought it interesting that Diana had planned every detail of her service, as if she knew it would occur soon. A shiver crossed Brooke's shoulders at the thought. No one would know for sure if her death was planned or a horrible accident.

After the minister said a few words and included standard readings from the Bible, Austin rose from his place in the front pew, walked to the dais, and faced them. He was a handsome, smart man, but when he began speaking, she could see the sadness of a child losing his parent.

When he was finished, he drew his eyes away from Livy and settled his gaze on his brother. There was a feeling of anticipation as Austin took his seat and Shane rose.

Facing the audience, Shane began to speak in a soft but determined voice. "My mother was a difficult woman. Those who might say otherwise didn't really know her. But there were times when she was at her best. That's what I'd like to remember today and going forward. I want to remember some of those better times, the way she'd make my brother and me laugh by pretending to be the queen of Spain, speaking in a silly accent. Ricardo loved those moments when she let her guard down."

"She came from a rough background, which is why she put on airs around people, afraid she'd be judged for her humble beginnings. I think many of us here can understand the need for her to do that, being married to someone like Ricardo Perez. While her life was glamorous, she was full of doubt, uncertainty, and pain. Depression was a constant trouble-maker."

"The lesson she leaves behind for me is to learn to forgive and be grateful for the family I have, including Charlotte Bradford whom I love deeply." He stopped and drew a deep breath before letting it out again. "Let us remember we are human and have failings. I hope you all appreciate the people you have in your lives. Let them know how much they mean to you. Thank you."

The entire chapel was silent as Shane walked back to his seat next to Charlotte and gave her a kiss.

Brooke dabbed at her eyes with a tissue, aware she wasn't the only one to do so.

Later, she noticed how close Charlotte stayed to Shane. She went up to him and then spoke to Austin to give them her condolences and congratulate them on their tributes to their mother.

Both men gave her a quick hug, and Brooke realized how

important this summer was to all of them, giving them the opportunity to know one another better.

She and the other cove kids joined the people invited to a light luncheon reception at a local restaurant, Le Petit, a favorite of Diana's. Small, elegant, and known for its classic French food, it was the perfect ending to a special service.

Served buffet style, the array of little bites of food was carefully chosen and prepared to be easily handled by guests. Brooke gathered a plateful of them and sat beside Livy at a small table.

"This is delicious," said Brooke. "Be sure and taste these miniature beef wellingtons."

Livy grinned at her. "I'm trying to taste as many different things as I can. I love these little bites for a crowd like this. Let me know which are your favorites, and I'll be sure to try it."

Brooke loved that her cousin was open to trying new things. But then, Livy was a foodie.

After Brooke returned to Gran's house, she took the time to call her mother. Shane's words had found a home in her heart, and Brooke wanted to be sure that all was right with her.

Her mother picked up after only two rings. "Hi, Brooke, how are you?" she asked in a cheerful voice.

"Fine. I just got back from a memorial service for Austin and Shane's mother, Diana. It was short, but lovely. How are things there?"

"Great. My new nurse is excellent. He has no trouble helping me with my exercises and doing other things for me."

"He? Are you telling me you have a male nurse? That's a surprise," Brooke said. In the past, her mother had refused to consider a male nurse.

"Yes, but when I got the call, I figured, why not? He's willing to run errands, as well."

"What kind of errands?" Brooke said as a shiver of warning raced through her.

"Going to the grocery store and all. Nothing big. But each little bit helps me a lot," said her mother. "Oh, here he is now. He wants to speak to you."

"Hello? Is this Brooke? I'm Jamie. No need to worry about your mother. She's in good hands. But feel free to check on her anytime."

"Oh, okay, thanks," she said, her mind racing.

"Brooke?" said her mother. "I've got to go. I'm working on a special project for work. Talk to you later."

"Goodbye, Mom. I'm thrilled things are going well for you. I'll talk to you later." Brooke ended the call and sat back on her bed. Her mother had sounded as if she didn't need Brooke anymore. That was such a switch. Lying there, Brooke decided she liked it.

She could hardly wait to visit the Sarasota Art Museum with Dylan. After a somber morning, it would be a relief to let past worries go and enjoy this new opportunity to learn more about art being shown in the area.

Dylan picked her up at Gran's house. "Ready to go? Do you have to be back for the Inn's social hour?"

"Not today. Livy is in charge."

"I'm glad, because while we're in Sarasota, we might want to try out a new restaurant I heard about. Nothing fancy."

"That sounds like fun." Brooke watched her weight, but a tasty meal was important to her.

On the drive to Sarasota, Brooke quizzed Dylan on his education. He'd attended college at The Rhode Island School of Design in Rhode Island, graduating from RISD with a BFA in painting. Listening to him talk about some of his teachers and classes, Brooke felt a pang of regret that she'd never pursued art. She'd loved it as a kid. But then, if she hadn't had her steady, practical job as an accountant, saving as much money as she could, she wouldn't be able to spend this time here in Florida.

The Sarasota Art Museum on the Ringling College Museum Campus was located in the Old Sarasota High building, an historic landmark.

As she followed Dylan inside, Brooke's heart pounded. She closed her eyes for a moment and then opened them, excited to simply be there.

For the next two hours she absorbed as much as she could of the different media, shapes, and colors. She loved an exhibit combining contemporary weaving with Native American traditions. At one point she sat on the wooden floor and just stared at a colorful painting.

Dylan walked over to her and sat down beside her. "What are you doing?"

"Staring," she said. "All these colors and the way the artist portrays his people. It's all so inspiring."

"Yes, and his social statements are important too," said Dylan quietly.

When other visitors entered the room, he held out his hand to her.

She took it and felt herself lifted to her feet, feeling as if she'd visited another world.

Dylan kept hold of her hand as they walked into another room and then released it, giving her freedom to walk around on her own.

Later, sitting in a small bistro not far away, Brooke let out a long sigh. "Thank you, Dylan, for bringing me to the museum. I loved every minute of it."

"Especially the time you spent on the floor?" he said, giving her a gentle smile.

A grin spread across her face at the memory. "That was the best, just feeling myself being drawn in. Your paintings tell a story too, but in a different way. I still think you should put your paintings in a gallery here in Florida."

"I like that you care that much, Brooke. Every artist needs someone like you behind them."

"I'm hoping to learn a whole lot more about the art world. Thank you for including me in yours," said Brooke, ignoring the stinging in her eyes.

"I know you'll be busy with Adam and Skye tomorrow, but after that maybe we can make another trip somewhere."

"That would be great." Brooke was happy to spend time with Adam and Skye, but she needed this time with Dylan too.

CHAPTER THIRTEEN

CHARLOTTE

On this early morning, Charlotte sat in a golf cart with Shane, pleased to have the time alone with him and his parents as they enjoyed golf. She'd never gotten into the game but knew how important it was to learn so she could play with her soon-to-be husband. Shannon told her that while Henry played with his friends, her ability to play with him as a couple was important to them both. Besides, how hard could it be? Seeing Shane with his father and stepmother brought a sense of relief to Charlotte. She had cried along with everyone else in the chapel when Shane delivered his remarks about his mother. She knew what it was like to win a parent's affection. She and her mother had formed a decent relationship, but it was nothing like the warm, accepting one she'd always wanted.

After their round of golf, the four of them sat in the clubhouse sipping coffee and eating a light breakfast.

Henry smiled at her. "It's a pleasure to have you with us, Charlotte. Did we destroy your wish to learn?"

She laughed. "I know it'll take time, but I love the idea of playing golf together."

"Okay, then," said Henry. "To start you off right, I'll be pleased to buy the equipment you need." Shannon murmured to him, and he said, smiling, "Anything, but the clothes."

They all laughed, but Charlotte felt warm inside at Henry's offer.

"Thanks, Dad," said Shane. "A nice gesture on your part."

"I expect Shannon and I will be visiting here more often, now that you and Austin are both spending time at the cove."

"Yes, that's the hope," said Shannon. "The kids at home keep us pretty busy, but we want to be with our Florida children, as well."

Though not another word was said, Charlotte knew they, like her, were comparing Diana to Shannon.

CHAPTER FOURTEEN

BROOKE

After helping with guests in the morning and working on the financials, Brooke headed over to Mimi's house for lunch with Adam and Skye. Afterwards, they were taking Skye to the Children's Museum in Tampa. Mimi had suggested it, and both Adam and she had readily agreed.

When they'd met in late May, Brooke was curious about him. She loved Skye and the idea of a family. But then, she was rediscovering herself in a new way and wasn't sure what she wanted.

Mimi fussed about lunch, offering a selection of sandwiches, homemade pickles, chips and cake that she and Skye had made together that morning.

"Everything's delicious. Thank you, Mimi," said Brooke dabbing the last of the icing off her lips. "This will do for both lunch and dinner."

"It's the least I can do. You're giving me the afternoon and evening off," she said, ruffling Skye's curls.

"Do you want to come with us, Mimi?" asked Skye looking concerned.

"Thanks, but I'm leaving this adventure to the three of you. See you later. Have fun," she said before leaving.

Adam stood and gave Brooke a wide smile. "Thanks for agreeing to come to the children's museum." He winked. "It should be fun."

"Actually, I'll enjoy it," she responded. "Sometimes I think

I should've been a kindergarten teacher. I love this age." She picked up her bag and followed him to the car.

"I hear you're interested in art. Dylan says you've got talent," said Adam, after she and Skye were seated in his rental car and he'd slid behind the wheel.

"I don't know about talent, but I'm definitely interested in art. You must be too. If you're a contractor, you're an artist too."

He looked surprised and then grinned. "Never thought of it that way. Brendan and I always built things as kids, so it seemed natural to set up business together. Now, though, he wants to buy me out."

"What do you think of that? Are you happy about it?"

"It might work out well. I'm thinking of moving here and starting my own company. Lots of work in the area, and it will be satisfying to be on my own."

"I know that idea thrills Mimi," said Brooke.

He cocked an eyebrow. "Guess whose idea it was?"

They laughed together.

"Daddy, when are we going to get there?" asked Skye from the backseat, where her car seat had been locked in.

"It won't be too long. Look out the window and tell me what you see."

"I'll help you," said Brooke.

After playing a game about letters they saw in signs along the road, they finally arrived at the museum.

Much later, Adam picked up Skye who was still playing in the Clock Factory. "Time to go, Princess."

Skye began to fuss but quickly settled in her father's arms. It had been a fun afternoon of interactive play, but they'd all had enough. Brooke wasn't surprised when Skye fell asleep on the way back to the cove.

A comfortable silence reigned in the car. Brooke was content to look out at the scenery, pleased that Adam wasn't someone who needed to fill the quiet with chatter.

"While I'm back here at the cove, I'm hoping to get to know you better," he said. "I was able to think about a lot of things while I was away, and I'm more open to moving on with my life. The fact that Skye is very fond of you is important to me."

"I'd like to get to know you better, too," said Brooke, hoping she didn't sound as awkward as she felt.

He reached over and clasped her hand. "It would mean a lot to both Skye and me."

"Yes, I know. She's a darling child," said Brooke with feeling. "You've done a nice job with her."

"Thanks. She's been my world."

"Yes, I can see that." The bond between Skye and him was strong, lovely.

Adam pulled into the driveway of Mimi's house and turned to her. "Thanks for coming with us. Would you like to go out to dinner tomorrow?"

Pleased by the idea, Brooke said, "Thanks, I would. It has to be fairly late because I'm on duty tomorrow."

He frowned. "That's right. I forget you're working for your grandmother this summer. Let's say eight o'clock and we'll go find someplace casual, maybe find some other cove kids. Okay?"

"Yes. I'll be ready. Thanks again. See you later." She got out of the car and headed to the Inn wondering why she was feeling so unsettled. Adam was a handsome man, a good father, and pleasant to be around. But she wasn't sure she wanted a relationship with him.

But the next afternoon when Adam strolled into the gathering as she'd suggested, her heart raced at the sight of him. He was a tall, broad, athletic man with brown hair that curled enough to be interesting and blue eyes that sparkled with mischief. As a kid visiting in the cove, he'd been a natural leader in the games they'd played. And fair to everyone. He still had that air of caring about him.

He saw her and walked over. "You have a big crowd tonight. Looks like your PR campaign is working."

"Yes," she said proudly. "We're getting more and more reservations for both short-and long-term stays. Charlie, Livy, and I are pretty excited about it."

Holly Willis, the young girl they'd hired to help with these evening parties, carried a tray of appetizers over to them.

Adam took one and then another. "Delicious," he said, smiling at Holly. "Thanks."

"You're welcome," Holly said as she moved away.

"Excuse me, Adam," said Brooke. "I see some new arrivals and need to speak to them." She walked over to a young couple who'd arrived with a baby. After making sure they had everything they needed for them and the baby, Brooke made her way through the crowd, speaking to as many people as she could. A captive, satisfied group was a real chance for scoring points and making PR inroads.

When the crowd had thinned, Brooke checked her watch. Time to change for her date.

On her way back to Gran's house, she bumped into Dylan.

"Just the person I wanted to see," he said. "Tomorrow I'm going back to the Dali Museum in St. Petersburg. Care to join me?"

"I'd love it," she said.

"What are you doing tonight?" Dylan said.

"Adam and I are going out, but why don't you join us? We'll see if Livy is free and she can come too. I'm sure Adam won't mind."

"Okay, sounds like a plan. What time?"

"Eight o'clock. I'll talk to Livy and let you know."

Brooke picked up her phone and texted Livy. In seconds, she had a positive reply. She noticed her mother had called but hadn't left a message. She let it go.

The Tropical Breeze Bar was similar to the Pink Pelican in layout with a less defined décor. A few shells, nets, and other seaside fixtures were placed on walls to give it some flavor but basically it was a simple bar with indoor and outside seating.

Tonight, the four of them decided to enjoy the cool air outside. They sat on the deck beside the sandy beach that had been cleared of debris for dancing. A few couples were already barefoot on the sand dancing to the music from strategically-placed speakers.

Their table was one of several that lined the edge of the deck where they could capture the onshore, salty breeze that was a blessing after the heat of the day. Brooke sat opposite Adam where she could get a look at him. He'd dressed in a light-green golf shirt and tan slacks. Next to him, Dylan wore a Hawaiian shirt in a bold green color and jeans. Livy, as usual, looked adorable in a lacy white top and a short denim skirt.

Brooke realized some of her old, plain clothes were boring and had spent some of her precious money on new, bright-colored items to liven up her wardrobe. Tonight, she wore a purple sundress that went well with her hair. No more beige, brown, and black for her.

They ordered beers and burgers and sat back and watched dancers on the sand.

While Livy chatted with Adam, Dylan leaned over to Brooke. "Want to dance?"

"Sure." This was another part of her plan for becoming the new person she hoped to be. No more shyness about dancing. She'd get out there and do her best.

Out on the sand, she moved to the beat and soon got into it, letting go, whirling and stepping to the music that flowed around her. She looked at Dylan and laughed for the pure joy of it.

The music suddenly shifted into a slow number. Dylan held out his arms and Brooke moved into them.

"You look beautiful tonight," he said into her ear.

A shiver of pleasure moved down her spine. He made her feel tingly all over. She stepped back and gaped at him, just as Adam tapped on her shoulder.

"Livy wanted to dance with Dylan, and I want to dance with you." Adam pulled her closer and swayed to the music, moving in rhythm with easy grace. His large, strong body wrapped around her made her feel small and protected, but there were no tingles.

The music ended, and they faced one another with smiles.

"Our food has arrived," Dylan announced, leading Livy to the table.

Brooke and Adam followed, and when they all sat down everyone seemed happy.

On the way home, the moon was a glowing globe in the dark sky. A perfect evening. She looked out at the passing scenery and admired the palm trees along the way. The setting was very different from what she was used to seeing, and she loved it. Her thoughts drifted to her mother and she promised herself to check on her soon.

Adam pulled his car up to Gran's house and turned to her. "Thanks, Brooke. Let's try to do this again."

She hesitated, not sure if he'd try to kiss her, but when he made no move, she hopped out of the car. "Thanks. See you tomorrow."

Livy and Dylan were standing outside talking.

Brooke hurried into the house, her emotions in turmoil. She wanted Adam to kiss her but didn't want their first kiss to take place inside a car with her friends hanging around outside it. Then she felt relieved that he hadn't even tried, because thoughts of Dylan and the way he made her feel kept interrupting.

In her room, Brooke lifted off her sundress and studied herself in the mirror. She'd lost a little weight, had gained a suntan, and looked the best she had in a long time. Her purple-streaked hair and the seashell tattoo above her ankle pleased her with their show of independence.

Livy knocked on the door and cracked it open. "You okay?"

Brooke turned to her. "Yes. Just a little confused."

"Want to talk about it?" Livy asked.

"Sure. Come on in," said Brooke sitting on the edge of her bed.

Livy walked in and lowered herself on the bed beside Brooke. "What's going on?"

"It's Adam and Dylan. I like them both. I thought Adam was going to kiss me when he brought me home, but he pulled back and I knew I should just leave. I wasn't sure if I was disappointed or relieved,"

"And Dylan?" Livy's gaze penetrated Brooke.

"I have so much fun when I'm with him. It just feels natural being with him. Exciting, too," Brooke responded. "But Adam and Skye need me. You know?"

"What I do know is that both men are attracted to you. My advice? Let things roll out the way they're supposed to happen."

"You're right. I've been stung by relationships in the past, I don't want to get caught again in daydreams that might never happen," said Brooke. "Is that why you decided not to get involved with anyone?"

Livy looked at her and glanced away. "Maybe. I don't think I want to be more than friends with any of the guys here. I had a bad experience with Wayne, and I have no desire to get in a relationship right now. It's too much trouble."

Brooke took hold of Livy's hand. "Anything I can do for you?"

Livy shook her head. "It's just going to take time. Being here this summer is perfect for me."

"I agree. Being here, helping Gran and John, is wonderful for me too. I haven't talked to my mother in a while, and she hasn't called. It makes me realize how important it is to have our own separate lives."

"Good for you," said Livy. "That's what we all wish for the two of you." She got to her feet. "I'd better get to bed. I have to be up early tomorrow."

"I haven't forgotten I promised to help you because Billy Bob has a day off." Brooke rose and gave her cousin a quick squeeze. "Thanks for your support."

"Of course," said Livy, and left the room.

As Brooke continued to get ready for bed, she thought of Livy and Charlotte. Having grown up in varying circumstances, the three were very different. But they'd had Gran bringing them together. Brooke would always be grateful to her.

CHAPTER FIFTEEN

BROOKE

Brooke was beginning to like the morning routine of greeting guests and making them feel welcome at the Inn. She'd always been a little shy, a little unsure around men she didn't know, and this activity was making her more comfortable with people. Another crack in her old image. One she was proud of.

After the last guest had been served breakfast, the last local map given away, the last restaurant reservation made, Brooke went into the kitchen to check in with Livy.

Livy gave her a quick wave as she wiped down the stove. Mary was handwashing some pots and pans. Juan had already gone home.

'I'm going to take a quick walk on the beach before heading into the office," said Brooke. "When is Charlie getting here?"

"This afternoon. On her way back from Miami, she's stopping at the printers in St. Petersburg to pick up business cards, letterhead, and envelopes with the new logo for the Inn."

"As soon as I get back, I'll check the website for new queries and reservations." Brooke felt as if with their hard work, they'd climbed a mountain together. "I can't believe how well our campaign is doing. We're getting new reservations almost daily."

"Charlie sure is talented. The website is irresistible with the new logo and photos and the new summer discount programs we're promoting."

"I wonder what Gran and John will decide about selling the Inn after seeing all these changes." Livy caught her lip. "I really don't want them to sell, but I'm not sure if I'm ready to manage the Inn myself. How about you?"

Brooke shrugged. "I'm not ready to consider it seriously. We have several weeks to go. The last email we got from Gran said they weren't sure when they were coming back."

"Even if Charlie continues to handle PR for the Inn, she won't be living here helping with the daily duties," said Livy. "There's so much to think about."

"I'm going to give you your own advice," said Brooke, nudging her cousin. "Let's just relax and enjoy ourselves."

Livy laughed. "You're right. We'll have plenty of time to worry later."

"I'll be back soon," said Brooke. "By the way, I checked with Beryl earlier. She and her crew are set to meet the housekeeping schedule. Bless her heart, she's such a treasure. Gran and John are lucky to have her and Amby. They're worth every penny they're being paid."

"Absolutely," Livy said. "I'll check in with you later."

Brooke left the kitchen and walked down to the beach. It was going to be another hot, steamy day, but for now, she intended to enjoy a pleasant breeze before heading back to the office.

As usual, she was drawn to her special shelling spot on the beach and walked right to it, as full of anticipation as she'd been as a child. There was something magical about finding a perfect little shell among the pile of shattered ones. She glanced down at her tattoo, thinking it would always be a reminder of this summer and the changes she was making.

At the sound of her name being called, Brooke turned. Observing Skye running toward her, she bent and opened her arms to her. Behind Skye, Adam strode forward with a smile on his face.

Skye hugged her tight as Brooke rose to her feet. "Are you looking for shells too?" Brooke asked Skye, aware that Adam now stood with them.

"Yes, my daddy said I could hunt for some pink ones. Mimi and I are making pictures with them," said Skye, wiggling to get down.

Brooke laughed and gave her a pat on the bum as Skye landed on her feet.

Adam gave her a look of approval. "You're very good with her."

"She's a special little girl," Brooke said, meaning it. "Thanks again for last night. It was fun."

"Yeah, I thought so too," said Adam. "Maybe tonight we could go out, just the two of us."

"That would be great," said Brooke. She wanted the chance to sort through her feelings about him. They were just friends. They'd never really had a date. Only when they were alone would she have a better idea about him.

Adam looked down at her ankle. "You got a tattoo?"

"Yes," she answered proudly. "Charlie and Livy got one too. It's a sign of our summer freedom. I've never wanted one before, but I figured why not?"

"Do I get a sense of rebellion here?" Adam said, his lips curving in such a way his entire face lit.

Brooke's breath caught. He was such a handsome man. But she wanted to know what was beneath that surface. She knew he was a nice guy, a doting father, but why had he been eager to get away from the cove, leaving Skye behind? Was it all business like he said or something more?

"My cousins and I wanted to do something to commemorate this summer and our bond," Brooke said. "It's just lucky circumstances that we're here supporting one another."

His brow wrinkled. "What did you used to call yourselves?"

Brooke laughed. "The three musketeers. We thought we were very cool."

"Nothing wrong with that. You're quite a trio, as Mimi says."

"It's been fun being here. That's for sure," said Brooke.

"From here to where?" Adam said.

Brooke shook her head. "I don't know. I'm leaving it open-ended."

"Daddy! Come look. I found a funny one," Skye called to him.

They walked over to check on her.

Skye held up a slimy piece of seaweed that had washed ashore.

Adam knelt beside Skye and held the seaweed in his hand as he explained what it was. Seeing him like that, a pang went through Brooke. Often as a child she'd wished for a father just like Adam.

He stood and faced her. "We could try the Pink Pelican or go to a Mexican place in Clearwater tonight."

"Let's try Mexican for a change," she said. She'd bought a silver and turquoise necklace that she'd wear with her new flowered long skirt and turquoise top.

He grinned. "Okay. I'll pick you up at seven. Skye should be settled for the evening with Mimi."

"Sounds great. Thanks. 'Bye, Skye."

Brooke turned to walk away and hadn't gone far when Skye ran up to her. "Kiss! I want a kiss!"

Laughing, Brooke bent over and kissed Skye on the cheek, wondering if this is what it would be like if things got serious between Adam and her.

###

Still thinking of Adam and Skye, Brooke returned to the office and decided to call her mother. She was startled when a male voice answered.

"Hello? Who is this?" Brooke asked.

"Jamie Murphy, her nurse."

Brooke's heart fell. "Is she ill? I thought she was feeling better."

"She's working and asked me to get the phone," said Jamie.

"If she's well and working, why are you there?" asked Brooke, unsettled.

"Jo says she always feels better when I'm here. I don't mind," Jamie said smoothly.

Alarm bells rang in Brooke's mind. All nurse's aides and nurses were friendly but maintained a professional distance. This didn't sound like that at all. "May I speak to my mother?"

"Hold on. I'll see if she'll take the call."

Brooke worried as she waited. She knew talking with her mother would calm her fears. After what seemed a long time, Jamie returned. "Sorry. Your mother says she's busy working and she'll call you later."

"Okay. Tell her I'm expecting the call right after she finishes her work. Thank you."

Brooke hung up, frowning. On a whim, she decided to call the nursing service.

When she was finally connected to the office of the director, Brooke was wondering if it was right for her to check up on her mother. This summer was supposed to be a time when they became independent of one another.

The director, Betty Hardwick, spoke in a cheery voice. "Hello, Brooke. It's been a while. Everything all right at home?"

"I think so, but I wanted to talk to you about one of your

nurses, Jamie Murphy. He's been helping Mom. When I called her, he said Mom was busy working and would call me back. I don't know. Something seems a little off."

"What did you say the nurse's name was?" Betty asked.

"Jamie. Jamie Murphy."

"Hmmm. He hasn't been working for us for several months. He went out on his own." Betty sighed. "It happens, but it isn't entirely honest to take a client list with you when you leave. How did your mother know to call him? Our records show that he was never assigned to her."

"I don't know," Brooke said, her throat becoming dry. What was going on with her mother?

"Call if you need us," said Betty. "Your mother is a lovely person. I'd hate for anyone to take advantage of her."

"Me, too. Thanks." Brooke clicked off the call and sat a moment, trying to think of what to do. She punched in her mother's number and waited.

"Hello," said Jamie. "It's you again."

"Yes, it's me again and I need to speak to my mother now. Not later, but now," she said, her voice as firm as she could make it.

"Hold on. She's in her office. I'll take the phone to her," said Jamie.

Brooke tapped her finger on her desk as she waited, growing more and more upset. When she finally heard her mother's voice, she drew in a deep breath. "Mom, I need you to tell me what's going on? You've hired a nurse who isn't with the agency we normally use. How did that happen?"

"Honestly, Brooke, what are you trying to do? Make trouble? Jamie called to see if I needed any help when I was feeling down. He's been with me ever since. With him around, I don't feel so isolated, so alone."

"What hours is he working?" Brooke asked, a suspicion

growing in her mind. One she didn't like.

"He's here pretty much every day," her mother admitted. "On his free time, we watch television together, and he's a great cook."

"You mean he eats dinner with you too?" Brooke lowered her voice. "Does he spend the night there too?"

"Heavens, Brooke. Where did you come up with that nonsense? We're friends," her mother said, a defensive tone entering her voice.

"We don't have a budget for friends," said Brooke. "We've set aside money for monthly medical bills. We can't spend more than we have."

"It's no longer *we,* Brooke. You've abandoned that part of our deal. Besides, I've told you, Jamie often spends hours here without charging. We enjoy one another's company," said her mother. "Now, if you'll excuse me, I must get back to work."

"But Mom ..." Brooke began and then realized her mother had already ended the call.

Brooke set down her phone, got up from her chair, and walked to the window. Looking out at the waves rolling in and pulling away, she felt her heartbeat begin to slow. Life would go on, if in a different way. This is what she wanted, wasn't it? Complete freedom from the care of her mother. How she wished Gran was here to talk to. But no matter how worried she was about her mother she wouldn't interrupt Gran's vacation with her concerns.

The office phone rang. Sighing, she picked up the receiver and forced cheerfulness to her voice. "The Sanderling Cove Inn. How may I help you?"

"Hi, this is Laura Benson. I live in Tampa and recently read about weddings at your Inn on your website. I know this is a long shot, but by any chance do you have time available in two weeks for a small one?"

Caught off guard, Brooke hesitated. Then, smiling with pleasure, she said, "As a matter of fact, we do. When would you like to meet with us to discuss it?"

"Can my fiancé and I come tomorrow?" Laura said.

"Of course. Why don't you come in the morning? Say, ten o'clock," Brooke said. Charlotte should be back from Miami and Billy Bob would be back from his day off. That should give them all time to work on this unexpected opportunity.

"Okay, see you then. I know this is a rush situation, and I really appreciate your willingness to take it on," gushed Laura.

"No problem. We're always happy to help guests," Brooke said, wondering how in the world they could pull this off.

CHAPTER SIXTEEN

LIVY

Livy sat in Gran's kitchen with Charlotte and Brooke, her mind spinning. A wedding cake and appetizers would be no problem, but if lunch or dinner was included, it might be another story. She'd never worked with the kitchen staff on such an undertaking.

"I knew changes to the website would bring results," said Charlotte. "This is a whole segment of business Gran and John have let go. We aren't equipped to do big weddings, but we certainly can put on small ones with style."

"It's helpful that the gazebo has been repainted," said Brooke. "We also need to make sure the side garden is at its best in case they choose a ceremony there."

"What about one on the beach?" Livy asked, aware that's where she'd choose to have a ceremony if the time ever came for her.

"Let me find Beryl and see what she knows about past weddings here," said Charlotte.

"Okay. This might be especially interesting for you, Charlie, in helping you to plan your own," said Livy.

"My mother thinks I'm going to get married in New York," Charlotte said. "The thought of it makes me queasy."

"Well, then, go find Beryl and let's get this organized," said Brooke.

Later, after they'd made a list of things including possible locations that needed some attention at the Inn, they started another that addressed food and drink choices, and still another with room selections and package prices, Livy got to her feet. "Okay, time for celebratory lemonades. Hopefully this is the beginning of something wonderful at the Inn." She wondered what Gran would think of all this. And if small weddings worked, would they be foolish not to try dinners at the Inn?

CHAPTER SEVENTEEN

BROOKE

Brooke took a deep breath as the time drew near to meet with Laura, the bride. Both Livy and Charlotte were busy with morning routines, so it was up to her to sell Laura on the idea of holding her wedding at the Inn. Earlier, she'd debated calling her mother and decided not to. Her mother had been less than happy about her call, and like everyone told her, it was time for them to be on their own.

When she finally heard Laura outside the office talking to Charlotte, she rose and went to greet her.

A tall, striking blonde, Laura Benson was accompanied by a dark-haired man taller than Laura by quite a bit, and Brooke wondered if he played sports.

Charlotte turned to her. "Brooke, this is Laura Benson and Jonathan Scott, her fiancé. This is Brooke Weatherby, my cousin, and the person you spoke to on the phone yesterday, Laura. She'll be handling the details for you."

"Thanks, Charlie," said Brooke. She led them to the sideboard in the dining room. "Please feel free to help yourselves to the coffee, tea, juice, and water. You'll definitely want to try our cinnamon sweet rolls. Then we can go to my office."

They all carried cups of coffee into the office, and then Brooke sat behind the desk and pulled out the questionnaire she and her cousins had prepared.

She wrote in their names and then turned to the couple.

"Laura, you said you heard about us online. Anywhere else?"

Laura and Jonathan looked at one another and shook their heads.

"We actually were looking for a place to stay after getting married at the courthouse. Then, when I saw you provided wedding services, we talked about getting married here," said Laura.

"Having one here is more like what Laura originally wanted," said Jonathan. He reached over and squeezed her hand. "The thing is our families don't support our wishes to get married."

A shadow crossed his face.

"Jonathan's parents don't approve of me because I'm divorced," said Laura. "They're devout Catholics."

"They also believe I shouldn't have broken off with my long-time girlfriend, the daughter of friends of theirs." He shook his head. "That relationship was never going to work."

"That's why we want a small wedding with just a couple of friends to join us. My parents are divorced, and it was going to be messy to choose who should be invited. Another reason to keep it low key."

"I'm sorry to hear that," said Brooke, "but I'm delighted that we can help you put together a really sweet occasion. Let me show you around, and then we can talk about what you want in depth."

Brooke introduced them to Livy in the kitchen. "She's the best baker I know. She can make a cake you won't believe."

"It's a pleasure to have you here," said Livy. "When the time comes, we can talk about food."

"Great," said Laura, smiling.

As Brooke walked them through the property, a sense of pride filled her. The Inn was lovely and even more so after the finishing touches the three cousins had added over the last several weeks.

When Laura saw the gazebo, she turned to Jonathan. “This is where I want to get married. How about you? Do you like the idea?”

He put an arm around her. “Whatever you want, honey. I just want you to be happy.”

Brooke sighed. They were such a sweet couple.

Once a place had been chosen, everything fell in line. They wanted a late morning ceremony, so they could get to Miami for the night. From there, they were going to the Bahamas for a couple of days and then back to Tampa and their jobs. Laura was a legal assistant, and Jonathan worked in an insurance office.

That afternoon, Brooke, Livy, and Charlotte all worked on the plan. Brooke arranged for flowers as Laura had requested, Livy worked on a simple luncheon menu to be served in the private dining room, and Charlotte worked on a plan to convert one of the guestrooms into a bridal retreat for Laura and her two friends who were going to stand up with her. Jonathan would be assigned to another room for the day so he, a brother, and a friend, along with the minister they’d chosen, would have a place to change their clothes and prepare for the ceremony. Having rooms available for daytime use only was something new they added to the budget of the package.

When Brooke got off the phone with the florist, she waved the others over. “Guess what? Rosalie Sweetwater, the owner of Tropi-Flowers, is willing to work with us on this wedding and others in the future. She suggested placing a floral rope along the gazebo’s balustrade. Laura gave us a budget that almost covers the cost. I say we pay the extra cost, take lots of pictures, and get her to place a recommendation on the website in exchange for the extras.”

"Excellent idea," said Charlotte. "That's how we can build this business."

"What if Gran and John want to sell the Inn?" Livy said.

"Proving how solid the business is can add a lot of value," said Charlotte, "but honestly, I hope we can work something out so it stays in the family."

"I'm excited about this," said Brooke.

"You're such a romantic." Livy shook her head.

"Brooke's right. This is a perfect place for a wedding," said Charlotte. "Shane and I have been talking about one on the beach sometime in the future."

"This year?" asked Livy.

"We don't know. Everything has happened very fast, and I just want to enjoy being engaged," said Charlotte. She held out her left hand and studied the diamond on her finger. "It all seems surreal."

"One small step at a time," said Livy. "So far, it's been a giant leap."

Charlotte laughed, and they all joined in.

That evening, Brooke was still feeling romantic when Adam picked her up to go out. She was touched to see that he wore what looked like a new golf shirt in blue that matched his eyes. His brown hair, still wet from a shower, curled softly around his face. Feeling giddy with excitement, Brooke wondered if their relationship would turn into something serious as it had for Charlie and Shane. But then, she reminded herself, Adam was a wounded man, not likely to trust something that moved too fast.

"Ready to go?" Adam gazed at her with approval.

"Yes, and thanks," she said, brushing a non-existent crumb off her new turquoise top. A long skirt with a pretty tropical floral design and new, turquoise high-heel sandals completed her outfit.

"Skye told me to tell you she's found a special shell for you," said Adam. He shook his head. "I don't know what the two of you have going on between you, but it's great. She really likes you."

"And I really like her," Brooke said easily. "She's a darling little girl who's sweet and well-behaved."

"Overall, she's an easy kid to be around. Once in a while we have our disagreements about how things should be done, but as long as I'm consistent, it works."

She looked at him with new respect. "That's cool. Where did you learn all that?"

"By doing and failing and doing again," he said, chuckling. "That kid never forgets a thing."

Adam helped her into his car and slid behind the driver's wheel. "Does the Mex Café sound okay? Their food is terrific."

"Yes, I'm looking forward to it."

They headed north on Gulf Drive into Clearwater Beach.

Adam pulled into a parking lot next to a small, unassuming place and turned to her. "Don't be put off by the appearance. I promise you the food is delicious."

"No problem. The food is what I'm interested in." Her stomach growled, and they both laughed.

"We'd better get you inside," teased Adam. "Wait right there."

Adam got out of the car, ran around the back, and opened her car door for her.

Brooke felt special receiving this treatment. There was a lot to be said for dating an older man used to doing things like this. And Dylan had done the same thing for her. Though the two men were cousins, they'd received the same kind of upbringing.

Inside, the interior walls were painted a bright golden yellow. Sombreros and plastic cacti hung from them added an air of gaiety with no pretense. It was all about the food. Smelling it, Brooke's mouth watered. It was easy to find TexMex food, not as easy to find the more authentic meals.

A waitress seated them at a table near the window where they could watch people walking by. After taking their orders for drinks, she returned with menus, nacho chips, and two bowls of salsa, one red, the other green.

The minute Brooke tasted the nacho with the green salsa, she let out a soft moan. "This is delicious."

Adam laughed. "That's only the beginning."

Brooke ordered a chicken mole dish. Adam chose a beef carnitas meal, sat back and sipped his beer, then gazed at her.

"I hear you're going to host a wedding at the Inn. My grandmother is letting Livy borrow some recipes."

"Mimi's a wonderful cook. Some of her recipes will be perfect for the small, intimate luncheon that will follow the ceremony." Brooke clasped her hands together. "It's going to be very romantic. The ceremony will take place in the gazebo."

"Is that what the table I'm making is for?" Adam said.

"Yes. We need something simple to hold candles, flowers, and a bible."

"I can do that for you and paint it if you like," said Adam. "I enjoy doing stuff like that. Sam Ensley has a great collection of tools, and Granny Liz has already given me permission to work over there."

"So, Dylan can keep his studio in Mimi's garage? Both of you are very talented," said Brooke. "It must run in the family."

"I hear you're pretty talented yourself. Dylan told me you have real color sense."

Brooke swallowed her beer and felt a sting in her eyes. It

felt so exhilarating to have this new side of hers recognized. It made her feel as if she was more interesting.

Their meals came, and while they ate, they chatted about Skye, her latest accomplishments, and what school choices there were in Florida for her if Adam decided to stay.

"I have a lot to think about, but moving to Florida is a real possibility," said Adam. "My ex is still around back home. I think it's healthier for both Skye and me to be gone."

"That makes sense," said Brooke. "After being away from New York, I definitely don't want to go back."

"How's your mother doing?" Adam asked.

Brooke set down her fork. "I'm not sure. She sounds different, acts more independent. She actually was annoyed with me for checking in with her."

"Wow. From what I've heard about the situation, that's a big change."

"Yes," said Brooke. "But it's all healthy."

"I guess so," said Adam. "She has some home care, doesn't she?"

"Yes. That's my concern. The nurse helping her is a man who quit the nursing service we normally use. He's gone out on his own and is using past clients of the service as his own. I talked to the owner, and she wasn't happy about it."

"That kind of thing happens, but it doesn't make it right," said Adam. "I'd keep an eye on things."

"I intend to," said Brooke, "but I also intend to keep to our new agreement and call her only every few days."

"One reason I'm considering the move to Florida is to be here for Mimi. She's aging and will need more and more help with the house. Like all the families in the cove, she doesn't want to leave there."

"That's because it's a special, close-knit community. It's amazing, isn't it, how we all get along," said Brooke.

"Yes," he agreed, lifting his glass of beer in a salute to her. "Very special."

Brooke took another bite of food, savoring its flavor and wondered what it might be like if both Adam and she continued to remain at the cove after the others left.

As if he sensed her thoughts, he smiled at her, sending a frisson of excitement through her.

Later, as they drove home, both Adam and she were quiet. But it was the kind of silence that was peaceful after sharing a wonderful meal. She looked out at the scenery loving the fact that it was far different from her hometown.

Adam turned to her. "I know it's fairly early, but you won't mind if I call it a night after delivering you home, will you? I have to get up early tomorrow. I promised Skye I'd go shelling with her."

Brooke shook her head agreeably. "I don't mind. I have to get up early too. We have lots of work to do to get ready for the weekend."

"I was sure you'd agree to an early night. We can do it differently next time." He cocked his eyebrows. "If you agree to one?"

"I'd like that," she said.

They pulled up to Gran's house.

Adam turned to her. "Thanks for a great evening." He leaned forward and kissed her briefly on the lips. "I'll call you to set another time."

"Okay," she said and was surprised when he kissed her again, this time a little longer. Before she could wonder what would happen next, he pulled away. "I like you, Brooke. A lot."

"I enjoyed tonight, Adam," she responded, turning to the door and grasping the handle.

"Hold on. I'll get that door for you," said Adam.

"No problem. I've got it, but thanks," she said, and climbed out of the car.

He gave her a wave and backed out of the driveway, leaving her standing there. Disappointed but relieved at the same time that his kiss hadn't been something more. She understood that dating Adam was going to involve a lot of time learning to trust one another.

CHAPTER EIGHTEEN

CHARLOTTE

Charlotte was thrilled with the idea of holding a wedding at the Inn. While they were working on Laura's, Charlotte was thinking of her own. Though her mother wanted a big New York social event, Charlotte didn't. Shane had money and social standing, but he was someone who, like her, detested that was how people wanted to identify him. He was a down-to-earth guy who wanted their special day to be everything she wanted, not her mother. For that, she was grateful.

On the morning of the wedding, Charlotte worked with Dylan photographing the cake Livy had made. They placed it in different settings with different lighting to get the best result. Three tiers with white, lacy icing, the cake was decorated with real tropical flowers. Though Laura and Jonathan hadn't asked for this in their package, they'd be presented with this one.

From there, Charlotte and Dylan moved to the gazebo where Rosalie Sweetwater and an assistant were draping floral ropes along the balustrade. Charlotte had already promised Rosalie several photographs for her own use. Brooke had selected pink, orange, and red flowers, which offset the white paint of the gazebo with stunning bright colors that matched the flowers Laura selected.

Jonathan walked over to them. "Wow, this is beautiful. Laura will be thrilled. She and her friend, Ginger, are getting their hair done, but when she sees this, believe me, she's going to cry."

Charlotte smiled at him. "We're very excited to have your wedding here. This is the first one my cousins and I are putting on, and we're going a bit overboard. But we're happy to do this for you."

"We appreciate it." He turned as a man with red hair walked toward them. "Here's my friend, Rob Clausen. He and his wife, Ginger, arrived late last night. They're standing up for us for the ceremony."

"How nice," Charlotte said. Introductions were made all around, and then the men left to get ready.

"Are you getting excited for your own?" Dylan asked her.

Charlotte's cheeks turned a pretty pink. "I don't know when it will be. Now that we're engaged, Shane and I don't want to rush into anything."

"I get it," said Dylan. He looked up when Brooke walked toward them.

Charlotte saw the way his entire face lit up and she wondered if anything was going on between them. She knew they painted together from time to time. But she also knew that Mimi was pushing for Adam to date Brooke seriously.

Deciding not to say anything, Charlotte lifted her arm and waved to her cousin.

CHAPTER NINETEEN

BROOKE

Brooke saw the smile that crossed Dylan's face and her lips curved in response. There was something irresistible about him. Probably because he was laid back, so easy to be around.

"The gazebo looks fantastic," Brooke said. "Rosalie, you've done a beautiful job with these flowers. Charlotte said we're going to do some cross promotion with you. Can't wait for people to see what you can create here."

Rosalie wiped a bead of sweat off her face. "Thanks. Our businesses just naturally fit together. Combined promos will be an excellent way to help us both."

"Yes, I agree," said Charlotte. "We've done photo shots of the cake with flowers. I'm making that part of the promo package I'm putting together for us."

Rosalie gazed around and sighed. "I've always loved The Sanderling Cove Inn. It's wonderful you women are adding new life to it. It's too beautiful a property to allow to fade away."

"We don't intend to let that happen," Brooke said, aware of the firmness in her voice, making her realize how much she wanted to stay.

"It's been part of the cove almost from the beginning," said Dylan. "Too important to let it go."

Brooke's gaze met his. His lips curved at the same time as hers.

"How are things inside?' Charlotte asked her.

"The breakfast for guests is over," Brooke said. "The private dining room is decorated and set for the luncheon. Livy has outdone herself with new recipes, but she wanted to try as many as she could. Luckily, we get to taste some of them."

"It will be a true test of how the kitchen does, as well as the serving staff," said Charlotte. "We might be putting on dinners sooner than we thought."

Brooke grinned at the idea. Gran and John were in for some surprises when they returned.

Charlotte and Dylan followed her inside the Inn to take photos of the dining room.

The table in the small dining room was covered with a white-linen cloth. Crystal glasses, shiny silverware, and silver-rimmed white dishes were part of the setting. In the middle, a small crystal bowl was filled with the same tropical flowers as those displayed at the gazebo. The look was both classy and relaxed.

Livy joined them. "I think this luncheon is going to work well. Nice and easy, but fancy enough to please everyone."

Brooke gave her cousin a hug. "Everything you make is delicious, Livy. Laura will be thrilled. For such a small group, it has everything most brides would want."

"Has the minister come?" Livy asked.

Brooke checked her watch. "He should be here soon. The ceremony is due to take place in just a few minutes."

Everyone left the dining room and waited for Jonathan and Rob to appear. A few minutes later, the two men walked into the lobby wearing matching white shorts, bright orange golf shirts, and sandals.

Brooke's surprise changed to approval. The guys looked great—comfortable and happy.

"I'll escort you to the gazebo," said Charlotte. "You're to

wait there for the bride and her matron of honor."

Charlotte departed with them, leaving Brooke and Livy to greet Laura and Ginger.

"I can't wait to see what the bride is wearing," said Brooke.

"Or her maid of honor," Livy said. "It's proving to be one of the coolest weddings I've ever seen."

"I'm getting lots of ideas for my own, if that day ever comes," said Brooke.

"Take it easy," said Livy with a playful grin. "Neither of us is even close to that."

"You're right," Brooke said, chuckling. Out of the corner of her eye, she saw movement and turned to face Laura. "Oh, Laura," she gasped with admiration.

Laura was wearing a sleeveless, ankle-length lace dress with simple clean lines. Her blond hair, pulled back into a bun of sorts, held a simple spray of red bougainvillea.

"And Ginger," exclaimed Livy. "I love your dress."

Ginger was wearing a multi-color, sleeveless muumuu with a ruffled, ankle-length hem. Her dress and colorful red hair were attractive additions to the tropical floral theme.

Both women twirled around, smiling at each other.

Dylan appeared. "Are you ready for me to take a few photos of you two and then some of the service?" he asked Laura.

"Please. Everything is lovely, and I want to have as many reminders as possible of this day," Laura said. She looked as if she was about to cry.

Brooke gave her a quick hug. "Okay, then. Let's do it." She stood aside as Dylan snapped several photos of Laura, Laura and Ginger together, and finally, of the two of them heading outdoors to the gazebo.

Livy grabbed hold of Brooke's elbow. "C'mon. I've got to see this."

They stayed in the background as Ginger moved into the

gazebo followed by Laura, but even from a distance Brooke saw the way Jonathan looked at Laura with such love her breath caught. That's what she wanted for herself.

She couldn't hear all the words being exchanged but when the minister announced Jonathan could kiss the bride, Brooke clapped along with the rest of the onlookers. Then she, like Livy, hurried inside the Inn to make sure all was ready for the luncheon. Charlotte stayed behind with Dylan to make sure more photographs were taken.

Later, after the luncheon had been cleaned up and Jonathan and Laura went to change their clothes and pack for their trip, Brooke joined Livy, Charlotte, and Dylan in the kitchen.

"I thought we and the staff would all celebrate by sharing the extra food I prepared," said Livy. "I made more than the luncheon needed just so I could try out recipes."

Dylan rubbed his stomach. "It's definitely a requirement for going forward, getting the approval from all of us."

Livy laughed then turned serious. "If anyone has any suggestions, please let me know. If we're going to launch weddings, we need to figure out what works and what doesn't." She offered them small portions of chicken breasts stuffed with a mixture of mushrooms, spinach, mozzarella, garlic, and thyme. While simple, it had color, texture, and taste. A light sauce made from the juices was drizzled on top. A lemon-herb risotto and a greenleaf lettuce salad with a balsamic vinegar and oil dressing accompanied the chicken.

Brooke was amused that after sharing what they could of the main course, everyone eyed the remains of the cake with grins. The top tier had been set aside for the bride and groom to freeze until they could pick it up after their honeymoon. But the rest was open to tasting.

The lemon cake with a raspberry and cream filling was one of the best cakes Brooke had ever tasted. The murmurs of contentment in the kitchen proved she wasn't alone. She glanced at Livy and wondered if she knew how talented she was.

Dylan caught Brooke's attention. "Good, huh?"

She laughed. "Delicious."

He moved closer. "I was wondering if you wanted to go out tonight. The Pink Pelican has a new band playing."

"Thanks. That sounds like fun," said Brooke, pleased.

"Great. I'll pick you up at seven. We can catch dinner there. Okay?"

"Perfect. The Inn's social hour should be over by then," said Brooke.

She headed into the office to meet with Charlotte and Livy. She and her cousins had talked about hiring someone in addition to Rico Torres to cover the desk for the evening hours. Maybe it was time to do so. The three of them wanted their evenings free.

That evening, waiting for Dylan to pick her up, Brooke filled with anticipation. Spending time with Dylan was always special. When he saw her in her tie-dyed top and blue jeans, he let out a slow whistle.

"Thanks." She still wasn't used to getting many compliments, but she liked it. After years of dressing in dowdy clothes, it was exciting to feel attractive.

They took off, and a short while later, Dylan pulled his red truck into the parking lot. Music from the restaurant filled the area with an exciting beat. After acting as hostess at the Inn, Brooke felt like letting loose. She climbed out of the truck and stood by as Dylan came around the back.

"Hey. I was going to get that door for you. Ready to go inside and have some fun?"

She grinned and held onto the elbow he offered her.

Inside, the place was crowded. They looked around for a spot.

Austin saw them and called out to them.

Dylan led Brooke over to Austin's table.

"Join us," said Austin. His date, a dark-haired woman, stared at them with curiosity.

When the noise softened enough to do so, Austin made the introductions. "Meet Aynsley Lynch, an old friend from the past," Austin said, smiling at her. "This is Brooke Weatherby and Dylan Hendrix, from my cove family."

Aynsley's dark eyes widened. "Dylan Hendrix, the artist?"

Dylan looked embarrassed, but he nodded.

"Oh my God. I love your work. You're showing some of your work at my friend's gallery." She beamed at Dylan and turned to Austin. "You must buy one of his pieces of art. You can afford it."

Austin gave Dylan an apologetic look. "When the time's right. I'm not even sure where I'm going to end up living."

Aynsley put her hand on Austin's arm and smiled at Brooke and Dylan. "I'm trying to convince him to buy his mother's house. It's gorgeous. And like I said earlier, he can afford it. He's one of Miami's most eligible bachelors. Too bad Shane is off the market. His fiancée must be a friend of yours from the cove. Right?" she asked Brooke.

"Actually, his fiancée is my cousin. Charlie and Shane are perfect together," Brooke said, feeling a need to defend Shane's choice. She studied Aynsley and noticed that the ring finger of her left hand was bare but a white circle in the midst of tan indicated a ring had once rested there.

She glanced at Austin, but he was smiling at Aynsley in a way that had her worried.

Dylan waved a waitress over to them. They all ordered drinks, and Dylan and she ordered dinner—a fried chicken sandwich for him, a Caesar salad for her.

"You know, you can order dressing on the side," Aynsley said to her, inspecting Brooke's body.

Brooke's brow furrowed. "Yes, I'm aware of that. I've had this salad here before, and I like it with a lot of dressing."

"Really?" said Aynsley, a look of surprise on her face. "I just worry about those calories. But, oh well, to each his own. So, where did you prep?"

"What?" Brooke said, confused.

"Where did you go to prep school? I assume all of you cove people prepped somewhere."

"Speaking for myself, I went to the local public high school in my hometown. It was a top school in the state."

"Oh," said Aynsley.

"Brooke is very smart," said Dylan, coming to her aid. "She won several school awards and a scholarship to Cornell."

Surprised Dylan knew that, Brooke glanced at him.

"What's all this business about prepping anyway?" Austin said, frowning at Aynsley.

Aynsley's lip thinned. "I just wondered...Geez, you guys are ... so protective of each other. Just relax."

"Here come our drinks and food," said Dylan, breaking the tension. "Can't wait to dig in. You should've been at the Inn today, Austin. The first wedding of the summer took place there. And we got to eat some of Livy's food. The cake was the best cake ever."

A fleeting look of envy, one Brooke almost didn't catch, crossed Austin's face, and she wondered what was going on with him.

CHAPTER TWENTY

LIVY

After the last breakfast had been served and she had time to herself, Livy wrote down some changes she wanted to make to procedures and to the recipes she'd served. She worked on figures. They'd done a lot of free things for Laura and Jonathan, but still made a profit. Seeing the facts and figures, she intended to tell Brooke and Charlotte that they needed to step up advertising for weddings. Done right, they were moneymakers.

She walked into the office and was surprised to see Jake sitting there. "Morning. What are you doing here so early?"

Jake set down the papers he held in his hand. "Just looking over financials Brooke left for me to review. She'll be here shortly."

"You didn't come into the kitchen to get a treat. Did you help yourself from the sideboard?"

He gave her a teasing grin. "Always the perfect hostess. Thanks, I'll get some coffee now. It was busy in the dining room, and I didn't want to disturb anyone."

Livy admired how considerate Jake was of everyone. No wonder his clients loved him. She watched him leave the room and thought there were other things about him to admire. The view was fantastic. She'd heard through Brooke he had a girlfriend, but if he ever asked her out, Livy knew she'd say yes. She was allowed her fantasies.

Brooke accompanied Jake back to the office. "Hey, Livy,

what's up?"

"I want to set aside time at our afternoon meeting to discuss weddings. I'm not an accountant like you and Jake, but holding them can bring in money. I want to do as many as we can."

"The way to make money with weddings is by putting heads into beds, as they say," said Jake. "But you're right, done well, they can produce some sizeable income. But you need to streamline the process with as little staff costs as possible."

"I agree, but we need to give top service, or we won't build our reputation for exceptional ones," said Livy. "I'll do more work on it and we can talk about it this afternoon, Brooke."

"All right," said Brooke, taking a seat beside Jake at his desk.

Livy left them, her mind whirling. Jake was right about selling guest rooms. Could a place as small as theirs work? She was lost in ideas as she headed to the beach. Walking the beach was a perfect way to think creatively.

She stepped onto the sand, took off her sandals, and wiggled her toes. There was something very satisfying in doing that, she thought, and looked out at the water. She loved seeing the waves rush in and pull away in a steady rhythm, settling her thoughts. Is this where she wanted to live? She'd been thinking about it more and more. But for all the pleasure that idea brought her, there was still an emptiness inside.

Adam walked out onto the beach with Skye.

Livy waved, then laughed when Skye came running to her. Everyone had fallen in love with Adam's daughter. Mimi and Adam's steadying hand kept Skye from being spoiled as others doted on her.

Livy hugged Skye. "Are you here to look for shells?"

"Maybe," said Skye. "Want to see the secret hiding place for them? Brooke showed me."

"How about later? I need to take a quick walk and get back to the Inn. I still have work to do in the kitchen."

Skye shrugged. "Okay. Maybe tomorrow."

Livy looked up as Adam approached. "Sorry I can't stay to spend time with you on a shelling expedition, but like Skye says, maybe tomorrow."

He laughed. "No worries. We'll be here every day. By the way, how did the table work out for the wedding?"

"It was perfect. I think we're going to need something like it but lighter to use on the beach for ceremonies there. Do you think you could make one for us?"

"No problem. The one I made was specifically for the gazebo, and I wanted it to look as if it was part of the building. Seen Brooke around?"

"She's working with Jake this morning," said Livy, pleased by the idea that Brooke and Adam seemed to be getting serious about one another.

CHAPTER TWENTY-ONE

CHARLOTTE

Charlotte sat at her desk looking through photographs. Dylan had a natural, artistic eye that captured the emotions of people, producing pictures that were very special. She uploaded a few on the website on a new page dedicated to weddings and let out a sigh of satisfaction. She'd work on the text and be ready to show Brooke and Livy at the meeting.

She and Shane had talked about their own wedding, and though they didn't want to do anything rash, they both agreed the sooner the better. Having made the commitment to one another, they wanted to buy a house together and settle down in it as a married couple.

It still amazed her that things had happened so quickly between them. But after facing the possibility of losing him in a drowning, Charlotte knew her feelings for Shane were deep and true. And the chemistry? Unbelievable. Even now, thinking of him, a surge of desire hit her, making her wish he hadn't gone back to Miami. While he was at the cove, he'd begun spending the night with her at Gran's, where they had more privacy. Granny Liz was okay with that now that they were engaged.

Charlotte focused once more on writing promotional copy. The Inn was a perfect place for a small wedding, and the words came easily.

Finished with her work, Charlotte stood and walked

outside. Clouds were starting to roll in, and the promise of a thunderstorm hung in the air, humid and heavy. Instead of walking on the beach which she often did to settle her mind, she walked over to Granny Liz's house. They'd become close since her engagement to Shane. Their conversations often turned to talk of Shane, and Charlotte found these talks helpful in understanding him.

Granny Liz met her on the front porch with a hug. "Good to see you, Charlie. How about a glass of fresh lemon water? It's going to storm in a while, and I find the drink refreshing on a hot, humid day like this."

"Thanks. That sounds good," Charlotte said. "I wanted to ask your opinion on something."

"Sure. Let's go into the kitchen and talk there," said Granny Liz, holding the door open for Charlotte to go inside.

Charlotte breathed a sigh of gratitude for the air-conditioned temperature as she followed Granny Liz into the kitchen.

Liz poured them each a glass of lemon water, sat at the kitchen table, and gave her a questioning look.

Charlotte set her glass down on the table and sighed. "My mother wants a big social wedding in New York. Neither Shane nor I agree. Do you think everyone would be upset if we eloped?"

"Eloped? Think of your cove family here, how we're all celebrating you and Shane being together. Weddings are a time of sharing a special moment and committing to each other in front of those you love."

Charlotte bit her lip and then nodded. "I see. We were all surprised and disappointed to know Gran and John got married without us but I thought this could be different."

"You have plenty of time to think about it. I know Ellie would be terribly hurt if you did anything like elope before she came home. Now, how did the wedding at the Inn go? I want all the details. Ellie is going to be pleased."

"You think so?" Charlotte asked. "Brooke, Livy, and I are going to discuss it this afternoon, but we all think the Inn is the perfect place for a wedding. And it can be a moneymaker too."

"I remember back when they were a big thing at the Inn. I think your grandmother will be proud of you girls for bringing them back."

Charlotte filled with pride. If they could do something to save the Inn, she and her cousins would do it.

CHAPTER TWENTY-TWO

ELLIE

From the inn in Naples, Italy, Ellie looked out at the Tyrrhenian Sea admiring the blue-green water. She and John had seen many beautiful things on their travels, but watching the waves, she was struck with homesickness. Still, she wouldn't mention it. Being away this long was all part of the plan she and the other grandmothers at Sanderling Cove had cooked up.

She opened her computer, hoping for an email message from Liz. Seeing one, she quickly clicked on it and, in her eagerness, leaned forward to read it.

> **"Hi, Ellie -Things keep moving along here at the cove. Your granddaughters, that marvelous trio of young women, are busy with the Inn making changes here and there, including hosting a wedding. Remember those days when we were younger and all pitched in to make weddings at the Inn special? Seems like Charlie, Livy, and Brooke are bringing them back. It did my heart good to see it.**
>
> **"As far as any other news, nothing exciting happening. But maybe soon. Adam is back at the cove looking to set up his own business here in Florida to keep an eye on Mimi. Of course, Karen is thrilled. She's still pinning her hopes on Adam and Brooke being together. But I'm not sure about that.**

Livy, sweet thing that she is, is playing the field. Just having fun, she tells me. We might need to give her more time to think of anything serious with any of the cove men.

"Keep sending news of your travels. It all sounds wonderful. *Ciao.* Liz"

Ellie closed the lid of her laptop and sat back in her chair awash with memories of those early days when she'd started with a simple B&B in her home and how the other four women living in the cove had rallied around her. At that time, unbeknownst to her, her recently departed husband had squandered money by investing in unstable stocks. His insurance and John's investment had given her the opportunity to build the Inn and grow her business, allowing her to live at Sanderling Cove.

Each woman living there was a treasured friend. Now they were working on a whole different project together.

CHAPTER TWENTY-THREE

BROOKE

When Brooke saw Austin siting on Granny Liz's porch, she decided to go talk to him. It bothered her that he was dating Aynsley Lynch, a woman she instinctively didn't like. A woman who seemed obviously into money. Austin might be rich, but she saw him as being a little vulnerable after breaking up with a woman out west and dealing with his mother and her death.

"Hey, Brooke, what's up?" Austin asked, setting down his mug.

"Just thought I'd come say hello. Thanks for sharing your table with Dylan and me the other night at the Pink Pelican."

"Sure, no problem. It was good to see you guys. Everyone is busy, and I haven't seen as much of everyone as I thought I would."

Brooke took a seat in a rocking chair beside him. "Are you dating Aynsley for real?"

He frowned. "Not as much as she'd like, but I'm not ready to get serious with anyone."

Brooke hesitated and then blurted out. "She's after your money, you know."

Austin's eyebrows shot up. "That's what you think?"

Knowing she had to follow through, Brooke added, "I'm sure that's not all of it. You're a great guy. But all she talked about was money and going to prep school and how she wanted to go to Europe. The common factor in anything she talked about was money and status."

He gave her a thoughtful look. "So, you're protecting me. Is that it?"

Embarrassed by his teasing tone, Brooke felt her cheeks heating. "Something like that. As she said, we cove kids take care of one another."

Austin laughed. "I like you, Brooke. Thanks for the input. But, as I said, I'm not going to move into any relationship anytime soon."

"You're like Livy," said Brooke. "Neither is she."

"Yeah, well, Livy has a lot on her mind, what with trying to decide if she's going to stay in Florida or not."

"True," said Brooke. "We all need to decide that, except for Shane and Charlotte. That's already a done deal. How do you feel about it?"

Austin's face lit with the smile that crossed it. "Shane and Charlie are great together. I've never seen my big brother so happy."

"I know," said Brooke. "Granny Liz is very excited about it."

"She and all the other grandmothers here," said Austin, chuckling and shaking his head.

Brooke stood. "I'd better get back to the Inn. I want to update the books, and I'm meeting with Beryl about the housekeeping staff."

"You really seem to like the business. Do you?"

Brooke thought a moment. "I really do."

"Then, maybe you'll stay in Florida?" he asked.

"I think so, but no decisions can be made until Gran and John return." She gave him a little wave and left the porch deep in thought.

As she walked toward the Inn, she pulled her cell phone out of her pocket and called her mother.

Her mother picked up on the second ring. "Hi, Brooke.

What's up?"

"I'm just wondering how things are going? Are you feeling better? Well enough to let the nurse go?"

There was a pause and then her mother said, "Actually, I'm giving Jamie a place to stay while he hunts for another apartment. In exchange for this, he does errands and other things for me."

Unease slithered through Brooke like a poisonous snake. "You're not involving him in anything personal, are you?"

"Brooke, stop treating me like a child," her mother protested. "Jamie and I are friends helping one another. That's all."

"Mom, I'm just concerned for you. You're a very nice person. Sometimes, too much so. I don't want to see you hurt. I love you."

"I love you too, Brooke. But I am your mother and will do whatever I want with or without your permission."

Brooke swallowed hard. "Okay. I get it."

"How are things going there?" her mother asked.

"Very well," said Brooke. "I'm seriously thinking of staying permanently."

"Ah, so you're making decisions for yourself, too."

"Yes, I guess I am," said Brooke, stung by her mother's attitude. "Well, I'd better go. Have a nice day," she said, ending the conversation on a more cheerful note.

"You, too," said her mother before she ended the call.

She went inside the Inn and to the office. Taking a seat behind the desk, she googled Jamie Murphy's name but didn't come up with anything that would cause her concern.

Pulling up the financials for the Inn, she was soon lost in the comfort of numbers. They were easier to handle than dealing with people.

When she received a call from Adam asking her if she

wanted to go to the late movies, Brooke was happy to say yes. The call with her mother had been nagging her with unease, and she was looking forward to relaxing. Besides she was anxious to see how Adam was on a more low-key date.

That night, Adam showed up in a pair of tan slacks, a golf shirt and loafers. He looked, well ... yummy. Better yet, he was beaming at her.

"Ready for some adult time?" he asked. "Sorry it's so late, but that's the only way I could do this."

She laughed. "You bet. Is Skye settled for the night?"

"Yes. She gave me permission to go out with you." He sobered. "Seriously, that's a big deal. Being here with Mimi and liking you has helped Skye from being as clingy to me." His gaze studied her. "Helped both of us, really."

"I'm glad," she said, pleased. "This summer has been good for all of us."

"Let's go." He cradled her elbow and led her to his car. "I didn't ask what movie you'd like to see. There's a "chick flick" that doesn't look too bad and an action spy movie. Take your pick."

The decision was easy for Brooke. "The spy movie. I need a good diversion. Anything to take away my worry about my mother."

He lifted his eyebrows. "Anything wrong?"

She stood by the passenger door and let out a long sigh. "I'm not happy that the nurse she hired is now living with my mother until he finds a new apartment. It doesn't seem right. But my mother is saying they're just friends, and she's allowed to make decisions of her own without my input." She shook her head. "Independence is a step in the right direction, but this is bizarre. There's a price for our new relationship. She's angry at me for being concerned."

"I can understand your worrying," said Adam, helping her into the car. "It doesn't seem very professional of the nurse."

"No, it doesn't. I'll keep my eye on things but Mom is right. It's her decision." Brooke stared out the window, wishing she felt better about the situation. She straightened in her seat determined to simply enjoy the evening. Maybe she'd have a better idea of how she and Adam might work out.

In the movie theater, which wasn't too full, Brooke chose center seats to help her become immersed in the film. She loved movies. They gave her a chance to forget about her worries and be transported into a different life. Often, she and her mother would see movies together as an escape from a sometimes-difficult life.

Adam handed her the bag of popcorn and placed a diet soda in the cup on the armrest between them. "It's ready for you anytime."

"Thanks," said Brooke. "I'm warning you right now that I'm a bit of a pig about popcorn. I'll share of course, but you might have to remind me."

Adam laughed. "Okay, something to remember. I like popcorn too."

Soon after the movie started, Brooke became involved with the plot. She knew there would be a satisfying ending, but it was the twists and turns to get there that gave her fits of anxiety.

At one point, Brooke grabbed Adam's arm. "Oh, my God."

He took hold of her hand and squeezed it. "It's going to be all right. Hang on."

She turned to him and then focused on the screen again, but she couldn't ignore the feeling of being protected.

Later, when the movie was over, they faced one another.

"That was excellent," she said, pulling her hand from his. "Thank you, for helping me through it."

"Anything for you," he said, smiling. "I have to admit, there were some pretty scary parts." He stood, and they made their way out of the movie theater and to Adam's car.

"Do you want to go out for a drink or get something to eat?" he asked her.

"Actually, why don't we go back to Gran's house? I can offer you both food and drinks," said Brooke.

"I'd like that," said Adam. "It's late, but I don't want the evening to end. I'd invite you to Mimi's, but we wouldn't have the privacy there that you have."

"Livy will be asleep, and Charlotte and Shane are in Miami, so we should pretty much have the house to ourselves."

"I was hoping for a chance to sit and talk. I want to know more about you, Brooke."

"Yes, we haven't had the chance to do that," said Brooke. "I've been meaning to ask you how your search for a house is going."

He led her to his car, helped her into it, and slid behind the wheel, leaving her question hanging in the air.

Inside the car, he faced her. "I'm looking at a few houses to fix up. I'm not positive this relocation is going to work out the way I want, and I don't want to get stuck with just any house. I'm handy and can upgrade a house and by doing so, make money."

"That makes sense. Then if things don't work out, your effort would pay off," said Brooke, unsure how she felt about his being unable to commit to anything more than a trial period.

###

They drove to Gran's house, where they each shared a beer on the front porch. Sitting with him, Brooke found herself totally relaxed. They'd had a pleasant time together, could talk easily about many different things, including some details about their childhood, and they both loved the cove and the people who lived there.

When Adam finished his beer, he set down the bottle on the end table and turned to her.

Brooke set down her bottle too. She knew from the intense look on Adam's face that he wanted to kiss her and she welcomed the idea.

Adam wrapped his arms around her and drew her close. Then his lips pressed down on hers.

Heat filled her body as his kiss deepened. She felt his hesitancy change into something demanding, and she responded.

Later, when he said it was getting late and he had to go, she walked him to the door filled with mixed emotions. She couldn't help comparing the time with Adam to the moments she spent with Dylan.

CHAPTER TWENTY-FOUR

BROOKE

Brooke lay in bed the next morning reliving the evening with Adam. There was no question that he was a nice guy, a great kisser, a super father, but she still didn't feel as if she'd really made a connection with him. She could sense he was holding part of himself back, and it bothered her. And then there was the problem of tingles.

When she looked at her phone, she saw that she'd missed a call from her mother. She sat up and blinked the last of sleep away. Her mother usually rose early and lingered over coffee. She pushed the button to return her call. It rang and rang without any answer.

Frowning, Brooke got out of bed. Her mother was adamant about the courtesy of responding to phone calls. Brooke dutifully left a message and clicked off. She didn't have time to wait for a response. She had to get to the Inn to help with the breakfast routine.

The morning was busy. It was amazing how what little advertising they'd done had boosted reservations. Though it could be hectic, Brooke enjoyed meeting the guests, getting to know them a little. She realized how isolated she'd felt in her job in New York. She had a natural way with kids and even liked to connect with them as long as they behaved.

She was refilling the coffee container on the sideboard in the dining room when Dylan walked in. "Okay if I get a cup of coffee? Skye is having some kind of meltdown and it's too early for me to cope with it."

"Sure. Help yourself to a muffin too. Most of the guests have finished breakfast. I'm just leaving these here for them for later on."

Dylan helped himself to a cup of coffee, took a muffin and sat down at the table. "Thanks."

Brooke sat down opposite him. "How's the painting going? I was hoping to have some time with you today."

His mouth too full to speak, he studied her.

"I'm worried about my mother," Brooke blurted, surprising herself and him with her words.

He set down his coffee mug. "What's going on? I thought things were going well with her."

Brooke filled him in on her unease about the nurse living there.

"It doesn't seem right to me," he said, "but maybe they have something going on."

"You mean actually 'living together'," she said, bracketing the words with her fingers.

He shrugged. "Why not?"

She sighed and shook her head. "I don't know. He seems shady to me, and you hear all kinds of stories about single women being scammed."

Dylan leaned forward. "I have an idea. I have a short trip to New York City coming up. A few of my paintings are being shown in a gallery there. Why don't you join me? You could help me out at the opening, and I could travel to Ellenton with you. A surprise visit that would give you a better idea of what's going on with them. Because I'd be with you, it wouldn't seem like spying on her."

"You'd consider doing that for me?" said Brooke, feeling a sudden sting of tears. The relief she felt was overwhelming. It had been difficult worrying in private, acting as if things were all right.

"Sure. We'd be helping each other. Besides, Brooke, you can ask me for help anytime." The intensity of his blue-eyed gaze warmed her.

"Thanks," she said softly and left the table in confusion. Dylan had looked at her in the same way Adam had before he kissed her.

Two days later Brooke sat next to Dylan on a flight to New York City. He'd insisted on paying for her ticket, telling her it was in exchange for being his date at the opening.

When she'd protested about the money, he said, "I hate these openings where I'm forced to talk about my work with people who sometimes don't even understand them. With you by my side, we can talk about other things."

"I'm happy to help. Besides, it'll give me a chance to understand your work better. I love your paintings, the colors, the balance, everything."

He grinned at her. "See? You'll be able to do a lot of the talking."

She laughed, pleased by the whole idea. She was curious about the art world he lived in. This would be a wonderful way to find out more about it.

She leaned back in her seat and closed her eyes. She hadn't realized how much effort went into running the inn, even though she shared those responsibilities with her cousins. Her admiration for Gran grew. Maybe working like this had kept her grandmother young, vibrant.

Dylan shook her awake. "Hey, Sleeping Beauty, we're getting ready to land."

A few moments later, the announcement came over the intercom system.

Grateful she'd had a few minutes to prepare, she stared out the window. As the plane circled, she stared down at the city, alive with people, places, and possibilities. She turned to Dylan.

"Always exciting, huh?" he said.

"Yes. There's no place like it. Thanks for inviting me."

"We'll make it fun. You did bring a little black dress. Right?" he teased.

"Oh, yes. And Charlie lent me dangly earrings, and Lily gave me a silk scarf to drape around my shoulders."

"Must be handy living with your cousins."

"Yes, it is," she replied, more grateful for them than he realized. Livy had trimmed her hair and Charlie had put fresh polish on her fingernails.

She discovered how easy it was to deplane from first class carrying just a small bag. And then, when they walked into the baggage claim area of Kennedy Airport and saw a limo driver holding a sign for them, she was even more impressed to be traveling with Dylan.

Though Ellenton was less than two hours away from the city, she hadn't spent much time in New York. Now, riding in the limo to their hotel, she wondered why.

When she learned she'd be sharing a suite with Dylan, Brooke was thrilled by the luxury of it. Growing up, she and her mother had been comfortable but without many extras. She'd never minded their situation, but she intended to enjoy every moment of privilege on this trip.

After the bellman had delivered their luggage, Dylan turned to her. "The master bedroom is off to the right from the living room. Why don't you take that? I'll take the smaller one."

"Okay," said Brooke, relieved he'd made things clear.

She walked into a large bedroom with a small sitting area.

Next to the bathroom was what she'd call a dressing room with closet space and plenty of mirrors. The bathroom contained a toilet, a bidet, a shower, and a soaking tub.

Dylan came up behind her. "Everything all right here?"

She turned to him. "I could just stay right here and have a great time. It's gorgeous."

He put an arm around her and beamed at her. "I thought you'd like it. But remember, you're here to work."

She gave him a mock salute. "Aye, aye, sir."

He pulled her to him and gazed down at her. "You're making this a lot of fun for me."

She was about to throw her arms around him when he stepped back. Feeling foolish, she looked away.

He caught her chin and turned her face toward him. "I'm very attracted to you, Brooke, but I don't want to get involved if you're with Adam. I wouldn't do that to either of you."

"But Adam and I aren't together," said Brooke. She took a deep breath, knowing she was right. "And I don't think it's going to happen. No matter how much Mimi wants it to." Being here with Dylan, she knew she was right. She felt connected to him in a way she hadn't felt with a man before.

"And Skye?"

"I love that little girl," said Brooke, "but you can't base a relationship on that alone."

"But you want children of your own?" Dylan asked.

"Yes, I do. I've always wanted a big family," she said honestly. That statement had turned off one of her dates, but she knew she had to be honest with Dylan. His response was very important to her.

He grinned. "Yeah, me too. As a kid, I always wanted a brother. Maybe two."

"And I would've taken either," said Brooke delighted by his response.

"Okay, then, Brooke Weatherby, do I have your permission to date you?" Dylan said, bowing before her as if asking her for a dance.

"Yes," Brooke said, playing along, knowing it was much more than that.

Dylan drew her into his arms and kissed her. A thoroughly satisfying kiss that held the promise of more to come.

Tingling from the top of her head to the tips of her toes, Brooke responded. When they pulled apart, Brooke simply stared at Dylan, too stunned to say anything.

He was quiet too as he caressed her cheek. "Wow," he said softly.

"Me, too," she murmured, rocked to the core. She knew Dylan was a sensitive, caring man, but the chemistry with him was something she'd never experienced.

"This trip to New York was a great idea," said Dylan. "I didn't want anyone else to know how I felt about you until I was sure you felt the same way."

"I do," she said, and quickly added, "feel the same way about you." The words "I do" sounded too much like a marriage ceremony.

Dylan checked his watch. "I'm sorry, but we can't hang around here. We have to get to the gallery unless you'd rather have some time alone to shop or such."

Brooke shook her head. "No, you asked me for your help, and I'm here to be with you."

The smile he gave her warmed her heart.

The art gallery, Galerie Claire, occupied part of a brownstone structure on the Upper East Side of Manhattan in a quiet section of the street. Large triple windows allowed light inside, and the sparkling white walls made a perfect background for Dylan's large, colorful pieces.

Claire DuBois, the owner, was a striking woman with gray hair pulled back into a tight bun behind her neck, exposing her classic features and dark, almost black, eyes that seemed to miss nothing.

Brooke remained quiet as she followed Claire and Dylan around the gallery while they discussed the placement and prices of his paintings. Brooke soon realized how shrewd a businesswoman Claire was as she informed Dylan of her guest list for the opening.

"We should be able to easily sell five pieces of your work," Claire told him. "When I saw what you've done, I could place one in at least three homes."

Dylan turned to Brooke. "We'll be here by four o'clock tomorrow, ready to do our job meeting your clients."

Claire's gaze settled on Brooke making her wish she'd chosen to wear something better than blue jeans and a knit top. "So, you are a painter too? *Oui*?"

Brooke shook her head. "Not really. I've dabbled with a few things at Dylan's studio in Florida."

Dylan placed a hand on Brooke's shoulder. "She might be a novice, but she has an excellent eye for color and a natural balance to her work. The day may come when you'll want to show her work."

"Ah, I see," said Claire, beaming at them. "You're in love, Dylan."

Neither Brooke nor Dylan knew what to say.

Claire impulsively gave Brooke a kiss on one cheek, then the other. "Adorable," she said in her French accent. "Stay that way."

"Thanks for your time today," Dylan said to Claire. "We're going to visit Brooke's family upstate, but we'll be back here tomorrow at four, as I promised."

"Good enough," said Claire. "*Jusqu'à demain.*"

"Yes, until tomorrow," said Brooke, surprising them both.

Out on the street, Dylan said, "Why don't we enjoy the rest of the afternoon walking around. Then we can go back to the hotel and change for dinner. Sound okay?"

"Yes. I'm open to seeing whatever you want. It's all a treat for me."

"We're not that far from Central Park. I have an idea. Do you trust me?" He gave her a devilish grin she couldn't resist.

Smiling, she said, "Sure. Whatever it is, I'm game." She waited while he stepped away and made a phone call, and then they walked toward the park.

As they approached the spot Dylan led her to, Brooke clapped her hands. "Really? A carriage ride? How sweet."

"Not as romantic as nighttime but nice nevertheless," he said.

A short while later, they sat in a white carriage with red seats gazing at the scenery around them. Their travel included Fifth Avenue stores, The Plaza Hotel, St. Patrick's Cathedral, and other tourist sights.

Feeling like a princess, Brooke returned waves from others until both she and Dylan were laughing so hard that they couldn't stop for several minutes. She couldn't remember having such fun.

Still laughing, Dylan put his arm around her and gave her a squeeze.

When the ride ended, Dylan tipped the driver, took her hand, and suggested they return to the hotel.

"I need to make a few business calls, and then we can go out to eat. There are several restaurants within walking distance of the hotel, but the choice is yours. I'm happy with most anything."

"Me, too," she said. "Let's keep it simple. But we have to

take note of everything so we can tell Livy about the food."

"No problem," he said agreeably.

Back at the hotel, while Dylan made some calls, Brooke decided to soak in the tub. After traveling and sightseeing, she wanted to feel fresh for a night out on the town with Dylan.

The bathroom contained a spa tub and a supply of fluffy white towels. Sighing with pleasure as she drew the water, she sprinkled some of the bath salts from a container the hotel had provided. She undressed and then slipped into the pleasantly hot water.

Brooke wondered what it would be like to have a life of luxury and realized that while she liked the idea, she didn't really need it. She wasn't sure where a relationship with Dylan would take her, but she knew she wanted to be with him. He brought out a side of her that no one else understood—the need to be the person she wanted to be; not the one that others expected of her. He loved her purple hair, encouraged the artwork she did, and found other words and ways to make her feel good about herself. With him, she was a more open person. She'd always be grateful to him for that.

Later, with a towel wrapped around her, she headed into her bedroom to get dressed. She wanted to wear something that could easily be dressed up or down,

She laid a pair of black pants and a purple knit top on the bed. She could add jewelry, a scarf, or nothing at all, depending on where they were going.

When she was dressed and standing in front of the mirror, she heard a knock on the door.

"Yes?" She hurried to answer it and faced Dylan.

"Beautiful." He let his gaze wander over her. "Any idea where you want to go for dinner?"

"I'll be happy with anything you choose," she said, pleased that he obviously liked her outfit.

"Let's decide later. A bottle of wine and a cheese and fruit platter have been delivered to the room, courtesy of Claire. We can start there."

"Do you always get this kind of service wherever you go?"

Dylan laughed and shook his head. "Claire really wanted me to show my paintings at her gallery. I agreed to do it as a favor for a friend of hers."

They walked into the living area and took a seat on the couch. The open bottle of wine and a cheese platter sat on the coffee table in front of them.

Dylan poured them each a glass of the wine and took a sip of his. "M-m-m, a silky Chandler Hill pinot noir from Oregon. I think you'll like it."

Brooke took a sip. "It's nice and fruity with a smooth finish," she said, remembering what John had taught her about wine.

Dylan's eyes widened. "I didn't know you knew so much about wine."

"John made certain all of us cousins learned about wine and excellent food. Not that I've had that much opportunity to do a lot of tasting. Life at home was pretty boring. This is the new me."

He set down his glass, put his arms around her, and drew her close. "I like the new you."

Smiling, she gazed into his eyes and let out a sigh as she set down her glass. "You make me feel wonderful."

"You *are* wonderful, Brooke. I've watched you all summer. Everyone at the cove loves you."

She caressed his cheek. "But you're the only one who really understands me. You don't know how much that matters to me. With you, I'm comfortable being myself, the real me."

"I think I know what you've gone through to get there. Because of my size everyone thought I should play sports, be a jock, all of that. But I've known I wanted to be a painter all my life. I've been called names for it, but my parents let me choose. I'll never forget what they did to help me be myself."

"I remember your parents. They were always very kind to me and my mother."

"Yeah, KK and Gordon are pretty cool. They were great about Grace being gay and marrying Belinda. I know they'll be happy to know we're dating."

"So, we've agreed we're dating," said Brooke. "Exclusively?"

"That's what I want. How about you?" Dylan said.

Noticing the vulnerability in his expression, Brooke said, "Yes. Definitely." She studied him. "I feel good about the two of us, you know?"

He grinned. "Yeah. Me, too."

She lifted her wine glass. "Here's to us!"

Chuckling, Dylan lifted his glass. "To us."

They each took a sip of their wine and then settled back on the couch.

"Tell me more about your childhood," said Brooke. "Growing up, I've seen you at the cove when our families visited, but what was your favorite school subject? Dessert? Did you go to camp? I want to know it all."

"Okay. I was born at an early hour on a September day, thirty years ago. My mother, who is artistic herself, was thrilled I loved to paint and draw from an early age. Grace, two years younger, uses her creativity in the kitchen. Dad says his creativity is used for fishing. He loves to go fly fishing. Growing up as we did in Colorado, we used to go on a lot of family camping trips. As for school, I preferred classes that didn't have to do with math. How about you?"

"I was always good in math. That's one reason I ended up an accountant. Numbers come easily to me." She held up a hand to stop him from speaking. "But, and this is a big but, you've helped me realize what things I really love doing. Things like art work."

"And working at The Sanderling Cove Inn," he prompted.

"That, too," she said. "I'm not sure what's going to happen when Gran and John get back, but if they keep the Inn, I'd be willing to help them."

He gave her a steady look. "So, you'd stay in Florida?"

"Yes. I don't want to go back to New York. You'll understand better after we visit my mother tomorrow morning."

"I don't think you should tell your mother we're coming," said Dylan. "We need to surprise her."

"I agree. If anything is amiss, I want to catch her off guard. And I've thought of the perfect excuse for showing up. I left a pair of dressy black heels at home. I want to wear them tomorrow night."

"Great. I'm getting hungry. Where do you want to eat?"

"How about Thai food? Know of any place nearby?"

"As a matter of fact, one of my favorite places is close. It's a small neighborhood restaurant. We should be able to get seated. Put on comfortable shoes and we'll walk there. It's a pleasant evening."

Delighted with the idea of a restaurant within walking distance, Brooke went into her bedroom and slipped on a pair of sneakers. She'd rather be comfortable than fashionable.

When Dylan saw what she'd done, he laughed. "Smart choice."

CHAPTER TWENTY-FIVE

BROOKE

Thai Garden was everything Dylan had suggested and more. A small restaurant conveniently tucked inside a large building on the corner of a street five blocks away, it served the best Pad Thai Brooke had ever tasted.

"It all has to do with the sauce," said Dylan. He'd chosen a sauteed basil curry seafood dish with a rich saffron-colored curry.

They finished their meal and, contented, walked slowly toward the hotel.

"How does a cold beer sound?" Dylan asked as he drew to a stop in front of Joe's Bar.

Intrigued by the simple name and the noise leaking from inside, Brooke nodded. They'd had only tea at the restaurant.

They walked inside, and Brooke felt as if she was on the set of the old television show, *Cheers*.

Dylan found them seats at the bar and ordered them each a beer as she gazed around with curiosity. Everyone seemed to know one another except for two pockets of people who appeared to be tourists.

"I forget the city is really composed of neighborhoods," said Brooke. "This is great." Sitting next to Dylan, she wondered what the future offered them. He hadn't mentioned staying in Florida. Would distance tear them apart?

The man sitting next to Dylan started talking to him. While they conversed, Brooke decided to check her email. She frowned when she saw a notice from her local bank manager asking her to call them. She thought of her mother. They shared a savings account for security purposes should her mother suddenly be unable to act on her own.

"What's wrong?" Dylan asked her.

"I'm not sure, but I'm very happy we're going to see my mother tomorrow," she said. "I got a message from our bank."

"Well, let's not waste an evening worrying about it," said Dylan, taking hold of her hand. "Let's go back to the hotel. It's getting late and we have to be up early tomorrow if we're going to Ellenton and get back in time for the gallery opening."

"You're right," said Brooke.

They finished their beers and headed out.

In their suite, Brooke became nervous. She and Dylan's kiss had proved their chemistry was out of sight, but she wasn't sure she was ready for the next step.

Dylan sensed her feelings and patted the cushion next to him on the couch. "Come say goodnight."

Relieved and grateful to know where he stood, she joined him. "Thanks for a wonderful day, Dylan. It was one of the best days of my life."

He turned to her. "For me, too. I figure tomorrow we'll be busy with your mother and then the opening, but I want us to have a special time after that. We have a late afternoon flight out of here the day after the opening."

"That sounds perfect," she said, cuddling up next to him. "What was your favorite part of the carriage ride?"

Dylan grinned. "That's easy. Kissing you."

She laughed. "I thought you were going to say something different, but that was the best answer ever." She reached up and cupped his cheek. "You're such an incredible man. You make me feel special."

"That's because you are," said Dylan. "Especially the way you kiss." He leaned over and placed his lips on hers.

Brooke felt herself soaring, overwhelmed by a feeling of joy. He made her feel so good about herself. She knew from the way he was kissing her, drawing her close, that he needed her too.

When they pulled apart, Dylan studied her. "I want you, Brooke, but I'm not rushing you into anything." He stood and held out his hand. "C'mon. I'll walk you to your room."

They'd just declared their exclusive status. Brooke knew he wanted more but she thought it was right to wait.

The next morning, she was awakened with a kiss. She rolled over and gazed up into Dylan's face.

"Hello, handsome," she murmured, reaching up for him. Dressed in boxers, he set down the cup of coffee he'd brought in and stretched out beside her atop the blanket that covered the bed.

She opened her side of the blanket. "Climb in. The bed's comfortable."

Grinning, he stood and slid beneath the blanket and wrapped her in his arms. "M-m-m...really comfortable."

She chuckled and then moaned softly when his lips met hers. She'd thought about being with him all night, had even dreamed about it.As their kisses deepened, Brooke knew she was ready to make this commitment. Even more, she knew enough about Dylan to understand she could trust him.

Later, lying together, she stroked his solid chest, feeling close to tears.

He tilted her chin up and gazed into her eyes. "Are you all right?"

The tears that had threatened now leaked at the corners of her eyes. "I've never felt this way before."

He cupped her face in his hands and kissed her long and hard. When he pulled away, his eyes welled with love. "I think I fell for you the moment I saw your new hair color." He fingered the strands. "You were walking on the beach, looking as if you'd just climbed a mountain with that pleased look on your face."

"Why didn't you let me know?" Brooke asked, surprised by his declaration..

"I couldn't say or do much with Adam in the picture. I knew this trip would either work or be the end of any thought of us being together."

Brooke smiled at him. "I'm very happy it worked."

"Me, too," said Dylan, pulling her on top of him.

After breakfast, all thought of romance fled as she and Dylan headed north to Ellenton in a rental car. On the way, she called the bank manager.

"Brooke, I'm glad to hear from you," the manager said. "There's been an incident with one of your accounts, and I needed clarification before I could proceed."

Brooke's heart sank. "Is it the savings account?"

"Yes, as a matter of fact, that's the one. A gentleman came through our drive-thru line and requested a withdrawal of $10,000 from the joint savings account you and your mother share. I thought it was unusual and blocked the funds. I tried to call your mother, but there was no answer."

"I've tried calling her too. Thank you for letting me know. I happen to be on my way to Ellenton now. In the meantime, I'm requesting you to remove all the funds from the savings account I share with my mother to the savings account I have in my own name. I'll explain what happened to them to her. There's something going on with my mother and the nurse who's been taking care of her. She doesn't know I've returned from Florida to check up on her here."

"No problem. I'm pleased we could talk about this situation. I'll take care of the transfer for you."

"Thank you so much," said Brooke, feeling sick to her stomach. Her mother was in trouble.

After she ended the call, she turned to Dylan. "We've got to get to my mother's house as quickly as possible. A man, I presume Jamie Murphy, the nurse, tried to withdraw $10,000 from a savings account my mother and I share. I haven't liked the idea of him working for her from the beginning."

"That's the nurse who suddenly appeared?"

"Yes, he used to work at the agency we've used in the past," said Brooke, feeling guilty that she hadn't pressed harder for her mother to get rid of him.

When they pulled up to the small, gray Cape Cod house, Brooke's heart thumped with dismay at the sight of the battered silver truck parked in front of the garage as if it had every right to be there.

She turned to Dylan. "Do you mind going in with me?"

"There's no way I'd let you go inside alone. The man could be dangerous."

They got out of the car and walked together to the front door.

Before she could ring the bell, the door opened and a gray-haired man peered out at them. "What do you want?"

"I don't know who you are, but I'm Brooke Weatherby, Jo's daughter. This is my home and I have every right to be here. You must be Jamie Murphy."

He stepped back. Brooke had a better look at him. He was of average height, well-built and with a bushy gray mustache above his lips. His brown eyes studied her.

She looked around but didn't see her mother. "Mom, where are you?" she cried.

"It's not one of her better days," said Jamie. "She's in her bedroom."

Brooke left Dylan with Jamie and hurried to her mother's bedroom. At the threshold to the room, she stopped and gasped. The room was a mess and her mother lay in bed on her back, her hair frazzled around her pale face.

"Brooke? Is that you?" her mother said in a trembling voice. "Your hair. Purple?"

Brooke rushed forward and held her mother. "Mom, what's going on? Are you having one of your spells?"

"I don't know. I feel so weak. I've been in bed for what seems like days."

Brooke looked at the bottles of medicine sitting on the bedside table. "Have you taken anything besides these medications?"

"I don't know. Jamie gives me what I need."

Brooke straightened, as angry as she'd ever been. "I need to speak to him."

Her mother took hold of her hand. "Don't be mad. He's been helpful to me. He really has."

Brooke didn't bother to respond. She hurried back to the front entrance to find Dylan standing there.

"Where's Jamie?" she asked.

"He's loading up his truck now. I think with the bank stopping his attempt at taking your mother's money, he must have suspected something. Looks like he was packed and ready to go."

Brooke tore out of the house and over to him. "Hey, you!

I'm going to report you to the police!"

Jamie faced her, hands on his hips. "What for? Taking care of an old lady?" The smirk on his face made Brooke fist her hands.

"Old lady? She's only in her 50's. Except now, you've made her all but bedridden. Was that it? Drugging her so you could steal her money and God knows what else?"

"You have no way to prove anything," Jamie said. "Ask your mother. She'll tell you I did a decent job of taking care of her."

"Why didn't she answer her phone? I've been calling her."

"She told me she didn't want to talk to you," said Jamie. "Don't you think you're a little out-of-line here, making all sorts of accusations you can't prove."

She turned as Dylan joined them. He held up a cell phone.

"I found your mother's phone. It was on mute," Dylan said. He narrowed his eyes at Jamie. "I suggest you leave while you can before we call the cops."

Jamie gave him an insolent shrug. "Can't pin anything on me."

"Not even the attempt to steal money?" Brooke said. "I know all about it."

Jamie shook his head and glared at Brooke. "You really are a bitch, like your mother says."

Blood rushed to Brooke's face so fast she thought she might faint. Dylan took hold of her arm to steady her.

"Get off this property now," Brooke said, gathering her strength.

She and Dylan stood back as Jamie got into his truck and roared away.

"I'd better go check to see what damage he might have done," said Brooke. Tears stung her eyes. "I should've been more attentive, should've protected my mother."

Dylan turned her around, facing him. "Actually, Brooke, that's not your job. Your mother is a grown woman who can make her own decisions. This was a bad one, but it was hers to make."

Brooke sighed. "I know you're right, but I feel I should've followed through on my bad feelings."

"Okay, let's see what we can do to help her now," Dylan said, his voice softened with concern.

They went inside.

"Did he go?" her mother asked when Brooke went to check on her.

"Yes. You won't be seeing him again. But, Mom, I want to call the nursing service and have them send someone to help you get your strength back. Do you mind?"

"No, sweetheart, I don't mind. Jamie would get very angry if I complained. I didn't dare ask for too much help. I think I need a nurse who does physical therapy."

"Okay, that's what we'll get," said Brooke, trying not to cry at how weak her mother had become. There had been days her mother felt awful, too sick to do much, too tired to be active. But seeing her like this was a shock.

Together, they made the call to the nursing agency.

Betty Hardwick, the director of nursing, took their call.

Brooke explained the situation. "What we need now is a nursing assistant who does physical therapy."

"I have someone in mind. Would your mother mind if it's a male?"

Brooke and Jo exchanged glances. "No, I don't mind," said Jo. "I trust people from your agency."

"Okay. Then I'll see if he can start this afternoon. Will that do?" said Betty.

"Yes," said Brooke. "I'll help my mother get dressed for the day, but I'll have to leave right after that. I have a commitment in the city that I can't break."

"That sounds fine," said Betty. "His name is Chet Brigham. He's a man about your mother's age, in excellent shape, and a real sweet guy. A favorite of our clients."

They finished making arrangements, and then Brooke helped her mother to the bathroom. While her mother took her time in the shower, Brooke quickly straightened the room and changed the sheets on the bed.

Later, after her mother had dried her hair and gotten dressed, Brooke led her into the kitchen.

Dylan got to his feet. "Hello, Ms. Weatherby. Do you remember me? I'm Dylan Hendrix, KK's son."

"Oh, my! Dylan, the artist. How wonderful to see you. Did you come with Brooke?"

Brooke helped her mother into a chair and then stood by Dylan. "We're dating," she said, unable to hide a note of excitement in her voice or the smile she felt spreading across her face.

"How lovely," her mother said. "And, Dylan, please call me Jo. Everyone does."

"Thank you," he said politely. "I'm sorry to have to whisk your daughter away, but soon we'll need to leave for the city. I have an opening at a gallery, and Brooke is going to help me."

"That's not a problem. Brooke and I have already taken care of getting a new nurse for me," said Jo.

"While you two chat I'm going to quickly straighten up," said Brooke. "I gather Jamie was sleeping in my room?"

"Yes," said her mother. "I hope it's not a mess."

Brooke left them and went to her bedroom expecting the worst. Instead, she found her room in order. Almost too much so. Before she'd left for Florida, she'd done a thorough job of cleaning out her room. She checked her closet. All was in order. But when she opened the top drawer of her dresser, she found a few pieces of costume jewelry missing. Thank heavens, she'd taken her good jewelry to Florida.

She searched for her dressy black heels and found them in a corner of the closet where she'd left them.

Gathering them up, she went back to the living room and took a mental inventory. Nothing seemed to be missing. Maybe by keeping things pretty much the same in the house, Jamie wanted to appear as if he wouldn't stoop to take money from a client's savings account. Just thinking of what he'd tried to do made Brooke angry.

When she walked back to the kitchen, she overheard her mother laughing and she silently blessed Dylan for being the kind man he was.

"I've been telling your mother about some of Skye's antics," he said.

"She sounds adorable. Mimi must love her," said Jo. "It certainly sounds like you all are having a great summer. I've received some emails from Gran. She and John are having a wonderful time too. I'm looking forward to feeling better and making the trip in the fall for the family get-together."

"I'll be anxious for you to see the Inn. Charlie, Livy, and I have done some upgrades and are working on booking weddings there. We've already had our first one, and it went very well."

"It's a beautiful place for one," her mother said, glancing from her to Dylan.

Dylan winked at Brooke as her cheeks heated. She'd thought the same thing, but it was much too soon to be even thinking about it.

Brooke hugged her mother. "Are you sure it's all right for us to leave you?"

"Yes, sweetie. Go! Now that my phone is working properly, I can call someone if I need help. Besides, Chet will be here soon. Enjoy your time in New York. Dylan tells me you're quite the artist. As a little girl, you used to love to paint. Somewhere we both lost sight of that. I'm happy you've found it again."

Jo shook Dylan's hand. "I'm pleased we've had a chance to talk. Take good care of my Brookie."

"I will," said Dylan, placing an arm around Brooke's shoulder and drawing her close.

If Brooke hadn't already fallen in love with him, she would've right then.

CHAPTER TWENTY-SIX

BROOKE

On the trip back to New York City, Brooke and Dylan talked more about her relationship with her mother. Brooke confided that Gran had hoped the summer apart would give Brooke more freedom.

"Has it?" Dylan asked.

Brooke thought about it. She'd sat or walked on the sand wishing for something different from her life in Ellenton, new work opportunities, and new, healthy relationships. She'd found them all. "Yes. I came to Florida hoping for changes in my life. I wasn't ready to think of making a commitment to anyone because I had to find myself first. With you, I've found a part of me I'd been missing. I will be forever grateful to you for giving me the gift of art and discovering that part of me."

He glanced at her and focused back on the road, but not before she saw the look of tenderness he gave her. It seemed strange to her to feel so much love for someone this quickly, but then she'd entered the summer wanting to be someone open to possibilities, love, and the joy of living. If only life would continue that way for her.

As soon as they returned to the hotel, they dressed for the opening at the art gallery. Along with the black heels, Brooke chose to wear a sleeveless black linen sheath with a funky, large-bead necklace in black, white, and red. Studying herself in the mirror, she thought she looked perfect for a gallery opening.

Dylan thought so too. He let out a low whistle when he saw her emerge from her bedroom.

She smiled, pleased with herself.

They took a cab to the gallery and arrived shortly after four. Claire had invited some special guests to the show before it opened to others, and as they entered the building, Claire rushed over to them. “I think two are sold already. But Dylan and Brooke, you need to mingle with these big buyers if we want to sell more.”

Dylan took hold of Brooke’s hand. “C’mon. Let’s make a few sales.”

She grinned and allowed him to lead her to a heavy-set, older man with a shock of white hair. He stood gazing at pictures while leaning on a cane.

“Hello, Laurence,” Dylan said, reading the name on a prominent name tag. “I’m Dylan Hendrix. Can I answer any questions you might have about some of these pieces?”

The man shook Dylan’s hand. “I’ve been admiring a few. I especially like the one titled ‘Beach Sunrise.’ There’s something about it that pulls me in.”

Dylan winked at her. “It’s a collaborative piece with my partner, Brooke.”

Shocked but pleased, Brooke allowed a smile. This painting was the one where she’d suggested placing a few colors.

Laurence beamed at her and turned to Dylan. “In that case, I will purchase it. I love stories behind various works. My wife will be pleased with this one.” He turned and said, “Margery, come here. I want you to meet the artists.”

A woman with a grandmotherly build walked over to them smiling. She held out her bejeweled hand to Dylan. “Hello, I’m Margery Veltmann. Laurence and I enjoy meeting the people behind the paintings.”

“Pleased to meet you,” said Dylan. “This is Brooke

Weatherby, my partner."

Brooke shook hands with Margery and stood silently while Dylan continued to chat with the Veltmanns. Still stunned by the turn of events, she wondered if she was perpetuating a lie. She wasn't a real artist. She just dabbled in paints. And though she and Dylan had made a commitment to date exclusively, they weren't real partners.

After the Veltmanns left them, she turned to Dylan. "I didn't really collaborate on the painting."

He looked surprised. "But you did. You offered an opinion of placement of colors, and I followed your advice. It made for a better painting. You might be just getting started, but, Brooke, you have a natural eye for color, balance, and texture. I wouldn't have listened to you if I didn't believe that."

Tears stung Brooke's eyes. "Really?"

He put his arm around her and kissed her cheek. "Really."

"Hey, you two," said Claire. "I have someone who wants to talk to you about the painting on the far wall."

Brooke followed Dylan to a young woman who stood gazing at another large painting. Tall, immaculately dressed in a long, flowing black skirt and black corset top, the woman whose tag read, Daphne Winston, wore huge diamond earrings that matched a diamond bracelet. Brown eyes stared at Brooke from a stunning, dark-skinned face.

Totally inhibited by Daphne's beauty, Brooke remained silent while Dylan introduced himself to her.

After they exchanged a few words about the painting, Daphne turned to Brooke.

"What do you think of this painting? Should I buy it?"

"Only if it speaks to you," said Brooke honestly. "I love it, but you have to love it too. Otherwise, why bother?"

Daphne glanced at Dylan and back to Brooke. A huge smile formed on Daphne's lovely face. "I like you, Brooke."

Chuckling, Dylan put his arm around her. "I do too. Brooke is as honest as they come. She has talent too."

"Really? Are you showing here?" said Daphne.

"Not yet," Brooke answered boldly, as surprised by her response as Dylan.

"Someday you will," said Dylan.

Daphne stood back and studied the painting once more. "I'm just not sure."

"How about the one next to it?" said Brooke. "It has some of the same colors but feels very different to me."

Daphne moved over to the painting Brooke had indicated. She studied it while Brooke and Dylan stood aside.

"You know, Brooke, I think you're right. This feels a little more exciting to me." Daphne smiled at her.

Brooke grinned. She liked this woman who wasn't afraid to be both outstanding and flexible, and vowed to be more like her.

Dylan left them, and in chatting with Daphne, Brooke discovered she was a model and was about to be on the cover of *Vogue*.

"I'll have to buy the magazine," Brooke said. "I know you'll be amazing."

"Thanks," said Daphne. "If you ever get a show here, let Claire know I want an invite." She started to walk away, turned back, and gave Brooke a bright smile. "You're right. I'm getting this painting. It will look perfect in my apartment. Thanks."

After Daphne departed, Brooke went to search for Dylan. She found him surrounded by an admiring group of women and decided to take a breather. She walked to a quiet corner where several comfortable chairs were placed, lowered herself into one of them, and let out a sigh. This evening was magical. She watched the crowd with interest, and when she could see them, she studied some of Dylan's work on the walls. It was Dylan's event, his time to enjoy his success. Yet, he'd shared that triumph with her.

"Having a pleasant time?" asked Claire, walking over to her.

"The best," Brooke said, rising. "Just giving Dylan a break."

"Daphne Winston spoke to me. She's buying a painting based on your recommendation. If you ever want a job with me, you've got it."

"Thanks," Brooke said with a note of pride. "But I'm busy working at my grandparents' inn in Florida."

"Ah, that's why Dylan has been working there. It's been good for him. We've had a very successful evening, in part because of you."

Dylan joined them. "Talking to my collaborator, huh?"

Claire shook her head. "You two, I don't know ... just adorable."

Brooke and Dylan looked at one another and grinned.

By the time they returned to the hotel after a quick dinner, Brooke was ready to unwind. She kicked off the heels and wiggled her toes on the soft carpet in front of the couch where she and Dylan had plopped.

She turned to him. "This was the best night of my life. Thank you. For everything."

"You were terrific," said Dylan throwing an arm across her shoulder. "I was very proud to be with you."

She straightened and faced him. "But Dylan, I'm really not your collaborator or partner in the business. You paint what you want to paint. And I'm not part of your business."

His blue-eyed gaze settled on her. "I wasn't kidding about your help with that painting. I want to work with you on many more. And as for being part of my business, I hope someday you will be."

She started to speak and stopped. If she tried to say something she'd break down and sob.

When he leaned over, drew her close, and pressed his lips on hers, she responded with a surge of love for him.

When they drew apart, Dylan gave her a questioning look.

Without hesitation, she stood and held out her hand to him.

Together they walked into her bedroom, where they discovered the magic of the evening was just beginning.

The next morning, after they'd ordered room service and stayed in bed enjoying their eggs benedict, Brooke finally rose. "I'm going to take a shower and then call my mother. I want to know how it's going with her and Chet."

"I'm going to call Claire and get some final figures on the sales. From what she said last night, we did well. We can even go out for lunch before we have to head to the airport to go back to Florida."

"That sounds wonderful. As magical as this trip has been, I can't let my cousins down. It'll be good to get back to help them. We've booked two more local weddings."

She left him and went to the bathroom. The shower, with two showerheads, was another bit of luxury. With water streaming down her body, caressing her, Brooke let out a sigh of happiness. She hadn't had that much experience with men, but Dylan had proved to her that they were right to wait until they knew for certain that what they felt was real. Because it wasn't just lovemaking, but a meeting of souls.

Just as she was about to step out of the shower, Dylan stepped in.

Laughing, she hugged him close. He was so much fun.

Later, when she called her mother, Jo picked up right away.

"Morning," Jo said, sounding brighter, clearer than she had the last time they talked.

"How are things going with Chet?" Brooke asked.

"Fine. He's such a nice man," Jo said. "Here, I'll let you talk to him."

"Hello?" came a deep voice. "Is this Brooke?"

"Yes, it is. How is my mother? She sounds much better."

"I believe she was given too much medication, which isn't healthy. But we're getting her back to normal. I'm doing exercises with her to strengthen her body after being in bed for too long. I've filed a report with our nursing agency, so Betty can notify other agencies about Jamie. He shouldn't be allowed to practice."

"No," Brooke said. "He tried to steal money from our savings account. If I could prove what he was up to, I'd bring in the police. But sadly, as he said, I can't prove anything."

"The important thing is your mother is fine. Don't worry, Brooke. I'll take good care of her."

"Please tell her to send pictures of the two of you to make me feel better about the situation. Dylan and I return to Florida this afternoon."

"Will do. Let me turn the call over to your mother," Chet said.

"Mom? Chet sounds really competent. I'm relieved you're feeling better and that you have someone there with you. As I told Chet, Dylan and I are returning to Florida today. But let's keep in touch."

"Yes. But don't worry about me. I'll be fine. I'm very comfortable with Chet. And, Brooke, your young man is wonderful. I've never seen you as happy as when I saw you."

"Thanks. I can't believe we've discovered one another. I haven't told him, but I love him, Mom."

"Aw, if you feel that way, go ahead and tell him. I saw how he was with you."

"Maybe, I will," said Brooke pleased by her mother's reaction.

Brooke accompanied Dylan to the gallery and kept busy looking at some of the work there while he and Claire made arrangements for any unsold paintings to be shipped to Florida following the closing of this exhibition of his art.

When he was through, they headed for the airport and the flight to Florida. Brooke was anxious to get back to work at the Inn. She couldn't do enough for her grandparents. They'd made it possible for her to get to know Dylan and fall in love with him.

CHAPTER TWENTY-SEVEN

CHARLOTTE

The minute Charlotte saw Brooke she knew something was up. "Okay, 'Cuz, what's going on? You look like you're dancing on air. Did you and Dylan finally see you're perfect for one another?"

Brooke stopped walking toward the Inn and faced her cousin. "What do you mean?"

Smiling, Charlotte shook her head. "I've been watching the two of you. When you're together, you're hot. Everyone but Mimi can see that."

"She wanted Adam and me to get together but it wasn't going to happen. I realized that on our last date."

"And Dylan?"

Brooke beamed at her. "Oh, Charlie, he's so special. He makes me feel talented, smart, and beautiful."

Charlotte hugged her. "That makes me happy. That's how Shane makes me feel."

"Hey, what's going on you two?" ask Livy, running to catch up to them.

"I'm in love," said Brooke, clapping her hands together. "Dylan and I had the most marvelous time in New York. He had the gallery opening, and I helped him. He even called me a collaborator on his work. He's serious about wanting me to do more painting. He thinks I've got talent. More than that he's such a fantastic ..." she stopped.

Charlotte and Livy looked at one another and gave her

teasing smiles. "He's that good, huh?" said Charlotte.

Brooke clapped her hands to her cheeks. "I didn't mean ..."

Livy put a hand on her shoulder. "Yes, you did. And it's all right. We won't say anything to him about it. It's too special. I'm really happy for you."

"Now, we'll have to find someone for you, Livy," said Brooke.

Livy shook her head. "I'm not ready for anything like that. I'm happy for the two of you, but I'm begging you not to set me up with anyone. I just want to enjoy this time."

"Okay," said Charlie. "I understand. Romances are popping up so fast it's hard to keep up."

"Yeah, something like that," said Livy. "Speaking of romance, we've got two weddings to plan."

"Sounds like we'll be busy," said Charlotte, and Brooke wondered when the time would come when they'd be planning her own.

CHAPTER TWENTY-EIGHT

BROOKE

Brooke looked over the checklist Charlotte had drawn up for wedding planning. As agreed earlier, Rosalie at Tropi-Flowers was giving them a discount in return for publicity. The two brides were as different in their choices as any two could be. The theme of one was bright tropical colors like the flowers in the previous wedding. The other had a color theme of pale pink and white. The first was on the beach, the other in the gazebo.

Slowly they went through each sheet, working out staff requirements, food and music choices, and any other details the weddings required.

"It's helpful that the number of people attending each one is small," said Livy. "It gives us time to decide how we want to proceed if Gran and John approve of what we're doing."

"And a better idea if dinners at the Inn are doable," said Charlotte. "A lot of that depends on you and what you decide for the future."

Livy nodded solemnly, pricking interest in Brooke. She seemed unnaturally quiet at times.

After they reviewed all the details and were satisfied that the plans would easily move forward, Charlotte said, "Guess what! Shane and I have put in an offer on a house. I'm not sure we'll get it, but I'm hoping we will."

"Tell us about it," said Brooke. "It's in Miami, right?"

"In Coconut Grove on Bayshore Drive. It's beautiful and

not too big. Three bedrooms, a study, two and a half baths."

"Do you have photos?" Brooke asked.

Charlotte lifted her phone and showed them the listing. Brooke was shocked at how much the house cost, but then she was used to real estate prices in Ellenton. If the time came for her and Dylan to find living quarters in Florida, what would they be able to afford? She scolded herself for thinking too far ahead.

After the meeting broke up, Brooke decided to go visit with Mimi. She wanted to make sure Mimi was aware of her feelings for Dylan. She didn't want to hurt Adam and still loved Skye, but being with Dylan, discovering a new side to herself was a gift she couldn't ignore.

When Brooke knocked on the door, Mimi answered it and held a finger to her lips. "Skye fell asleep in the family room on the couch and I'm not moving her. But come in, Brooke. I'm glad you're here."

Brooke followed Mimi into the kitchen and out to the back lanai.

"Care for anything to drink?" Mimi asked.

Brooke shook her head, suddenly nervous. "No thanks. I want to talk to you about Dylan."

Mimi indicated a chair for Brooke and took a seat in one facing her. A short woman who was a fabulous cook, Mimi showed the result of her talent in her bulk. Her face showed her usual warmth as she said, "Brooke, I need to apologize. I've been pushing Adam and you together when I should've realized how right Dylan is for you. He came to me this morning to tell me how he feels about you."

"He did?" Brooke was surprised but pleased.

"Yes. He told Adam, too, that you and he are dating exclusively. Adam understood."

"Oh, I'm glad. I didn't want any hard feelings," Brooke said, relieved. “Adam’s a great guy, and you know how I feel about Skye, but it wasn’t going to work.”

“I’m pleased for you. Apparently, Dylan told his mother, and KK is thrilled. Dylan is a very special man as are you a special young woman. I’m very happy with the way things are turning out.” Mimi stood and reached down and hugged Brooke to her. “Love you.”

“I wonder what Gran would think of all she’s missed here at the cove,” said Brooke.

Mimi laughed. “Oh, we all keep her up-to-date. I’m sure she’s going to be very happy with the latest news.”

CHAPTER TWENTY-NINE

ELLIE

While John took a nap in the hotel room following a delicious lunch of different flavored *arancina*, the iconic Sicilian dish of creamy risotto that's breaded and deep-fried, Ellie took out her computer and checked for emails.

During these quiet times, she liked to know what was going on at home. Her absence was due, in part, to the plan she and the other grandmothers had concocted. It had worked with Charlotte and Shane. Who would be next? She opened the email from Liz and read:

> **"Good morning, afternoon or night wherever you are, dear friend. I hope you're well and having a wonderful time with John. Hearing about all your travels has made me wonder if that's something Sam and I should do.**
>
> **"But enough chatter. On to the news. Brooke and Dylan are together and it looks serious. Mimi said she's never seen Dylan so content. He's such a dear young man. Kind and generous to others. Brooke is like a different person. The purple hair and tattoo she thought would change her can't match what Dylan has done to make her believe in herself. Remember how she used to like to draw and paint as a kid? Well, she's begun doing it for real, with Dylan's**

encouragement. Of course, she's still busy working on the Inn.

"You'll be pleased to know that Brooke saw Jo during a quick trip to New York and things are better there. Jo has a new nurse helping her and she and Brooke have worked out a new communication plan that's better for them both.

"Enough from this end. Sending hugs and wishes to you both to stay well and travel safely.

"Hugs, Liz"

Ellie rose from her chair, walked over to the window, and stared out at the old buildings that told a story of their own, not seeing them but her home at Sanderling Cove.

Brooke and Dylan? How wonderful. Why she hadn't thought of them as a couple. He'd always been one of her favorite boys, a bit shy but sweet. But then his mother, KK, was such a live wire she'd put anyone in her shadow.

She thought back to Brooke's childhood. Why hadn't she encouraged Brooke to continue with art? She'd shown such promise as a child. It was a shame when practical matters took over, leaving other things behind.

CHAPTER THIRTY

BROOKE

A few days later, when Brooke saw Adam and Skye on the beach, she decided to walk over and say hello. As happy as she was about her relationship with Dylan, she wanted no hard feelings with Adam. She knew what it was like to have someone just seem to disappear.

Skye saw her and came running over to her. "Hi, Brooke. Come see what we found."

Laughing, Brooke allowed Skye to tug on her arm, and began to run to catch up to her.

She waved to Adam and stood aside as Skye poked at a gelatinous mass with a stick. "Daddy says it's a jelly fish. A storm blew it on shore."

"You need to be careful with it," warned Brooke.

Adam approached and said to Skye. "Why don't you walk farther up the shore and see what else last night's storm washed ashore."

"Okay," said Skye, dashing away from them.

"I'm pleased we have a chance to talk," said Brooke. "I want you to know how much I enjoyed getting to know you."

"No problem, Brooke. Things have a way of working out. My ex-wife and I have been in touch, and I'm thinking about giving her another chance."

"That's great. Right?"

Adam nodded though no smile appeared on his face. "We'll see. If it works out, it would be good for all of us. But she's let

Skye and me down before."

"Would you still stay in this area to be close to Mimi?"

"Yes, that's part of the deal. Maybe this location will be better for us. At the very worst, Mimi will be here for Skye if anything goes wrong. I've already talked to a construction company, and I'll start working with them soon, allowing me the opportunity to discover where a company of my own could fit in."

"It sounds like a lot of changes in a few days. I'm happy for you, Adam."

"Thanks. I'm happy for you too. You and Dylan. I think you make a great pair. Hope it all works out for you."

"Me, too," said Brooke, remembering the kisses she and Dylan had shared this morning.

Brooke hurried through the early morning coolness to the Inn. The bridal group was coming in today. The bride, who lived in St. Petersburg, wanted rooms for all ten couples who'd be attending her wedding. Getting one set of guests out of their rooms and another into them was going to take coordination between Beryl, the head of housekeeping, and her.

After the first set of guests left, the rooms would be cleaned. Then staff could place special gift bags in the guests' rooms, along with a bottle of wine and a fruit basket that they'd ordered from a gourmet food store down the road, at the bride's request.

Ambrose "Amby" Pappas, Beryl's husband and the Inn's landscaper and handyman, was erecting a small white tent on the beach. Unless the wind kicked up, tropical flowers would be wound around the tent poles, even though the ceremony would take place out on the sand. Then the Inn would serve glasses of champagne from the tent before the guests assembled for dinner in the private dining room inside the Inn.

With the advertising that Charlotte had done, room bookings were up, which meant more work. However, whenever Brooke was free from duties at the Inn, she was painting with Dylan. He allowed her free rein with his supplies, and she was learning how to prepare canvases as well as mixing colors and trying different brush strokes. She'd never been happier.

When she got to the kitchen, Livy and Billy Bob were already preparing breakfast for the few guests who'd requested an early meal. Brooke grabbed a cup of coffee and went to speak to Beryl.

Beryl and Amby had been working for Gran for many years and were a mainstay in the Inn family. Gran and John loved them dearly. It had been a little awkward for Brooke to take over Gran's position with Beryl, but it had worked out. Brooke didn't tell Beryl what to do, and Beryl kept Brooke informed.

Beryl greeted Brooke now. "We've got extra housekeepers on today and tomorrow to take care of wedding guests."

"Great," said Brooke. "If things go smoothly for this one and the next, we'll be comfortable asking Gran and John to continue to grow the wedding business."

"Seems to me you girls have planned each one carefully," said Beryl. "Your grandmother would be proud of you."

Pride filled Brooke. She and her cousins wanted to keep the Inn in the family; they just weren't sure how that would play out.

By the time the wedding party arrived, all but one room was ready for them. The bride was sharing her room with her maid of honor and her sister. Though the group was small, the excitement was still there. And like most of these occasions, a few last-minute crises had to be addressed.

When at last the wedding guests were assembled on the beach, and the groom and best man were in place, Brooke, Livy, and Charlotte awaited the arrival of the bride and maid of honor.

As the bride walked into the lobby, Brooke's breath caught. Her long white gown was stunning. Sleeveless and with a heart neckline, the lacy bodice clung to her trim figure. From there the tulle skirt billowed like a cloud of fabric.

Brooke noticed Charlotte's interest. Though Charlotte had much more reason to do so, they both had weddings on their minds.

The bridesmaid was dressed in a long, satiny dress in deep pink, which went with the tropical color theme. Brooke loved the idea that though the wedding was small, every detail had been addressed.

The bride's father helped her leave the Inn and onto the grass leading to the beach. Then the bridesmaid took the lead. They stopped at the edge of the grass, and with music from the guitar player the family had hired, the bridesmaid walked onto the sand, followed by the bride and her father.

Brooke didn't realize tears were glistening on her cheeks until Livy turned to her with a questioning look. "It just struck me. Who's going to walk me down the aisle when it's my turn?"

"I suppose John will," said Livy softly. "Or your mother can, or you can walk down the aisle alone. Don't worry about that now. You'll make the choice when the time comes."

"You're right," said Brooke. She watched from a distance as the ceremony took place. Then, while guests began to clap for the bride and groom, she and Charlotte went to the tent and poured champagne into tulip glasses to hand out to the guests, while Livy hurried back to the Inn to oversee the dinner.

Later, after dinner was over and cleaned up and the group continued to celebrate in the pool and spa, Brooke sat with her cousins in the kitchen.

"Looks like another successful wedding," said Charlotte.

"The first two have been very different but sweet," said Brooke. She turned to Livy. "Was it harder making dinner than lunch? Is that something we have to consider?"

"Not really harder, just different. Lunches will have lighter food," Livy said. "But the same amount of care goes into both."

Dinner had consisted of grilled beef tenderloins, a vegetable mélange, and potatoes au gratin everyone had raved over. For the one non-meat eater, a grilled portobello mushroom was served in the place of beef.

"As long as we can serve the food the bride requests, we'll be fine," said Charlotte.

"I'm thinking we should offer a bridal package that includes a set menu. Maybe offer three different choices for lunch and three for dinners," said Livy. "That way we can have some sort of control over bridal meals."

"Smart idea," said Brooke. "The easier things are for us, the better."

"I'm going to grab something to eat and then get to bed early," said Livy. "Tomorrow, we have breakfast for our regular guests, along with the special breakfast buffet for the wedding guests."

"I'm leaving too. Shane and I are going to have a light supper at Granny Liz's, and then we're sleeping at Gran's house," said Charlotte.

Left alone, Brooke sat in the kitchen, deep in thought. Through the years it had bothered her that she didn't have a father to take her trick or treating or to do other things that many of her friends took for granted. But until now, she hadn't realized how much she missed the idea of having her father walk her down the aisle on her wedding day. Livy was right. She didn't have to follow tradition, but she wished her father hadn't died. She wished she'd known the love of a father. She wished he wasn't just a picture in a frame.

Her cell phone rang. *Dylan.*

She eagerly clicked on the call. She loved him, knew she was special to him, but he still hadn't said those three magical words. She knew it was silly to be bothered by it because he'd shown her in every way that he did. Yet, it mattered to her.

"How did it go?" he asked.

"Good, but we're all tired. I'm thinking of taking a swim at Gran's pool to relax. Interested?"

"Can't. I'm babysitting Skye while Mimi has dinner and goes to a movie with Grandma Pat. Why don't you join me here?"

"Okay. For a while," said Brooke. "Where's Adam?"

"He flew back home to talk with his ex-wife. They're trying to work things out, and he doesn't want Skye to know what's going on until he feels more certain about it."

"Makes sense," she said. "I'll walk over, but I'm not sure how long I'll stay. We're doing a special wedding party buffet, along with our regular guest breakfasts in the morning, and I need to be at the Inn early."

"Deal. I just want to see you. It's been a while," said Dylan.

She laughed. "Yes, about five hours." She loved that he wanted to spend time with her.

She headed across the lawn, hearing laughter from the pool area. As usual, Rico Torres would be on night duty at the Inn. A college student who needed the money, he was the perfect person to tend to guests until midnight. After that, guests could call Gran's house for any assistance. That was a rare occurrence. Luckily, it hadn't happened this summer.

Dylan greeted her at the door with a wide smile and pulled

her into his arms. "Thanks for coming over. Skye's asleep, and I'm about to watch a movie. Thought you might like it too. It's about soldiers who rescue works of art from Nazis."

"Oh, that does sound interesting. I'll watch it with you, and then I'll have to leave," said Brooke.

"Okay. Want a beer? Coke? Water?"

"Ice cold water sounds delicious," she said, taking a seat on the living room couch.

Dylan returned to her with a glass of water for her and a cold beer for himself. A bowl of popcorn sat on the coffee table in front of her. Seeing it reminded her of the evenings she'd shared with her mother, and she reminded herself to call her in a couple of days. Chet sounded polite and eager to help, but she needed to know for herself that her mother was better. Maybe they'd Facetime one another.

Dylan took a seat on the couch next to her and placed an arm around her. "Great to see you," he murmured, lowering his lips to hers.

Brooke responded to the need that captured her.

"We've got to find an excuse to get away soon. Those times in New York ..." His voice drifted off but Brooke knew exactly what he meant. She'd dreamed of their lovemaking, awakening with a need to be with him. She didn't know how Charlotte and Shane managed to live separate lives while he worked in Miami and she stayed at the cove to help with the Inn.

They stretched out on the couch and Brooke nestled up against him, loving the feel of his strong body close to hers. With him, she felt complete.

They cuddled and talked about the day, and then sat up.

"Guess if we're going to see the movie, we'd better get started," said Dylan, his breath a little shaky.

Brooke sat up, and waited for him to start the movie.

As they sat together, she nibbled on popcorn and focused on the movie. Observing the precious works of art shown on the screen, she marveled at how quickly she'd become engrossed in all art. It was if, by doing without it for so long, she couldn't get enough exposure to it ...

The next thing Brooke knew she was being shaken awake.

"Hey, sweetheart, you fell asleep," Dylan said softly. "Maybe you'd better go home. I'll help you."

Brooke sat up and rubbed her eyes. "No, no. I'm all right. You stay here with Skye. I'm not far away from Gran's. I can do it on my own." She stood and threw her arms around him. "'Night. Thanks for having me here."

He hugged her tight. "I'm glad you came." He kissed her and led her to the front door and then stood watching her from the front porch as she made her way across the lawn to Gran's house.

After she got ready for bed, she climbed under the light cover and hugged her pillow, wishing it was Dylan.

CHAPTER THIRTY-ONE

LIVY

After tossing and turning most of the night, Livy awoke and quietly dressed. An early morning walk on the beach would, she hoped, help her cope with the feelings of loneliness she'd been struggling with. She was happy for Brooke and Charlotte, pleased they'd found the men each wanted to build a life with, but she couldn't help the emptiness that filled her at the thought of being left behind. Still, she knew she wasn't ready for a serious romance.

As she crossed the lawn, little droplets of dew glistened like diamonds on the threads of grass. She kept going, wanting to feel the cool sand beneath her feet, hear the cries of the birds above her, the sound of the waves hitting the shore as if reaching for a hug.

Livy stood at the water's edge. The frothy foam licked at her ankles sending a chill through her. Her life was a mess. She'd hidden too much, and though she knew she'd have to deal with it someday, she couldn't, wouldn't face it now. Tears escaped her. Tears she normally kept in check. She didn't know why but seeing her cousins this happy made her future seem so bleak. She'd thought she had it all planned out. Now, she wasn't so sure.

She felt movement behind her and quickly swiped at her face before turning to face Austin.

"Hi, what's up?" he asked, giving her a look of concern.

"Just allergies," she lied. "I couldn't sleep, so I came out here hoping a fresh breeze would help."

"I see," he said. "I couldn't sleep either. They say a tropical storm is coming. Nothing too bad. Maybe a lot of rain."

"When?" she asked, worried about the next wedding.

"Who knows? It's somewhere off the coast of Africa. It could take days or weeks to get here. You know how those things work. They seem to go nowhere, then suddenly they're here."

"Yes, it sometimes seems that way," Livy agreed. "Brooke said you're dating someone new."

"What? Dating? Not really," he said.

Livy let it go. Brooke had told her how upset she was about Austin being with Aynsley Lynch. But if Austin didn't want to talk about it, that was fine with her.

"I'll see you later," she said to Austin. "Guess I'll bake some cinnamon rolls this morning to add to the breakfasts we're serving."

"Sounds great." He grinned at her. "Are you willing to let me sneak one?"

"You'll have to talk to Billy Bob about it. If he says okay, it's fine with me," she teased.

"Aww, come on, play fair. He's one scary dude."

Livy laughed. "I'll speak to him about it."

"That's a promise. Right?" Austin said, playing along.

"For you, yes," she countered before turning and jogging away.

CHAPTER THIRTY-TWO

BROOKE

Brooke awoke to a quiet household. Checking the clock on her bedside table, she sucked in a breath of dismay. It was late.

She scrambled out of bed and went about her morning routine, hurrying as fast as she could. She didn't want to let her cousins down.

As she left her room, she checked Livy's room and Charlotte's. Both doors were open showing emptiness inside.

She rushed to the Inn and into the kitchen.

Billy Bob and Livy turned to her.

"You're late," said Livy. "See if Charlotte needs help setting up for the wedding party. The rest of the guests should be coming into the dining room soon."

"Sorry," said Brooke, helping herself to a cup of coffee from the coffee maker in the kitchen. She gulped down a couple of sips and went to the small dining room. Charlotte was there, setting silverware at places along the white-clothed table.

Tropical flowers from yesterday's ceremony now sat in three small vases placed in the middle and at two ends of the long table.

"Sorry I'm late," said Brooke. "Where do you want me? Here or in the main dining room?"

"I've got it covered here," said Charlotte. "Why don't you take my place welcoming our guests to breakfast in the main room?"

"Okay, done," said Brooke. She found it easier and easier to make small talk with the guests. It was fascinating to learn about them—where they lived, why they'd come to this part of Florida, and other pieces of information they gladly shared with her.

When the bride and groom walked into the private dining room to the sound of applause, Brooke couldn't help the sigh that escaped her. They looked so happy. She could hardly wait for the next wedding. It was all very romantic.

After the activity at the Inn had died down, Brooke naturally headed to Mimi's and Dylan's studio. He didn't work every day, but when he was there, she enjoyed working on art projects of her own. He told her he liked the company because she didn't talk as they concentrated on their projects, though they usually shared a few kisses.

Today, Dylan wasn't there. Restless, she decided to take time to wash her hair, do her nails and read a book. As she often did, she thought about the idea of staying at the cove and helping Gran and John run the Inn. Now that she and Dylan were together, she wondered how he'd feel about that.

When she returned to her room, she Facetimed her mother. Jo answered smiling.

"You look much better, Mom," said Brooke. "How are you feeling?"

"Wonderful since Chet has helped me. We're going to continue physical therapy for a while. He says it'll help me stay healthy."

"Great. He sounds very professional."

"He is. Very kind, too. We have a lot of friends in common, and we've even had a few of them here to socialize. Chet thinks it's important for me."

"He sounds delightful, Mom. I'm thankful you're feeling better. Let me know if you need help with anything." When they said goodbye, Brooke ended the call filled with relief. She hadn't heard her mother sound this happy in years.

Later, when Livy walked into her room, Brooke told her about her mother. "How is *your* mom?" Brooke asked her.

"Same as always. Summer means dances and dinners at the golf club," said Livy. "My mother loves that kind of thing, but I detest it. I can't tell you how happy I am to be here at the cove. It's always been my safe haven."

"The three of us cousins have all had different lives, but here we can just be ourselves. I think Gran always worked hard to keep it that way."

"I agree." Livy picked up the bottle of dark-pink nail polish. "Okay if I use some?"

"Sure. Come sit with me. Want to watch a movie together. A real chick flick?"

Livy grinned. "Okay. I'll make the popcorn."

Brooke's thoughts flew back to the night before when she'd seen a movie with Dylan. Waking up to see his face smiling at her was an image she'd loved. She hoped the time would come when that would happen every day.

That night, as they were cleaning up from entertaining the guests, Dylan came to the Inn to find her. "A gallery in Naples wants me to show some work there. I thought I'd drive down there tomorrow. Any chance that you could come with me?"

"Let me check with Charlotte and Livy. I'm off breakfast duty but I need to know they'll cover the evening social time."

"Okay," Dylan said agreeably.

Neither Charlotte nor Livy had a problem with her taking time off. So, the next morning, Dylan picked her up at eight o'clock, and they headed down the coast to Naples.

On the way, she and Dylan talked about his gallery in Santa Fe.

"How often do you have to be there?" Brooke asked.

"I've taken more time off this summer than ever before, but it's working out well. I'm going to take a short trip there at the end of the month. Summer brings a lot of business, and though I have the best gallery manager ever, I need to make an appearance now and then. My accountant is on top of the books, but I need to socialize with potential customers just like I did in New York."

"I understand. It's all part of the business," said Brooke.

"Exactly," said Dylan.

Naples was an upscale town with a charming downtown area. The gallery, Gallery 535, was a relatively small but well laid-out space with the ability to showcase paintings beautifully. Located on Fifth Avenue, it received steady traffic. Better yet, the owner, Henry Rousseau, was a friend of Claire's and a fellow enthusiast of Dylan's work.

After a delicious lunch of French cuisine in a nearby restaurant, Henry and Dylan made arrangements for several paintings to be shipped from Santa Fe to the gallery.

"I see by the work shown on your website that you've been busy," said Henry. "It's always a pleasure to see such a productive artist."

Dylan placed an arm around Brooke. "It helps to have a muse."

"But of course," said Henry, beaming at them. "Young love always helps any cause."

Brooke glanced at Dylan, pleased that once more he'd drawn her into his world.

Between working at the Inn and dabbling with artwork with Dylan, the days passed quickly. Soon, it was time for the next wedding. This one was in contrast to the colorful beach one held recently.

The pink-and-white color scheme was quiet in comparison. The bride, herself, was quiet but had been very particular about what she wanted. The groom, a strikingly handsome man, told them his fiancée could make all the arrangements. From Tampa, the bride and groom elected to stay overnight at the Inn. Most of their guests, however, had decided not to book rooms. It was a disappointment not to be able to get heads in beds, but Brooke agreed with her cousins that the Inn was still getting good exposure.

Dinner was going to be served buffet style to accommodate all fifty guests. Amby and his nephew, Rocco, moved the long dining room table which normally sat in the middle of the room to one side, removed the smaller tables, and set up five tables, rounds of ten, in the room. Brooke was as surprised as the others to see how well the room handled that size.

The bride, Jillian Parker, and the groom, Anderson Tremblay, arrived with a small group of their friends after lunch.

Charlotte greeted them while Brooke raced to the two rooms set aside for them to make sure everything was in order. The bride wanted sparkling water, fresh fruit, and cookies in each room. Satisfied that all was in order, Brooke stood aside as Charlotte led them to their rooms.

The guys, three of them, entered the groom's room and closed the door.

Jillian ushered her two girlfriends into the bridal retreat. "We'll relax here," she said to them. "Then we'll get ready. Mother will lead the rest of the wedding party here one-half hour before the ceremony so people won't get their clothing all mussed up in the humidity."

Brooke marveled at how controlled the bride was, as if she were simply going to host a dinner.

In the kitchen, Brooke spoke to Livy. "Anything I can do to help?"

"Pray the steamship roast doesn't get overcooked. The bride's mother made a big deal about it. Ham is easy. The rest will take care of itself."

"The open bar is set up in the gathering room, where the bride wanted it. The bartender has already called to confirm."

"If he's acceptable, we'll make a deal with him to help in the future," said Charlotte coming into the kitchen. "Why does this wedding seem so ... quiet?"

"It feels a little off to me too," admitted Brooke. "Aren't brides supposed to be giggly and happy?"

"Maybe she has to get married," said Livy. "It happens."

"Still, we have to make this a memorable occasion, as lovely as possible," said Charlotte.

"You're right. The wedding guests should be here soon," said Brooke.

With guests arriving, the occasion seemed much more exciting. One of the young men was acting as an usher, taking people outside to sit in chairs set up by the gazebo. The bride's mother had rented a house nearby where everyone congregated before coming to the Inn for the ceremony and dinner. People arrived in bunches.

After the commotion had settled down and people were seated outside, Brooke waited for the bride and bridesmaid to appear.

Jillian, the bride, looked stunning. Her dark hair was pulled into a bun on top of her head and was encircled by a tiara, which held her veil in place. Her sleeveless, white silk dress clung to her curves and fell in soft folds to her feet. Her two-bridesmaids, who looked like sisters, were dressed in pale-pink silk and were a lovely complement to the bride.

One of the bridesmaids peered out the window of the gathering room. "Is everyone here?"

"I believe so," said Brooke. "I just came from the kitchen, but people are seated and waiting."

"How about the groom and best man?" the other bridesmaid said, looking worried.

"I can't see from here," Brooke said. "But I can go and check for you."

"Please," said the bride in a quivering voice.

Brooke walked out onto the lawn and stood behind the seated guests. The minister was standing behind the white table, but no one was at his side. She turned, saw Charlotte rushing toward her, and hurried to meet her.

"What's wrong?" Brooke asked, though a sinking feeling had already settled at her feet. "Is it the groom?"

Wide-eyed, Charlotte nodded. "He and one of his friends went out through the kitchen, got into a car, and drove off. What are we going to do?"

Guests were stirring in their chairs and cast curious looks at them.

"We'd better let the minister know," said Charlotte. "He can inform the group." She left Brooke and walked into the gazebo and spoke quietly with the minister.

"There's been a delay," said the minister. "Please remain seated while I go check with the bride."

Charlotte led the minister inside the Inn and to the gathering room where the bride was waiting.

Brooke followed, feeling sick. This was any bride's worst nightmare.

As Brooke walked into the gathering room, Charlotte finished talking, and Jillian let out a shriek that Brooke would never forget.

"Let's go back to your room," said one of the bridesmaids to Jillian, who'd crumpled into her arms.

"I'll tell Aunt Prudence," said the other bridesmaid, looking pale. "She's going to be furious."

"I told her I shouldn't marry him," sobbed the bride. "Now, look what's happened." She left the room.

Brooke and Charlotte turned to the minister.

"Will you make the announcement?" said Charlotte. "I'll speak to Jillian's mother about dinner."

Livy came out of the kitchen wearing an apron and a chef's hat. "I'm ready to serve the meal at the proper time. I'm going to pull the roast from the oven and hope for the best."

"Let's make sure we have plenty of refreshments here at the bar," said Charlotte. "I have a feeling we'll need more than we thought."

Later, Brooke marveled at the composure of the bride's mother. Having paid for the dinner, she was determined that her friends enjoy it. Jillian couldn't be talked into joining them until later after she'd obviously had plenty to drink.

Still in her wedding gown, which she refused to take off, she finally collapsed on a chair by the pool. Then with pure defiance, she jumped into the water and started crying again.

Brooke was finally able to coax her out of the pool and back to her guestroom where the angry, embarrassed woman finally fell asleep.

Shaken by all that had happened, Brooke joined her cousins who were trying to make the best of the situation. She thought of Dylan and Shane and felt sure neither man would do something as cruel as this.

Long after the wedding guests had departed, Brooke,

Charlotte, and Livy discussed the events of the day.

"We're lucky Prudence Parker honored her commitment and paid for everything. I offered her a discount," said Brooke. "The extra booze served will more than make up for that."

"Shane and I have talked about eloping like Gran, but Granny Liz made me realize that would be unfair," said Charlotte. "And then I've always dreamed of a small wedding here."

"Shane is not about to leave you at the altar," said Livy.

"I know, I know. But I won't feel the same way about the gazebo until we have another happy ceremony there," said Charlotte.

"Well, then, we can start planning yours there," said Livy with a note of impatience.

"Right," said Brooke. "Any ideas about when we should start?"

Charlotte laughed and lifted her hands in defeat. "Okay, okay. I know how silly that sounded. We won't let this bad experience destroy the atmosphere inside the gazebo. It's still the perfect place for a wedding."

"Good thing," said Livy. "Because we received a call requesting a wedding here at the Inn next week."

The three of them high-fived one another. Something was always happening in this business. Some of it better than others.

CHAPTER THIRTY-THREE

CHARLOTTE

When she could get away from the Inn, Charlotte walked over to Granny Liz's to find Shane. He was having dinner with his grandparents, and she needed to talk to him. She was still shaken by the wedding disaster. Granny Liz greeted her at the door. "C'mon in. Shane and Sam are sitting out back. I heard about the disaster you had at the Inn. What happened?"

"I'm not sure. I overheard a lot of conversation. Brooke and Livy didn't think things were right from the beginning. The bride didn't seem the least bit excited. Then during dinner, I heard whispers about the bride being pregnant, which forced the marriage. Obviously, it wasn't something the groom really wanted."

"Poor girl," Granny Liz said. "They should've determined that before going through all the motions. How was the bride's mother?"

"Funny you should ask. I think the proper word is stoic. The groom's parents didn't stay, of course, but the best man did because he's dating one of the bridesmaids. Nevertheless, it was awkward."

"I can well imagine," said Granny Liz. "We won't have to worry about anything like that with you and Shane. He told us he's pretty excited about the day you two become official."

Shane was such a dear man, Charlotte thought, feeling extra lucky.

CHAPTER THIRTY-FOUR

BROOKE

Brooke was more shaken by the wedding disaster than she wanted anyone to know. She and Dylan had agreed to date exclusively, but that was a far cry from getting married. They were still discovering things about one another. What if he decided at the last minute that dating her wasn't what he really wanted?

When he phoned her that evening, she quickly picked up the call. "Hi. What's up?"

"Thought it would be nice to sit and relax for a while. Are you at Gran's house?

"Yes. I'm sitting on the porch reading. Come on over."

When he arrived, he gave her a kiss and took a seat in a rocking chair next to hers.

"I guess you heard about the wedding mishap," she said, curious to see his reaction.

"Yeah. Crummy of the groom to run off like that. He must not have wanted to get married after all."

"I guess," she said.

He studied her. "Hey, you're not thinking I'd do anything like that to you, are you? If we decide to take our relationship to that level, I wouldn't hurt you like that."

She let out a sigh of relief.

He reached over and clasped her hand. "I don't play around with the truth. I'll be totally honest with you."

"Okay, thanks," she said, eager to move onto another topic.

"How are sales going at Claire's gallery?"

"I've sold one more painting. It's been terrific exposure for me. That, the gallery in Miami, and now the one in Naples showing my work means better chances for me to sell. I'm grateful that things are going well."

"Me, too. You deserve it."

He grinned as he asked her, "Are you going to be able to work on some of your own paintings this week?"

"I should be able to, though we have another wedding next week." She loved that they could work together, each on a project of their own.

"You're an inspiration to me," he said.

She laughed. "I don't know why, but I love it." She yawned. "Sorry. It's been quite a day."

"Look, I'll go. With Skye around, we get up early at Mimi's house. Especially with her father gone."

"I understand. I'll see you in the studio right after the breakfast crowd goes." She stood and sighed as Dylan rose and wrapped his arms around her.

"See you tomorrow." His lips met hers and all sense of time evaporated as she was carried away on a sea of longing. He did that to her.

The next day, as soon as she could, she hurried over to Dylan's studio. She'd put on her painting clothes—a pair of shorts, an old pair of sneakers, and a yellow T-shirt she'd bought with a picture of a dachshund painting in front of an easel. She loved all dogs; but dachshunds were her favorite.

He looked up from working on a canvas he'd laid on the floor, a red paintbrush in his hand. "There she is, my partner in crime."

She laughed. "It's going to feel wonderful to do some work

here. The stress of the weekend has rattled us all."

He kissed her. "Every day is better with you here."

She threw her arms around him, careful to avoid the paintbrush, and nestled against his chest. She could hear his heart beating a rapid pace. She loved that she could affect him in that way.

They pulled apart smiling at one another.

Dylan's cell rang. He put down the paintbrush and answered it.

While Brooke pulled out her work and began mixing paints, she couldn't help overhearing his end of the conversation. It was Claire, and it didn't sound good. She set down her palette knife and moved closer to him.

His face had lost color, and he looked upset.

"What's wrong?" she whispered.

He held up a finger. "Claire, are you accusing me of being dishonest with you? That's not how I operate. I'm going to put you on speaker so Brooke can hear you too."

"Okay," said Claire. "I'll start at the beginning. I just got a call from Laurence Veltmann, who bought your 'Beach Sunrise' painting. He and Margery were at a dinner party over the weekend, and the hosts proudly showed them a painting they had recently bought. It is almost identical to theirs, and he was upset. The artist's name is listed as yours, but the other party paid half the price of 'Beach Sunrise'."

"My name was on it? Where did they get the painting?" asked Dylan, looking stricken.

"From a gallery in the Caribbean where they were vacationing," said Claire. "I need to ask you if 'Beach Sunrise' is part of a series that you did? You told me it was the only original."

"Yes," said Dylan, his nostrils flaring. "That painting is the only one. I don't do series. Not with the size and scope of each painting. Did you investigate the gallery?"

"Sadly, the gallery has closed," said Claire. "But I'm having a friend check out the space. It's on the French side of St. Maarten. Where would anyone have been able to find information on that painting, enough to reproduce it?"

"You think someone was forging Dylan's painting and then selling it as his own?" said Brooke aghast.

"I do. My friend will take photos of other paintings for sale in the area to see if any resemble Dylan's work. It could be that if he's talented enough, the painter could be forging other artists as well."

Dylan's voice was low, shaking. "I think I know where someone could have seen a photo of this particular piece. Not entirely finished but done enough so that it could be copied except for the final touches I made with Brooke."

Brooke turned to him.

"My friend, Austin Ensley, is a computer guy, and he did some work on my website," said Dylan. "We showed a photo of the painting almost done with a story about my painting process. If this person was trolling for ideas, he could've come across it. Otherwise, there was no way other people could have seen it. I keep them pretty close until I'm ready to show them."

Brooke felt sick. Austin would be horrified to learn that he may have contributed to someone stealing Dylan's work.

"I'll get back to you with more information as I uncover it," said Claire. "I'm asking Laurence's friend to look at your printed portfolio to see if they recognize other works of yours at this gallery." She hesitated. "Dylan, I'm very sorry this has happened. Forgery is not unknown in the art world. Usually at a higher, more professional level, but it happens. People want to make easy money, no matter how they get it."

"Should I report it? Call the police? What?"

"At this time, there's nothing that can be done without

more information. As I said, I'm hoping this is a one-time thing. I'll call Laurence and reassure him," said Claire.

"Can you please send me a photo of the painting his friends bought?" said Dylan. "I need to see it as clearly as possible."

"Will do," said Claire. "Sorry to have to give you such bad news, but I'm thankful there are no issues with your work. I will reassure Laurence and Margery on that point."

"Thanks," said Dylan. He ended the call and faced Brooke. "Guess I'd better go talk to Austin. We need to fix my website. I want people to know about me but don't want to show any of my works-in-progress online. I didn't realize that could be dangerous."

"Austin is going to feel terrible," said Brooke. "Want me to come with you?"

"Yes. It's not his fault. He was just trying to help me."

Together, they went to find Austin.

He was at Granny Liz's packing some boxes.

"Where are you going?" Dylan asked.

"Are you moving out?"

Austin shook his head. "No. I bought a little place down the beach to use as my office. It's too crowded here, and this way when my parents and siblings visit from Atlanta, there'll be more room for them. I bought it as an investment. I can always rent it out if I decide to move back west." He grinned at them. "What are the two of you up to?"

"We need to talk about the website you updated for me. There's been a problem." Dylan went on to tell Austin about the forgery and how they figured whoever it was that did it had seen the painting on his website and the story of how Dylan put together a painting.

As Dylan talked, Austin's face grew grim. "I'm sorry, Dylan. It never crossed my mind that someone would want to steal your ideas or recreate the painting itself. That's awful!"

"Claire, the gallery owner in New York, said such thefts are not unheard of, but I'm sick about it," said Dylan." I'm still working hard to get noticed."

"Apparently you've succeeded. I suppose it's a compliment that someone wants to imitate you, imitation being the height of flattery," said Austin. "But I don't like it. Unless you find the person or persons who did it, I don't suppose there's anything you can do about it."

"I guess they've come and gone. The gallery closed. Who knows what they told the owner to get my painting shown there?"

Brooke froze. "Do you think they presented himself as you? That's weird enough to make my skin crawl."

"Or maybe it was the kind of place that took things on consignment, sort of like an estate sale store," said Austin. "We just put some paintings from my mother's house in a store like that."

Dylan rubbed his chin. "We'll be getting more information from Claire. In the meantime, let's take that part about the painting and my style off my website. It was a great idea that went very wrong."

"I doubt it's going to happen again, but who knows? Now that this character made it work once, maybe they'll try it again somewhere else," said Austin.

Brooke and Dylan exchanged horrified looks.

"How about as soon as I get to my office, I'll take care of that for you," said Austin. "Most of my equipment has been set up at the cottage already. But I need to get these boxes out of here. My little brother is coming for a visit sometime, and he's going to use my old office space for his bedroom."

"Okay, thanks," said Dylan. He took Brooke's elbow and they walked away.

"You can't let this ruin what you're working on now," said

Brooke. Dylan looked like a broken man. "If anything, make it spur you to put out more work."

Dylan turned to her. "What if this ruins my reputation? People might get the wrong idea about my integrity, especially if the press gets hold of this and twists words like they sometimes can do."

"I'm sure Claire knows the importance of handling things quietly. But if you feel the need to speak to her again, go ahead and call."

"I think I will. I'll see you later. I'm going to call it quits for the day. Stay here in the studio if you want."

"I'll work a little bit and then clean up," said Brooke. She felt a need to keep busy because thoughts were flying inside her head. In Dylan's case, someone copied his painting, signed his name to it, sold it, and took off. She supposed if they could find the person who did it, he or she would claim they didn't know it was a fake and blah, blah, blah. Impossible to prove. The only positive thing to come out of this was the idea that someone believed Dylan's work was valuable enough to copy it. Interesting.

Brooke added a few strokes of color to the painting she was working on, wanting to get just the right balance. She knew she was a long way from anyone wanting to copy her work. Still, it gave her satisfaction to work on a painting.

She was cleaning up the studio when Dylan came in. "I'm going to New York to see Claire. I don't know how long I'll be gone. I need to be able to talk to the Veltmanns and their friends in person. Both Claire and I would feel better if I were there."

"I understand," said Brooke. "Anything I can do for you here?"

He shook his head. "No, just keep on doing what you're doing, giving me moral support."

"Of course." She stepped forward and wrapped her arms around him. "Everything's going to be all right. Even if you never find the person who did this to you, the Veltmanns and their friends will understand you're an honorable man."

"Yes, that's what's important to me. I can't have my reputation sullied by some opportunistic, immoral son-of-a-bitch." Dylan's brow creased with anger.

"Do you want me to take you to the airport?" she asked.

"Thanks, but Austin is going to do it. Hopefully, you can pick me up when I return." He caressed her face with his broad, talented hands. "I'm going to meet Austin out by the gate. I'll call you tonight."

He left, and Brooke wondered how everything could change so quickly. She understood how angry Dylan was, his need to go to New York. Integrity was very important to him. It was one of the many qualities she admired about him.

When she returned to Gran's house, both Charlotte and Livy were there.

"What's this about some kind of trouble Dylan is in?" Charlotte asked. "Shane was supposed to meet Austin, but he said he had to take Dylan to the airport, that he was having an issue with one of his paintings."

Brooke sighed and told them the story. "He just wants to make sure everyone understands how upset he is, how he'd never cheat an art patron by selling something of his for far less at another gallery. His reputation is in question, and he doesn't like it."

"I know Dylan well enough to understand he'd never play games like that," said Livy. "Do you think they'll ever catch the person who did it?"

"Doubtful. Shady person, shady gallery," said Brooke. "The gallery suddenly closed. Who knows what other paintings were sold there? Maybe they all were fakes."

"Pretty lousy. People on vacation thinking they were getting a bargain don't often check too carefully on those things," said Charlotte. "It can happen."

"Well, let's hope Dylan doesn't get too discouraged. He's really coming into his own," said Livy. "And I'm happy for him." She looked at Brooke. "Both of you."

Brooke gave her a hug. She could always count on her cousins for support.

CHAPTER THIRTY-FIVE

LIVY

Livy headed for the Inn with Charlotte and Brooke. With more and more guests in-house, they all decided to work that social time when they could. It had already proven to be a great way to build reputation and reservations for guest rooms. Besides, Livy liked meeting different people. Owning a bakery had been a lot of work, but it had also provided her with a day full of seeing other people. She loved everyone at the cove but needed to feel as if she had her own space too.

She'd met with Grace Hendrix at her restaurant, Gills, in Clearwater to see about possibly setting up a business arrangement to supply them with cakes and other sweets. But until Gran and John returned, she couldn't really make any decisions. As the summer wore on, she liked the idea of working at the Inn more and more but wanted to keep her options open.

Having choices was important to her. It was one reason she was determined just to keep things casual with any of the dates she went on. Eric, Adam, Kyle, and Austin, the eligible men at the cove, were all friends and good company, and that's how she wanted it left.

She'd taken to walking on the beach as often as she could to sort her thoughts. The ability to do that most days was another reason for her to consider staying.

Livy entered the kitchen and set to work organizing the

appetizers. They'd experimented with a lot of different things but often came back to the same baked cheese puffs, stuffed mushrooms, and assorted veggie or meat trays that everyone loved. The salt-air and lazy days in the sun tended to increase their guests' appetites, and she and her cousins were more than willing to hand appetizers out if it resulted in future business.

Livy was chatting with a guest when Kyle Worthington walked into the room. Melissa and Morgan's brother was an agent in Hollywood, dealt with a lot of stars, and was surprisingly unassuming. With dark straight hair, chocolate brown eyes, a wiry body, and an easy manner, he was as handsome as he was charming. She still remembered him as a cute boy her age on the rare times they'd vacationed at the cove with their families simultaneously.

As usual his appearance drew attention.

Livy waved to him and waited while he headed her way.

"Welcome back to the cove. Are you here for another short visit?" she asked.

"I'm hoping to make it longer," he said. "I promised Grandma Pat I would. She said a lot has happened since I left soon after you arrived."

"I'm sure you've heard that Shane and Charlie are engaged. Dylan and Brooke are exclusive now. That about sums it up," said Livy.

"And you?" he asked, his gaze resting on her.

Livy shrugged. "You know I'm enjoying my time here, but not looking for romance. Once the summer is over, I'll have to decide where I want to live while I set up my own business."

"I see," said Kyle. "How about going out with me tomorrow night? We can head to Clearwater. I want to try out Grace's restaurant."

"Hmmm, that does sound like fun," she said, giving him a

teasing smile. For all his stature in Hollywood, he was just a cove kid to her.

CHAPTER THIRTY-SIX

BROOKE

After having nibbles in the kitchen with her cousins, Brooke returned to Gran's house feeling exhausted. She knew it was due, in part, to worrying about Dylan. She'd just changed her clothes and was heading to the porch to read when her cell chimed. *Dylan.*

"Hi. How's it going?" she asked forcing cheer into her tone, intending to lift his spirits.

"Claire and I are meeting with the Veltmanns tomorrow evening. I've set aside time in the morning to go visit your mother if you'd like. It might make you feel reassured about her working with Chet."

"Would you do that for me? That would be wonderful. I haven't called much, but I'd be relieved to know everything's fine, after her putting up with Jamie."

"Okay, then I'll go tomorrow. But unless you want me to tell her ahead of time, I'll just appear at the house so I can see what her situation is really like," said Dylan.

"Please don't warn her. She'll understand, I'm sure," she said, touched by his offer. "How's everything else going?"

"I've decided to go on to Santa Fe from here. I want to make sure everything is in order there. I'm in touch with my manager every day, but I need to put my feet on the ground there, so to speak."

"I understand," Brooke said, tamping down her disappointment. She'd grown to love their time together.

"And I might visit my parents in Idaho at their summer home. I'm trying to work that out now. Might as well take advantage of the time away to take care of personal things." Dylan's voice softened. "But I miss you, Brooke."

"I miss you too," she said, realizing all over again how much he meant to her.

"How are things there?" he asked her.

"Good. The Inn is almost fully booked, the social gathering went well, and Kyle Worthington showed up. He looks terrific. He and Livy are going out tomorrow night. That should be interesting."

Dylan laughed. "No matchmaking. Our grandmothers are taking care of that."

She joined in the laughter. "Who knew such well-respected women would stoop to that?"

"Hey, I'm glad they decided to get us all together. How else could I have gotten to know you this well?"

Brooke sobered. Dylan was right. She'd be forever grateful to all the grans for the opportunity to be with Dylan.

They chatted about little things, using it as a way to stay connected, but then Dylan ended the call with a promise to call after a visit to her mother.

The next day, Brooke was sitting in the office at the Inn reviewing income numbers when her cell rang. *Her mother*.

Not sure what her mother's reaction had been to a surprise visit from Dylan, she hesitated. But after more chiming, she decided to pick it up.

"Hi, Mom. What's up?"

"Are you spying on me?" her mother said in a stern voice, then laughed. "Your man, Dylan, surprised me this morning. He's such a doll. 'Said he just wanted to check up on me."

"Yes. He's back in New York on business and suggested a visit to you. How are things going?"

Her mother sighed. "I think I'm in love."

"What? What are you talking about? In love? With whom?"

"Don't worry. We're not going to do anything rash, but both Chet and I are attracted to one another. We've spent a lot of time talking. He's a very genuine person and we have a lot in common. His wife died two years ago, and he's just starting to think of being with other women."

"You haven't ..."

Her mother laughed. "Brooke, you know me better than that. I'm looking for someone I can be comfortable with, someone who knows the real me. What is developing between us is very sweet, very special. And, yes, sexy too."

Astonished, Brooke collapsed in her chair. *This was her mother?*

"Well?" said her mother.

"If this is for real, I'm happy for you, Mom. But please don't rush into anything. And please be careful financially."

"I'll pretend I didn't hear that last remark," said her mother. "Chet Brigham is as honest as they come." Her voice softened. "We're adults and don't need advice from anyone. But we're smart enough not to hurry this along. We want to take our time, see if this is what we really want." She giggled. "But I already know how I feel about it. Surprising as it is, I love him."

Her mother giggled? She actually giggled? Brooke was speechless.

"I hope you're not upset," her mother said. "It's always been you and me."

"Mom, I'm delighted for you. Can you believe that during this crazy summer we've both found someone to love?" Brooke started to laugh.

Suddenly they were both laughing over this, over the possibilities ahead.

"One day at a time," her mother finally said. "Your young man is perfect for you. But he's going through a tough time right now."

"He told you about the forgery?" Brooke asked, surprised.

"Yes, he told me all about himself, how you and he can work together, and ... and all," her mother said.

"Before things get too serious with you, I'd like to spend some time with Chet," Brooke said, feeling protective.

"No problem. He wants to have time with you, too. Dylan suggested that at the end of summer you both come and spend some time with us."

"In the meantime, send pictures, and we can do Facetime."

"That sounds like a smart plan," her mother. "I've got to go. Chet is outside with Dylan. But he'll soon be ready to do some exercises with me, and I want to freshen up." Her voice held a lilt to it that Brooke had never heard, and before she was aware, her eyes prickled with tears of happiness for her mother.

After they ended the call, Brooke sat still, stunned by the conversation. Her mother falling in love? It was such a fabulous surprise,

A few minutes later, her cell chimed again. *Dylan.*

"Hi, Dylan. I just got off the phone with my mother. She says she's in love with Chet."

"Looks that way," he responded, and she heard the smile in his voice. "Chet is a great guy, and the chemistry between them is definitely there. They're both aware they can't rush into anything, but they have a connection. I didn't realize your mother was such a pretty woman. She's positively glowing. Chet admitted he's never met a woman he's been interested in since his wife died."

"And he's been a nurse for some time?" Brooke asked.

"Yes, he'd been doing this for most of his career, after deciding he didn't want IT work," said Dylan. He laughed. "I got as much information as I could in such a short visit."

Brooke grinned. "I really appreciate it. What a fabulous turn of events. Who would've thought it?"

"It's all new, like us, but real," said Dylan. "Look, I gotta go. I pulled off the road to talk to you, but I'm blocking someone else. Talk to you later."

"Good luck tonight," Brooke said. "And thanks again."

She clicked off the call and hurried into the kitchen bursting to tell someone the news. But Livy wasn't there.

She left the Inn to check for someone at Gran's house and saw Livy and Charlotte down by the beach.

"Guess what," she cried, running up to them.

They turned to her.

"My mother is in love," said Brooke, breathless from her sprint.

"What?" said Charlotte, smiling.

"My mother is in love," said Brooke, unable to hide her excitement. The words came tumbling out, how the nurse was a cool guy who was a widower who connected with her mother.

"For real? This one isn't after money or anything?" said Livy.

"Nope. Dylan met him and talked to them both and says there's something very real there. Neither one is in a rush, but isn't that the best news? Now I won't have to worry about my mother."

"Hold on," said Charlotte. "One step at a time."

"I know it's early in the relationship, but I have to believe my mother finally is getting a break."

"Well, then, let's celebrate," said Livy. "Group hug."

With her cousins embracing her, and her hopes high, Brooke sent a thank you to the skies above. She'd made many wishes sitting on the sand looking out at the water, but this wish had ended with the biggest surprise of all.

CHAPTER THIRTY-SEVEN

BROOKE

Brooke waited anxiously to hear from Dylan about his meeting with the Veltmanns and their friends. He'd told her he was worried about it, but she felt because he was always honest both parties would understand that it was an unfortunate situation out of his control. Still, because he cared so much, she did too.

She was in bed reading when he called her. "How did it go?" she asked eagerly. "Did you see the painting?"

"Good and yes," he said. "The fake was surprisingly like mine color-wise, but the textures and brush strokes were off. Laurence Veltmann noticed that too, but his friends didn't. I suspect his friends aren't real collectors. But it bothered me that someone was happy with an inferior product and, of course, I hated seeing my name on it."

"It's awful to have people think you'd release something that wasn't up to your standards," she agreed.

"Claire stepped right in and explained to the friends that while some of my pieces may look easy to reproduce, the quality wasn't there, and that as a student of art, I created works of art that not only spoke to me, but told a story of their own through color, texture, and balance."

"Exactly," said Brooke. "I'm happy she was there to support you. Any news of the gallery or other paintings shown there?"

"Actually, there is. Another customer bought a painting from there, but when they had it appraised, they discovered it was a forgery. As far as Claire knows from her research into the matter, no other paintings were listed there with my name. Guess this person or persons did just single works of art, put them up for sale, and took off. According to the gallery's printed matter, the paintings shown there were originals. But we know at least two weren't."

"I guess you should be flattered," said Brooke trying to add a note of levity to the somber situation.

"I'm not," Dylan said. "I'm pissed. Claire has encouraged the Veltmanns and their friends to keep this to themselves to prevent other activity of this kind. She did offer a little discount on other works of mine at her gallery. That might actually work. They seemed interested."

"When are you off to Santa Fe?" Brooke asked.

"I'm staying one more night in New York, and then I'll fly out there. But, Brooke, I want you to join me. I want to show you my gallery there and have you meet my manager. Do you think you can get away?"

"I don't know. We have a wedding coming up, and I'd have to make sure Livy and Charlie are okay with it."

"Please ask," said Dylan. "It would mean a lot to me."

"Okay, I will. I'd love to see Santa Fe and your gallery. You've said your newer works are a little different from those done in the mountains."

"They are. Let me know if you can make it, and I'll arrange flights for you. I wish you were here. Claire and I are going to dinner, and then tomorrow I'm going to check out some other galleries."

"I miss you, Dylan. Have fun tonight. I'll let you know tomorrow if I can come to Santa Fe."

"Okay. I'd better go. 'Bye." Dylan clicked off the call and Brooke sat for a moment. She'd waited for Dylan to say more, hoped he'd say those three famous words. Scolding herself for rushing things in her mind, she got up and went to talk to Charlotte and Livy.

She knocked on Charlotte's door. Shane was in Miami, and with no date for Livy, it had become a "Girls' Night" at home.

Charlotte answered the door, a towel around her head. "Come in. I just washed my hair and am going to dry it. What's up?"

"Let's go to Livy's room, and I'll explain."

When they knocked on Livy's bedroom door, she called out. "I can't move right now."

Brooke and Charlotte opened the door to find Livy atop her bed applying nail polish to her toes.

"What is this? A party?" she said, grinning. "I'll be through in a second." She held up the bottle of nail polish. "Eggplant purple. What do you think?"

"I like it," said Brooke.

"Can I borrow it?" Charlotte asked.

'Sure," said Livy. "What are we gathered for?"

"I need your agreement for me to take a short trip to Santa Fe. Dylan wants me to see his gallery and to meet his manager," said Brooke. "I told him I'd have to ask you two for the time off. We've got a wedding coming up, and I want to do my share."

"Hold it," said Livy. "He's asking you to join him in Santa Fe? This sounds serious, Brooke."

"Well, it is," said Brooke. "But Dylan hasn't told me he loves me yet. I know it's still early, but my thoughts keep reminding me of that, and I just hope I'm not jumping into something too soon. Maybe he just wants me in his business, acting as his Florida manager or something." She hated her insecurity.

Charlotte gave her a steady look. "Brooke, I've seen the way Dylan looks at you, the way he acts around you, and I think business is the last thing on his mind." She reached out and patted her back. "I know you've been hurt before, but this is the real deal. Relax and enjoy. And if you want to go to Santa Fe, I'll cover for you."

"Me, too," said Livy. "This is a big step forward. Dylan is a sensitive guy who isn't about to hurt you. Go and have a good time."

"Thanks." She suddenly felt teary as she studied them. "I grew up wanting a sister. I'm very grateful I've got you two in my life—my sisters in spirit." She hugged them both, being careful not to mess with Livy's toes or Charlotte's wet hair.

They ended up watching a movie together, with Livy providing popcorn as she usually did.

As Brooke closed her eyes in bed later that evening, she knew how lucky she was.

Two days later, Brooke sat aboard a plane heading west. This was another adventure the summer had brought about, and she was as excited as a five-year-old awaiting her birthday party. Aside from the cost, a trip like this was almost impossible growing up because of the care of her mother. She gazed out at the clouds outside her window. She'd talked to her mother this morning. She'd babbled with pleasure about the things she and Chet were doing together when he was off-duty. Her mother and Chet realized they'd met briefly earlier and knew a lot of the same people, making Brooke feel more at ease about their sudden love. But then, she was as new to love as her mother and didn't doubt that it could happen.

Her travel was uneventful, but Brooke was glad when the flight approached the airport in Albuquerque. She could hardly wait to see Dylan and discover the area. Dylan told her the drive from there to Santa Fe was about one hour unless you took the Turquoise Trail, which would add about forty minutes to the drive.

Heart beating with excitement, Brooke walked into the baggage claim area where they'd agreed to meet. She eagerly scanned the area looking for Dylan. When their gazes met, the space around her seem to disappear as they moved toward one another.

He pulled her into his arms and hugged her tight before lowering his lips to hers. When they pulled apart, pleasure lit his eyes. "I'm happy you're here. I can't wait to show you around. There's something magical about Santa Fe and this area."

She smiled up at him. Here, his man bun seemed appropriate as did the turquoise and silver necklace he wore inside the collar of his blue sport shirt. He pulled a brown silk bag from his pants pocket and showed it to her.

"This is for you, to help you feel loved and protected," he said, lifting a necklace of turquoise and silver beads out of the bag and placing it around her neck.

"It's gorgeous," she said, loving the heavy weight of it settling against her chest.

"There's so much I want to show you. Are you still game for the ride home on the Turquoise Trail, or are you too tired from the trip?" asked Dylan.

"I definitely want to go on the trail," she said. "I read about it, and it looks fantastic. I love Native American arts and crafts. It touches me in a way I can't define."

"I get it. Me, too." His blue eyes seemed to take on a different color as if the bit of turquoise he wore added its hue to them.

As soon as her bag appeared on the luggage carousel, Dylan grabbed it, and they headed to his car.

"I'm glad you made it." Dylan slid behind the wheel of his

SUV. This vehicle suited him better than the red truck in Florida, and Brooke realized he was as much at home here as he was in Florida. Maybe more so.

As they began the trip on State Highway 14, Brooke marveled at the mountains around them.

"Another day, if you like, we can take a tram ride in the Sandia Mountain Cibola National Forest. The view is spectacular," said Dylan. "I wanted to give you a colorful introduction to Santa Fe, but we can come back and spend more time here if you want. Right now, driving along this road you're going to see old mining towns, a ghost town, llamas, historic churches, a bit of everything. In Madrid, there are a ton of galleries, arts and crafts shops, restaurants, and the like. I thought we could grab a late lunch there and then after you get a look around, we'll head into Santa Fe."

"It sounds delightful. I've never been out west, as odd as that may sound," said Brooke. "We never had the money to travel, and with Mom needing extra help, we stayed close to home. But now, I can't wait to see everything."

Dylan took hold of her hand and squeezed it. "I have so much I want to show you."

"Thank you. I want to see it all."

When they pulled into Madrid and Dylan parked the car, Brooke stared at the conglomeration of colorful painted wooden structures nestled together along the street. She could imagine what lay inside each shop filled with intriguing gifts. Even the wooden trim on adobe buildings was painted in a variety of bright colors.

As they walked, she noticed a few art galleries and shops tucked behind greenery and picket fences.

"Thought we'd eat at the Mine Shaft Tavern. It's more colorful at night, but the food is good, and it's an historic building. They have a Hatch Green Chile Basket that is great and something different for you to try. The fish tacos and the enchilada plate are tasty too."

"I'm going to let you order for me," Brooke said, smiling at him. "I trust you."

He laughed. "Wait until you see Santa Fe. You'll fall in love with it."

She smiled but wondered if he was going to tell her that he didn't want to return to Florida.

They were able to get a seat inside, and Dylan quickly ordered the items he'd mentioned and an IPA for each of them.

Brooke was happy to go with the flow and concentrated on taking in as much as she could of the interior and other visitors. She and her mother had traveled along the east coast going back and forth to Florida but had never made the more difficult trip to the west. Maybe Chet would encourage her mother to see more of the country. Knowing he was a nurse she trusted, her mother might feel more comfortable traveling with him.

After a delicious lunch, they walked around the town a bit, getting a feel for the funky art area with its small, brightly painted wooden shops lining the street.

From Madrid they drove through Cerrillos, another interesting town, and then they were on their way to Santa Fe.

"It took a while to take the trail, but I hope you thought it was worth it," said Dylan.

"Oh, yes. I already have a flavor for the area," Brooke said.

Dylan chuckled. "I think you'll find Santa Fe quite upscale in comparison. But there's the same kind of enthusiasm for the arts."

Brooke couldn't wait to see it for herself.

CHAPTER THIRTY-EIGHT

BROOKE

Dylan drove through the plaza area of Santa Fe and east to Canyon Road. "I have a little casita in this area, not far from the gallery where my work is shown," said Dylan. "This is just one section full of galleries. The Railyard area holds a number of galleries too."

"How does it work? Do you own the gallery or are your pieces of art part of a collection shown for sale?" Brooke asked him.

"I own a piece of the gallery with a couple of other artists who exhibit and sell their work there. We invite other artists to show their artwork, which gives us an opportunity to keep refreshing the collection."

"Is that how they all operate?" She was thinking of Florida and wondering if something like this would be successful there.

"No, it's an unusual agreement, but it works for me and my fellow artists. We couldn't do it without our manager, Karin Keith. She's terrific at supervising us and handling the staff. An excellent saleswoman too. I can't wait for you to meet her."

She gave him a steady look. "You mentioned me handling your paintings in Florida. Is that why you wanted me to come here?"

"Partly," he said, and clasped her hand. "I want you to know more about me and my life here."

"Okay." she said, pleased by his answer. It wasn't all

business. He made a left turn and drove through an open, wrought-iron gate attached to a tan adobe wall that encircled a small property and a one-story, tan adobe house. After he pulled to a stop, Dylan turned to her and grinned. "*Mi casa.* You know what they say, '*Mi casa, Su casa*'."

She laughed. "Thanks. I can't wait to see it."

They got out of his car, and he led her up the stairs to the wide porch that lined the front of the house. A couple of wooden rocking chairs sat on the porch along with two turquoise-colored pots that held flowers and were placed on either side of the carved-wooden front door.

"Come in." He opened the dark-stained door and waved her inside. "It's small, but perfect for me."

Brooke stepped inside and onto a stained Mexican-tile floor that extended as far as she could see. A living area with a fireplace tucked into a corner was filled with a comfortable-looking, brown-leather couch, two large over-stuffed chairs in a neutral fabric, a coffee table in front of the couch, end tables, and an assortment of lamps. But it was the painting above the fireplace that caught her eye. Bold swipes of brown were accompanied by burnt-orange, red, and turquoise. She blinked, feeling as if all the sights she'd viewed that day were there before her in different forms.

She approached it, automatically reaching out as if to touch it, and pulled her hand back.

"Do you like it?" Dylan asked quietly.

"I love it," said Brooke. "It captures this area completely."

He grinned. "Even if it's mine, I have to say I like it too." He took her elbow. "I'll show you the rest of the house. There's not much to see, but it's home."

Beyond the living area, she walked into a modern kitchen with black-marble countertops and the latest stainless-steel appliances. The cupboards were painted a pale turquoise. A long, wide wooden table with bench seating sat to one side of the galley-like kitchen. Beyond the table French doors opened up to a side patio that led to the walled-in backyard planted with flowers and a variety of cactus plants.

"Lovely," Brooke murmured.

"The two bedrooms and baths are on this side of the house," said Dylan, indicating a doorway off the kitchen eating area.

Brooke followed him into a hallway.

"The guest room is up front and the master bedroom suite is at the back." He'd carried her suitcase inside and now headed to the guest room with it.

Brooke was both relieved and disappointed to see him do it. For the time being she'd let him set the pace between them. It was, she thought, best that way.

After he set down her suitcase, he turned to her and drew her into his arms. "I didn't want to presume too much."

She blinked in surprise and couldn't hold in her laughter. "I was thinking the same thing about me."

"Great minds think alike. Should I take your suitcase into the master bedroom?" His gaze drove into her, begging for a response.

"I think it might save a little time," she answered saucily.

He laughed. "Okay, then. That awkward moment is past." He lowered his lips to hers and she drowned in the feelings that only he could arouse in her.

They were both a little breathless when they pulled away.

"I'm sorry, we can't linger. We have an appointment with Karin, and then we're taking her to dinner. I hope that's okay with you."

"Give me time to freshen up and unpack, and we can be on our way," said Brooke.

She stopped at the threshold of the master bedroom and

studied the king-size bed, end tables, and big closet, and liked what she saw. Another large painting was hung above the bed, this one in sunny bright colors that added color to the light-gray walls. The house was small, but very-well laid out, including the master bedroom, which, to her delight, had a skylight.

"Perfect," she said, looking up through the skylight.

"It was here when I bought the house," said Dylan. "But it's cool to be able to lie in bed and look up at the night sky."

Brooke unpacked, finding room in the closet for her things. She discovered the master bath had dual sinks and placed her toiletries on the one that didn't look in use. All in all, the house was very comfortable. She noted the large shower with two different showerheads.

She washed her face and brushed her hair and headed out to the kitchen.

Dylan was there talking on the phone. "Yes, I'll ask her. Yes, I'll do my best. Talk to you later, Mom." He turned to her. "My parents have asked me to come to Idaho to their summer cabin before returning to Florida. They want me to bring you. Are you game?"

"How much longer will that extend my time off?" she asked, thinking of Livy and Charlotte handling the Inn.

"We'll cut short our time here by one day, fly into Boise from here and then head back to Florida. My parents can meet us in Boise if that makes it easier."

"Sure. I'd like to meet them," said Brooke.

"Great. I don't like to disappoint my mother. She's my biggest supporter. She's the one who gave me my first set of crayons."

"I know I'll like her," said Brooke.

"I'll always be grateful to her," said Dylan. "When other kids were outside playing, she allowed me to stay inside and paint. She's a graduate of the Rhode Island School of Design, too, and encouraged me to go there." He slipped his phone into his back pocket. "Ready to head over to the gallery?"

"Yes, I'm anxious to see it and to meet Karin," said Brooke. She already loved the feel of the town and wanted to see more.

Dylan's house was tucked in among other houses and galleries. The short walk to The Collab Gallery took around fifteen minutes. It could've been shorter, but Brooke's gaze kept her stopping at different places along the way.

The Collab Gallery was in a white-painted stucco building with two wide windows in the front, allowing a passerby to get a glimpse inside to see a few of the treasures.

Dylan led her to the door, gave her a little bow, and said, "You may enter."

Laughing at his playfulness, she stepped inside and almost bumped into a tall, dark-haired woman rushing toward them.

"Dylan, you're back. I'm happy to see you. You've been ignoring my texts and phone calls," said the woman throwing her arms around Dylan.

Dylan glanced at Brooke, unwrapped the arms around his neck, and stepped away from the woman facing him. "Hello, Tina. Meet Brooke Weatherby, from Florida. Brooke, Tina Martinson is one of the permanent artists here who's known for her metal work."

Tina frowned at him, glanced at Brooke, and faced him. "Is *she* the reason you've stayed in Florida for too long? If so, we need to talk."

Dylan's ears turned pink. "We have talked, Tina, for several weeks before I left for Florida. There's nothing more to say. What little we had going on has been over for months. Don't make this more difficult than it has to be."

"But ... but ..." Tina whipped around and faced Brooke. "You may think it's all fine between you, but it isn't. Dylan and

I were dating exclusively before you came along."

Brooke swallowed hard and glanced at Dylan.

He shook his head. "Not true, Tina. You know it."

"We'll see." Tina pushed past him and out through the door, leaving Brooke feeling shaky.

"What was that all about?" Brooke asked, settling her gaze on Dylan.

He faced her. "I'm sorry about that. Tina and I dated briefly, and I knew early on that it wasn't going to work. I told her, but she refused to believe it. She's dated several men in the area, and I'm not the only one who has walked away. That was one reason I decided to spend the summer at Sanderling Cove as Mimi asked."

"Okay. Thanks for telling me," said Brooke, feeling better.

He cupped her face with his hands. "Brooke, I promise you that's the truth. Tina and I weren't dating exclusively, and I told her early on it wasn't going to work." He kissed her.

She was still in his embrace when a musical voice behind her said, "Welcome back, Dylan."

Dylan pulled away and grinned. "Karin, meet Brooke Weatherby, a special person in my life."

A woman of average height, with gray hair and classic features, Karin smiled at her, bringing a light to her tawny-color eyes. Holding out her hand, Karin said, "A pleasure to meet you. Sorry you had to hear that nonsense from Tina. She's a little confused, obviously."

Brooke shook Karin's hand. "Thanks. It's a pleasure for me too. Dylan has told me many nice things about you." Brooke couldn't help staring at the large crystal hanging from a silver chain around Karin's neck.

"Dylan, move closer to Brooke for a moment," Karin said, squinting at her through half-closed eyes.

Dylan threw his arm around Brooke's shoulder.

"Oh, yes, there it is. Auras in symmetry." Karin held up her hands as if embracing the image of them together. "Dylan, you've made such a wise choice. I see many happy years ahead for the two of you."

Brooke turned to Karin. "Are you a fortuneteller?"

She laughed. "Sort of. I see auras and can sometimes tell the futures of people. Sorry if I made you uneasy," said Karin, giving her a friendly smile. "Moments occur when I can't hold back."

"I've told Brooke how well you manage the gallery," said Dylan. "I'd like you to show her what you can about doing that. I want to place her in charge of my paintings in Florida."

"Oh? You're going to divide your time between Santa Fe and there?" said Karin.

"Yes, I'm definitely thinking of it," Dylan said. "Why don't we go out for drinks and dinner? We can talk more then."

"I'd love to. It's late enough we can close the gallery for the day. After six o'clock people can call for appointments."

They left the gallery and walked closer to the plaza to a restaurant called The Story Teller. Inside the tan adobe building, beamed ceilings, tile flooring, and wooden tables and chairs gave a southwestern flair to the décor. Dylan gave his name to the hostess, and they were led to a back dining area where the tables were covered in white linen. Blue-rimmed glassware sat on the table along with a centerpiece of a small, potted cactus sitting beside a pottery figure that had been placed on a ceramic disk.

Brooke was seated opposite Karin with Dylan between them.

She glanced around, absorbing the desert colors and textures in their surroundings, and studied the figure in the middle of the table.

Karin noticed and said, "That's a storyteller. See how the

figure has a round open mouth and is holding two children in her lap? Originally, female figures with children in their arms were created and called "Singing Mothers." Today, the term storyteller refers to any human or animal figure that is covered with smaller children or animals. They have become one of the most collectible and sought-after forms of clay art."

"I love it," said Brooke. "Very clever."

"The Navajo storytellers are a little more detailed than the Pueblo ones, but each artist makes their clay figures a little differently, giving them a distinct identification," said Karin. "There's a lot to see and admire about the artistry in various pieces here. You must go to the plaza market when the artists bring their wares to sell to the tourists. You'll see some remarkable work with silver and turquoise."

Brooke reached up and touched her necklace. "Dylan gave me this. I love it."

"You should," said Karin. "It's a lovely necklace. But then, Dylan has excellent taste."

The waiter came, took their drink order, and handed them menus.

Brooke studied the unusual items and chose Venison Carpaccio for a starter and a crispy fish entrée. Since being on her own, she'd made an effort to try as many new things to eat as possible. She and her mother were good cooks, but their meals consisted of rather plain food in comparison to a menu like this.

As they sipped wine and talked, Brooke wondered what it would be like to live here. Then she thought of Gran and John and decided not to allow herself to jump ahead. Dylan still hadn't told her he loved her.

After dinner, Dylan and Brooke walked Karin back to the

gallery to check on a few things, and they continued on to Dylan's house.

"It's a beautiful evening," Brooke said. It had been pleasantly warm during the day and was cooling off nicely.

"Yes, this is a perfect time of year to be here," said Dylan. "Something to think about going forward if I'm to have two different offices."

"I understand," said Brooke. "Santa Fe is totally charming. But I love life at Sanderling Cove, too."

"Me, too," said Dylan, wrapping an arm around her and pulling her close as they moved forward.

They entered the house and went into the kitchen. "Care for a nightcap? I'm thinking of a cold beer."

"I'll just have ice water," Brooke said. "I'm still enjoying the memory of my meal. It was delicious."

Dylan grabbed a beer, fixed her a glass of ice water, and they went outside. Two chairs sat on the back edge of the patio, away from the grilling area. They each took a seat, facing one another.

"I'm sorry about Tina," Dylan said. "I don't want you to get the wrong idea about my dating her. I will always be honest about my feelings for you."

"Okay," she said. "Tina obviously still cares, but if you say it's over, I believe you."

"Thank you," he said. "That's important to me."

Brooke clasped her arms against the colder air.

Dylan noticed and jumped up. "It's getting cold. Ready to go inside?"

"Yes, and if you don't mind, I'm ready for bed." The minute the words left her mouth, her cheeks turned hot.

Dylan looked at her and laughed. "I realize what you meant. I'm ready too." He didn't look the least bit tired or sleepy.

A frisson of excitement traveled through her. She felt like a different person from the one she'd been in New York and boldly walked inside, hoping she wasn't reading Dylan wrong.

At the threshold of the master bedroom, she paused and then entered aware it was more than sleep on either of their minds.

She went into the bathroom, washed her face and hands, brushed her teeth, and ran a comb through her hair. As she left the room, Dylan entered wearing just his boxer shorts.

Brooke's pulse raced, and she hurried to change out of her clothes and into the sexy, black-silk pajamas Charlotte had insisted she take with her.

As soon as she slid under the duvet on Dylan's bed, he emerged from the bathroom smiling.

He dimmed the bedside lights and slid in beside her. "Look up at the sky, Brooke. You can see the stars."

She lay on her back and stared through the skylight. The stars seemed to wink at her as if they knew how tingly she felt all over.

Dylan turned her toward him and kissed her on her nose. "Thank you for coming to Santa Fe. I want you to love it as much as I do."

She could smell the minty toothpaste on his breath, and when his lips met hers, she responded, loving being with him.

He moaned and pulled her toward him.

She melted in his arms ...

CHAPTER THIRTY-NINE

BROOKE

Brooke awoke with a sense of anticipation. She was going to learn more about the place Dylan called his home. So far, she'd loved Santa Fe with its southwestern flavor, beautiful setting, and abundance of art.

Beside her, Dylan stirred. She planted a kiss on his cheek and bounded out of bed. She wanted the chance to walk around town in the early morning coolness before tourists overran the area.

After she freshened, she tiptoed into the bedroom.

Dylan lifted up on an elbow and stared at her sleepily. "Where are you going?"

"I'm leaving to take a walk. I'll bring you back some coffee and breakfast treats."

"Want me to join you?" he mumbled.

"No, thanks. I won't be too long. Just wanted to catch the morning light on the buildings and sneak a few glances into store windows without a crowd. Go back to sleep."

"Okay," said Dylan. "See you later. Take your phone."

She held up her cell and stuffed it into the back pocket of her jeans before grabbing a sweater and slipping out the front door. The early morning sun cast a golden glow around her. Staring at her surroundings, she felt as if she were in a dream. She'd seen pictures of Santa Fe, of course, but photographs couldn't capture the sense of excitement she felt. Since being and working with Dylan, she was aware of color, shade, and shadows in a new way.

She walked briskly, slowing in front of galleries and shops that beckoned her. In the plaza, a number of vendors were spreading their blankets on the ground in front of them. Some were spreading silver pieces atop them. Others were standing with cups of coffee talking in groups with other artists.

Brooke waved to them and kept walking but would return to their irresistible wares.

She passed the Cathedral Basilica of St. Francis of Assisi, and the Georgia O'Keeffe Museum, determined to return and spend time there, along with the New Mexico Museum of Art. She felt as if she were a candy addict dipped into a pot of melted chocolate, and she silently thanked Dylan for asking her to come for a visit.

She stopped and got cups of coffee and muffins for each of them and hurried back to his house.

When she entered it, she found Dylan in the kitchen sitting on a bar stool wearing a pair of jeans and nothing else. She observed the muscles that crossed his chest and shaped his arms, set down the coffee and muffins on the counter, and moved into his waiting arms.

"Good morning," she said. "It's a beautiful day out there."

"Yes. We'll take advantage of it and do a little sight-seeing so you can get a better look before we leave for Boise. While you were gone, I changed our flights. We'll leave tomorrow morning to give us another night here."

"Your parents were okay about driving into Boise?"

Dylan grinned. "They will be. I sent my mother a message explaining the situation. She'll be very pleased to meet you."

"Does she know we're dating?" Brooke asked.

"Yes. Mimi told her, and then she asked me about it," said Dylan. He reached for a cup of coffee, and they dug into the muffins.

Brooke couldn't help wondering if Dylan would've told his parents about her if Mimi hadn't already mentioned it. Shaking off her self-doubt, she bit into a chocolate-chip muffin and decided not to think about it.

For the rest of the day, Brooke moved in a dreamworld of paintings, silver, turquoise, antique buildings, and works by Georgia O'Keeffe. They had a simple lunch at a local café between their stops.

By four o'clock they were ready for a rest. They went to a local bar and took a seat.

"There's one more place you have to see," said Dylan. "Meow Wolf is unlike anything you've ever experienced before. We'll have a snack and something to drink, and then we'll go. Okay with you?"

"Sounds fascinating," said Brooke.

"It's cool. The House of Eternal Return is a mind-bending art experience. You can explore it as you go through it."

After leaving the bar, they went to Dylan's house to pick up his car.

Meow Wolf was about five miles west of Santa Fe Plaza.

"Be prepared," warned Dylan. "It's a trippy escape into a world filled with scenes and settings worthy of sci-fi movies. There are hidden doorways, portals to other worlds, mysterious hallways, strange music, and fascinating artwork."

"I've honestly never done more than smoke a little weed, but this sounds exciting," said Brooke.

Later, with bright colors flashing in her mind, Brooke left the exhibit intrigued by all she'd seen and heard.

"Artwork can take many forms," said Dylan. "I like coming here and being reminded of that."

He took her elbow and led her to his car. "Let's relax tonight. We can order in. Okay with you?"

"Perfect," said Brooke. Her mind was spinning from all she'd seen. She glanced down at the silver and turquoise bracelet she'd bought earlier at the plaza and rubbed the stone. It was beautiful. The Native American who'd sold it to her said it would bring prosperity and health.

Back at Dylan's house, Brooke changed out of her running shoes and into a pair of flipflops that felt fabulous on her tired feet. She vowed to do more running and walking when she returned to Florida.

Dylan handed her a cold coke and sat down on the couch beside her. "How about pizza? A place near here has a chicken pizza that's great."

"That sounds delicious," said Brooke, wiggling her toes, relieved she wouldn't have to dress up for dinner. She was already a little nervous about meeting his parents. She'd been tempted to call her mother to find out more about Dylan's mother. They'd played together as girls. But Brooke wanted this moment to be hers. No one knew of her trip to Boise, and she wanted to keep it that way.

Dylan ordered dinner, and they sat sipping cold drinks and talking about all they'd seen.

"I can see why you love it here," Brooke said to Dylan. "It's gorgeous and very interesting. Does it mean that after the end of summer, you'll move back here?"

"No." He picked up her hand. "I want to spend time in Florida too. I'm trying to work out a plan to do both." He kissed her on the lips, enveloping her into his embrace.

A waft of joy swept through her. She loved his kisses, the way she felt protected being so close to him.

After they pulled apart, he smiled. "You'll be the first to know of my plans."

When they crawled into bed that night, all her insecurity fled when Dylan took her in his arms. He might not have told her he loved her, but he was showing her how much he cared.

The next morning Brooke awakened to an empty bed. She got up and padded into the kitchen. Dylan was there, talking on the phone. He saw her, waved, and said, "Okay, Mom. See you this evening." He clicked off the call and turned to her. "Good morning, sleepyhead."

"What time is it?" she asked and stretched. It was late when they finally fell asleep and she hadn't checked her clock this morning.

"It's almost nine. We have to leave for Albuquerque in an hour to get to our flight. I've hired a car to take us."

"Okay, I'm going to take a shower," said Brooke, giving him a quick kiss before leaving.

She'd just stepped out of the shower when he came into the bathroom and stripped off his clothes. They grinned at each other, enjoying their views, and then the moment was lost when he stepped into the shower.

"Later," he said, giving her a teasing grin.

She laughed. They'd already shared one shower together and it had been, well ... delightful.

Later, she placed the last of her things into the small suitcase she'd brought. She was pleased she'd packed a simple black dress for dinner. She wanted to look her best for Dylan's parents.

"Ready? Let's go. The car is here," Dylan said, entering the room and lifting her suitcase.

Brooke followed him out to the small limo and settled into

the backseat, sorry they'd had to cut short their time in Santa Fe.

The ride to the airport was quiet, comfortably so. Dylan checked his email and she looked out the window at the passing scenery, mentally reviewing her trip. She reached inside her purse and pulled out the turquoise jewelry she bought for Charlotte and Livy.

"Good beads," said Dylan. "Beautiful colors."

"The artist and I chose the two most unusual," she said, pleased. She fingered her necklace. "But, of course, I like this one the best."

"It suits you."

She studied him. Though his features were pleasant enough, his face took on a special, irresistible glow when he smiled. His man bun added to his uniqueness, especially because it seemed natural on him. And when he released it, he was sexy as hell.

The plane ride was smooth, uneventful once they landed in and departed from Phoenix for the direct flight to Boise. She dozed a bit. When the announcement came that they'd land soon, she eagerly opened the shade on the window and peered out.

She could see the city below and noticed the foothills to the north, interesting in their tan color. She turned to Dylan with a look of surprise.

"People forget Boise is high desert. Though it's known as the city of trees, there are plenty of reminders of it being desert. On the ground, you'll be amazed how green it is. It's a beautiful city with plenty of parks and the Boise River running through it."

"Another surprise," said Brooke, loving the idea of being in a place brand-new to her.

The airport was small and efficient. In no time, they had their bags and were outside waiting for a cab to take them to their hotel. They were meeting his parents for dinner at Chandler's restaurant. She was both excited and nervous.

Once they were settled in their room and had changed their clothes and freshened up, they walked down to the restaurant. They'd agreed to meet his parents in the bar, where they could talk before dining.

When they walked into the bar, Brooke's attention was immediately drawn to a stunning redhead woman who, when she saw them, waved and stood to give Dylan a hug.

"Dylan, I'm thrilled we could meet. It's been too long." She gave Brooke a smile and turned back to him. "And how exciting that you're dating Jo's daughter. One more hug, and I'll let you go."

A gray-haired man stood quietly aside. "Dylan, great to see you, son." He turned to Brooke. "And very nice to meet you, Brooke."

"Hi, Dad," said Dylan, giving him a man hug. He wrapped his arm around Brooke's shoulder. "Brooke, meet my mom and Dad—KK and Gordon."

KK studied her. "I see a little bit of Jo in you. How is she? I haven't seen her in years, but I looked up her number and called her yesterday to tell her I'd be meeting you today. She sounded surprised. I hope I didn't spoil anything. Dylan knows I can never keep exciting news to myself." She smiled at Brooke. "Your mother told me she was dating a nice man. I'm happy for her."

Brooke glanced at Dylan, wondering if his mother was always full of life.

He laughed. "There's no stopping Mom. We all have to be on our toes to catch up to her."

"That's for certain," said Gordon, smiling. "There's only one KK. We love her just as she is."

"Don't worry," said KK to Brooke. "I sometimes need to get everything out in a hurry. It got me into all sorts of trouble in school. That reminds me that Jo told me she remembers our times together at the cove. We had a lot of fun together. She's such a dear person."

"Brooke, how did you like Santa Fe?" Gordon asked her after offering her a chair.

"I loved it," Brooke replied honestly. "It's beautiful, and the artwork everywhere is stunning."

"Dylan told us you're quite an artist yourself," said KK, smiling at her.

"I'm just dabbling in oils and acrylics," said Brooke. "I don't have formal training."

"But she's talented. She even collaborated with me on one painting that sold to a buyer in New York," said Dylan sitting next to her.

A waitress took their order, and in addition to wine, Gordon ordered a cheese plate. "We don't want to spoil our dinner. The food here is excellent."

"Tell me, Brooke, how are you and your cousins doing with the Inn? Ellie and John have done such a lovely job with it over the years," KK said. "I'm sure they're grateful for the time away you three are giving them. Are they planning on selling as I've heard?"

"We don't know what Gran and John plan to do when they return," said Brooke. "Until we know, my cousins and I can't make too many plans. Though you must be aware that Shane and Charlie are engaged."

"Oh, yes," said KK. "My mother told me all about it. Such sweet news. She told me that Henry and Shannon visited Granny Liz too. It's too bad about Shane's mother, but she was always a difficult woman. Henry's a great man, though, and the couple of times I met Shannon, she seemed a very sweet woman."

"Life at Sanderling Cove is always interesting," said Gordon. "For the five families to remain so close through the years is quite remarkable. KK has told me of many happy memories of growing up there."

"Where did you grow up?" Brooke asked him.

"Outside of Boston. Now, I'm a real westerner. We live in Arizona most of the year and summer and do some winter skiing at Sun Valley."

"It sounds like a perfect plan," Brooke said. His parents were charming, very down-to-earth.

Their wine came.

Brooke settled back and listened as Dylan told his parents about the painting that had been forged.

"It's a shame these things happen. I have an author friend who's had her books pirated. It's such a nasty business," said KK. "I'm relieved you were able to make the buyers understand."

"Me, too," said Dylan. "I can't have my art underrated, or I'll soon be out of business."

"You said you're showing in new galleries in Florida," said Gordon. "Diversification is a smart idea."

"Grace and Samantha are going to join us in Arizona for Thanksgiving this year. I hope the two of you can join us too," said KK.

Brooke swallowed her wine and waited for Dylan to say something.

"Yeah, me too," he said, giving Brooke's hand a squeeze.

She was relieved by his response. She'd never had a long-term relationship and didn't want to assume anything.

The waitress came to the table and announced that their

dinner seating was available. They followed her to a booth, and Brooke slid onto the plush-cushioned bench beside Dylan. His parents sat opposite them.

"Please excuse me," said KK. "I have to freshen up. Brooke, want to join me?"

"As a matter of fact, I do," Brooke said and then wondered if it was a ruse to get her alone.

But nothing was said between them until they were washing their hands.

"I'm pleased to meet you, Brooke," said KK, studying her in the mirror. "It makes me happy to see Dylan's way with you."

"Thank you. Dylan is very special to me. He's given me a whole new life with painting. I've been very practical all my life, have needed to be, and now a new world has opened up to me. I'll always be grateful to him."

KK's eyes were shiny as she turned to Brooke and gave her a quick hug. "You're pretty special yourself."

They smiled at one another, and with new confidence, Brooke followed her back to their table.

Dylan gave her a questioning look.

"I think your girl suits you, Dylan," said his mother, sliding into her side of the booth and smiling at Brooke.

"Yeah, I think so too." Dylan laid a hand across Brooke's shoulder and she leaned into him for a moment before straightening.

They ordered, and later when their food came, the raw oysters, salad and steaks were as delicious as any Brooke had ever had.

"I think I'm becoming spoiled," she said to his parents. "Thank you for including me. I'll remember this when I'm greeting guests at the Inn or working in the office."

"Running a property like The Sanderling Cove Inn isn't for

sissies," said Gordon. "I once worked at a hotel on the Cape for a summer and decided I didn't want to go into the hospitality business. I'm much more suited to working with numbers."

"I thought I was too, until Dylan helped me with some painting. He still encourages me to try new things. It's made my life much more exciting." Brooke turned to Dylan. The love she saw in his eyes caught her breath.

That night, as they crawled into bed, Dylan drew her in his arms. "My parents love you. That means everything to me, Brooke."

"They're wonderful people. I liked them too."

When he kissed her, Brooke imagined she felt something different in the way he was holding her. And later, as they made love, she was grateful for the special time they'd had during this trip.

CHAPTER FORTY

BROOKE

Brooke awoke with a sense of disappointment knowing her time in Boise had been too short. After dinner, she and Dylan had walked through the downtown area, loving the fun, active vibe of the city. She saw a lot of blue and orange shirts representing Boise State University and loved the support people of all ages gave to the football program and other local sports teams. It was like a real community, not just the capital of the state.

After they'd both showered and repacked, they went downstairs for breakfast and then grabbed an Uber to the airport. Once there, Dylan called his parents while waiting for their flight to take off. "Sorry we couldn't meet for breakfast, but as I explained last night, Brooke has to get back to Florida. There's a wedding coming up in a few days, the second in a week, and she has to help with the event because Charlie and Shane are going to be away for a few days."

When Dylan hung up, Brooke said, "They understand?"

"Yes, but they hope to come to Florida sometime soon to see for themselves all you and your cousins are doing at the Inn."

"It'll be nice to have them visit. I know Mimi will be ecstatic."

"I'm sure before the morning is over, she and my mom will have talked. I'm pleased that my parents like you."

Brooke smiled. "My mother sent me a text early this

morning. She likes you a lot and told your mother how sweet you've been to her. So, I guess we don't have to worry about our families."

"Nope, not at all," said Dylan. "Time to board the plane. Let's go."

The trip, with a plane change in Dallas, took most of the day. Late afternoon, when she saw Livy and Charlotte at the airport waiting for them in the baggage claim area as planned, Brooke's eyes stung with tears.

She waved and moved forward to embrace each one as Dylan went to find their luggage.

"It's great to see you," Brooke said. "It feels as if I've been gone for weeks, not days. You won't believe all the things I've done, what I've seen, and, Livy, all the interesting food I've eaten."

Livy laughed. "I'm always up to listen to that. I love your necklace. That's new."

"You'd go crazy at all the beautiful jewelry in Santa Fe. And then we stopped in Boise to meet Dylan's parents. It's been a whirlwind trip, but wonderful."

"I vaguely remember Dylan's parents. His mother is a real live-wire," said Livy.

Brooke laughed at the memory of her first impression of KK. "She's a lot of fun and very kind. Gordon, Dylan's father, is a sweetheart. I like them both."

"That's really important," said Charlotte. "I'm thankful I like Shane's father and stepmother. His mother was a disaster and could've made things very unpleasant for us."

"I'm glad you won't have to deal with that," said Brooke. "How are things at the Inn?"

"The wedding over the weekend was a smashing success," said Livy proudly. "The next one should be a lot easier because of it."

"I think we have it down to a system. It too will be a late morning ceremony. That timing seems to work best—the service and then a lovely luncheon before the bride and groom leave for their honeymoon, and the rest of the wedding party unwinds at the Inn," said Charlotte.

"From Tampa, one can fly almost anywhere easily," said Livy. "Or even better, from Miami."

"I still think we need a special bridal suite with privacy," said Charlotte. "It would be lovely if we could have a small, separate building on the property, just for that."

"Let's work on a plan," said Brooke, turning as Dylan approached with their bags.

"Already at work?" Dylan teased.

She laughed, but it felt good to be back.

That evening, she and Dylan discussed sleeping arrangements and decided that Dylan should stay at Mimi's, but they'd carve out time to be together at Gran's house where there was a better chance of privacy.

"Feels like I just took fifteen years off my life," Dylan grumbled. "But I see Mimi's point. With Skye in the house, we have to be careful. She doesn't miss a thing."

"We can be together as often as we can work it out," said Brooke.

When Brooke wasn't working at the Inn, she spent as much time with him in the studio as possible. It seemed as if once she started painting, she couldn't stop. Ideas and colors flew around her. A blank canvas was no longer a challenge, but an invitation.

But work beckoned to her too. The upcoming wedding was a bit of a challenge because the groom was a veteran of the

Afghanistan conflict and had trouble walking. But he wanted to be married on the beach.

Brooke quickly turned to Adam, who'd returned to Sanderling Cove with his ex-wife, Summer, and asked him to build a walkway to a platform they could move to the sand for the ceremony.

"Sure thing," said Adam. "This will give me a chance to keep busy while Summer and Skye have time to be together to begin to heal."

"Sounds like a good plan," Brooke said, giving him encouragement. But she, along with Charlotte and Livy, were wondering if the self-absorbed woman who acted younger than her years would stick around. Livy had already had one run-in with her about Summer demanding catering service to her home during breakfast hour with the guests. Another time, Charlotte had to explain that the Inn wasn't there for the cove families' use unless they were paying guests.

The time for the wedding drew near. With fifty guests, the Inn would be fully booked. A late morning service, followed by a lovely lunch, was the beginning of a party weekend for the guests. The bride and groom had opted to spend their wedding night at the Inn to party with them.

Brooke helped Livy prepare frozen appetizers for their regular guests for the two evenings the wedding party would be in-house. They didn't want to do anything to annoy their regular guests by cutting back on service. Extra staff was on standby, ready to serve.

Brooke handled the financial details while Charlotte followed the check list they'd drawn up for it. Livy, bless her heart, stuck to food preparation. Instead of a regular wedding cake, the bride wanted an assortment of cupcakes with fancy icing in different colors and flavors. The cupcakes could be made ahead of time and frozen, but the icing was a different story. Livy easily made rosettes and all kinds of designs. But she wanted to do something special combining both design and taste.

Brooke and Charlotte joined her in the kitchen one afternoon to help her.

"I need your advice," said Livy. She'd made a number of icing flowers in different colors and placed them on a tray. "Some of the flavors make it a little harder to flow from my pastry bag. See which flavors you like best."

"You want us to taste the flowers?" Charlotte said with a gleam in her eye.

Livy laughed. "Go for it! I want to get it down to four different flavors and styles."

Brooke took a finger and swiped at a yellow flower. The taste of lemon filled her mouth. "I'm just getting started but I definitely vote for the yellow flowers."

"I like the orange ones," said Charlotte licking her finger.

"Those two are easy," said Livy. "Taste the others."

In the end, they kept the lemon and orange, and then went with a pineapple flavor and a white mint one.

"The cakes are white, chocolate, and orange," said Livy.

"It's such a fun idea," said Brooke. "Perhaps one for your wedding, Charlie."

Charlotte smiled. "We'll see."

"I'm feeling a little lonely, guys," said Livy. "Charlie, you and Brooke are getting settled. But I haven't even met someone I'm interested in."

Brooke cocked an eyebrow. "What about Eric? You're spending a lot of time on his boat."

"We're just friends," said Livy. "That's how I want to keep things."

"When you're ready, the guys will line up," said Charlotte, placing an arm around Livy's shoulders.

"Yes," agreed Brooke. "You're the one all the guys like."

"Maybe," said Livy. "I do make a mean cookie."

Brooke and Charlotte laughed, and soon Livy joined in.

CHAPTER FORTY-ONE

LIVY

Livy spread the icing on the cupcakes, preparing them to receive their sugary flowers. She'd made a few wedding cakes as part of her bakery business, but it hadn't been her specialty. She was better known for her breads, pastries, and pies for every day.

Maybe, she thought, a wedding cake business would be enough. One project at a time without worrying about day-to-day stuff. It was ironic, though, that while she was falling in love with this aspect of baking, she herself had no intention of getting married for years to come. Yet, she sometimes felt lonely when she saw how happy and busy Charlotte and Brooke were with their men.

Her mother was wondering what plans Livy had when the summer was over. Livy had no idea. Maybe Gran could help her decide. She bet Gran was thrilled about Brooke and Dylan. Who wouldn't be? They seemed perfect together.

CHAPTER FORTY-TWO

BROOKE

During preparations for the wedding, Brooke's mother called her.

"Hi, Brooke. I just had to call you."

"Hi, Mom. Is everything all right?"

"KK Hendrix and I just had a conversation. She said she had dinner with you in Boise and fell in love with you instantly. Is the situation between you and Dylan really serious? She seemed to think so."

"Yes, I think it is," Brooke said caught off guard. "I ... I love him."

"You *think* it's serious?" her mother said.

Tears stung Brooke's eyes. She hated to make the confession, but she had to be honest. "He hasn't told me he loves me, but I'm pretty sure he does. He shows me in many ways how much he cares."

"That's what matters," said her mother. "I'm very happy for you. I hope to spend more time with him when we come to the family party this fall."

"How are things with you and Chet?" Brooke asked.

"Excellent. Perfect, actually," her mother said and then let out a sigh. "He's such a wonderful man. He's agreed to come to Florida with me."

"Wow. Things are serious then," said Brooke. She waited to hear more, but her mother simply said, "Yes."

"Did you ever think this would happen to us?" Brooke said.

"In just a few months, we've each fallen in love."

"I hoped it would happen for you, but never imagined it would happen to me," her mother said. "Honestly, I still can't believe it."

Love for her mother welled inside Brooke. "I'm happy it's working out for you, Mom. You deserve it."

"Oh, sweetie, I feel the same way about you."

"I've got to go, but I'm pleased that we've talked," said Brooke. She clicked off the call grateful for the changes in their lives. A lot of her time had been devoted to caring for her mother. It seemed strange to think she didn't have to worry about her anymore.

Smiling, she went to Dylan's studio to tell him the news.

The wedding party arrived on a Friday night. They planned to celebrate the rehearsal dinner at Gavin's at the Salty Key Inn, but even so, Brooke and her cousins were busy making sure their rooms were ready for them, and they were ready for socializing with all the guests.

Brooke raced to Gran's house to change for the evening. She and her cousins had agreed it was more professional to dress properly for that time.

Later, Brooke was among the crowd chatting with hotel guests when she looked over at the entrance to the room and almost dropped the tray of hors d'oeuvres she was carrying.

Carefully she set the tray down and walked over to greet the newly-arrived guest.

"Tina, what are you doing here, all the way from Santa Fe?" she asked.

Tina gave her a satisfied smile that irritated Brooke. "Dylan invited me. He thought I should stay here before we travel to Naples together."

"What? He didn't mention it to me," Brooke said, willing her heart to start pumping again.

"I think it's some sort of surprise. He's introducing me to Henry Rousseau at Gallery 535 in Naples. He thinks I'm a perfect match for the gallery. Dylan's such a sweet guy. We always have such fun together."

Brooke swallowed hard and then managed to say, "Please join the other guests."

After Tina left her side, Livy came over to Brooke. "What's going on? You look like you've seen a ghost. Is it that woman?" She turned her gaze to Tina, who was joining the crowd.

"That's the woman Dylan used to date. Dylan made it plain in Santa Fe that their relationship was over, but now, I'm not sure. He invited her here to the Inn." All her past confidence about her relationship with him evaporated. She felt sick.

Livy's brow wrinkled as she studied Brooke. "That doesn't sound like him. I wonder what's really going on."

"You and me both," muttered Brooke. "But we can't let her ruin the party. People in this group are talking about another wedding in the future."

Trying to cope with her feelings, Brooke gamely picked up the tray of hors d'oeuvres she'd been holding and went back to chatting with guests. But she kept her eye on Tina.

Tina Martinson was a beautiful woman. Tonight she was wearing a low-cut blouse and a Hawaiian print wrap skirt that barely covered her butt. More than one male set of eyes kept her in their sight.

Watching her, Brooke felt a little sick. Her purple hair and shell tattoo seemed like feeble attempts to draw attention to herself.

When Dylan arrived, she quickly went over to him. "Tina is here. She said you invited her."

"Yes, I did. She and I are going to talk to Henry Rousseau

at the Naples gallery about a special show. I thought it best that she stay here at the Inn."

Brooke wanted to stamp her foot, tell him it wasn't fair, that he'd hurt her with his actions, but she said nothing. Dylan didn't owe her a thing. They may be exclusive for now, but that didn't mean he planned a future with her. She'd been a fool. Crushed to the core, she turned and walked away.

Dylan followed her, but she moved faster, needing to put as much distance between them as possible. She worked her way into the crowd. She had to be professional, had to act as if she didn't care, had to get through this weekend.

After most of the guests had departed for dinner elsewhere, Brooke helped with the cleanup, her mind whirling. She knew if she confronted Dylan, it wouldn't go well. The best she could do was to quietly disappear, tell her cousins she had a migraine and couldn't be disturbed.

She told Livy she wasn't feeling well and why, and then she slipped out the kitchen door. Maybe he and Tina were just friends. But the fact he hadn't told her about the visit made her heart crack.

In her room, she allowed tears to fall and then she marched into the bathroom, washed her face, and stiffened her spine. She would not, could not, allow Dylan or any other person to control her happiness. She'd just broken away from her situation at home with her mother. She wouldn't be trapped in another unhealthy relationship.

She lay down on her bed, clutched her pillow, and waited for darkness to fill her room.

Much later, there was a soft knock on her door.

Brooke tensed.

Livy opened the door, came in, and quietly said, "Is there anything I can get you?"

"No," said Brooke. "But thank you. I'm going to have to deal with this on my own."

"I hope you feel better," Livy said and walked away.

After the door was shut, Brooke buried her face in her pillow and sighed.

The next morning, she was in the kitchen sipping a cup of coffee and trying to get into a healthy frame of mind when Dylan appeared.

"Hey, how are you feeling?" he asked, and sat down beside her at the kitchen table. He gave her a look of concern.

Brooke sighed. Dylan wasn't a bad guy; it was her own fault for believing they had something more. "I'm okay. Just a little confused."

"What's wrong?" Dylan's eyes rounded. "Is this about Tina being here?"

"In part," Brooke said honestly. "But we need to be sure of what each of us wants."

He gave her a steady look. "I think you know very well what I want."

"But ..." He didn't get it. Maybe he never would. She needed to hear those three words from him. But she'd never tell him that. They had to come from his heart.

"Tina said you're going to Naples together. When are you leaving?"

"This morning," said Dylan. "We have a meeting with Henry, and then he's arranged for us to join him at a gala fundraiser to meet potential clients for my work and hers. In the future, all the artists in our Santa Fe Collab group might do a special show at Henry's gallery. That's what Karin is hoping."

"So, she knows about Tina's trip here?" Brooke asked. She didn't know whether she felt better about that or not. In either case, she needed to take care of her emotional health.

"Yes, Karin's in favor of our getting established in Florida," said Dylan.

"Well, good luck with it. I have to get dressed and over to the Inn. The wedding is today, and we'll all have our hands full."

Dylan studied her. She knew he wanted to kiss her but she turned away. "You'd better go."

"Okay, I'll see you later. I hope you feel better." He lifted a hand and caressed her cheek, then walked away, leaving her feeling bereft.

She headed upstairs to get dressed for the day, relieved she'd be busy for most of it. Brooke had no doubt Tina would try to take advantage of her time alone with Dylan. She was a determined woman. Even though she'd been rebuffed, Tina had managed to work out a deal like this.

The bride looked as beautiful as the other brides at the Inn had been. She wore a sleeveless white dress that fell to her ankles in lovely, silken folds. Her two bridesmaids wore soft-green dresses, and the groom and the two groomsmen wore khaki shorts and green golf shirts in the same shade as the dresses.

As the groom made his way down the newly constructed boardwalk to the ceremony site, Brooke studied his legs misshapen by scars and wondered at his bravery. For all the effort he had to put in to moving around with crutches, he seemed pretty determined to make light of it. She was deeply touched by that.

Standing aside with her cousins, she listened to the vows being exchanged with a sense of awe. In a clear voice, the groom said, "You're the best thing that's ever happened to me,

Jenn, I want the whole world to know it. I love you."

Brooke didn't realize she was crying until Charlotte handed her a tissue. "It's all very romantic, isn't it?"

Brooke bobbed her head, too emotional to speak.

Later, she stood aside as the wedding guests enjoyed a light lunch of gazpacho, a plate consisting of a trio of salads—chicken salad with a pineapple champagne dressing, steak salad with a blue cheese dressing, and a garden salad with a balsamic dressing. French bread and fresh fruit accompanied the meal.

They'd hired a bartender and three waitresses for the event in addition to using their usual staff to run the Inn, and everything was going smoothly. It pleased Brooke to see how easily the Inn accommodated different kinds of weddings from casual to more formal occasions.

She tried not to think of Dylan with Tina, but the thought kept intruding.

Charlotte elbowed her. "What's the matter? You look upset."

"Nothing I should really be worrying about," she responded, and realized it was true. If Dylan wasn't going to move forward as she hoped, it was better to find out now.

They went into the kitchen.

Livy was arranging cupcakes on three separate cake plates, making sure each had a variety of taste and color.

"Livy, everyone is loving the lunch. I don't know how you do it, but you've taken simple salads and made them look as if each plate is a masterpiece," said Brooke.

"We're lucky you're such a marvelous chef," said Charlotte.

"It's fun to try different things, but as we've discussed, it might be easier to offer a choice of menus to prospective brides so meals are a little more coordinated and professional," said Livy.

"Okay, I'll work on that with you," said Charlotte.

"And I'll work on the costs for each item you come up with," said Brooke. "We can still offer a reasonable selection, but as long as we're putting in the same amount of effort for each wedding, we want to make it work financially."

"Who knew the three of us would end up in this crazy business together," said Livy. "Even if it's only for a short time, it's been a great experience. Group hug."

Brooke looked at her cousins, feeling such love for them she couldn't speak.

After the festivities were over and the group had taken over the swimming pool and the beach, Brooke went back to Gran's house to change her clothes. With Dylan gone, it would be a good time to work on some painting ideas.

She walked over to Mimi's house and let herself into the garage. She stared at some paintings Dylan was working on and went over to a few of hers that she was using as studies for mixing colors and using different brushes for varying effects. She liked that Dylan encouraged her simply to play around to learn. She didn't think she'd ever become a professional, but she loved the idea that she had an outlet for her newfound creativity.

She stepped outside to get a bucket of water from the faucet near the back of the house and stopped when she overheard Summer saying, "No, Skye. We aren't going to wait for Daddy. We're going to the beach now. From now on, you're going to do things with Mommy, not Daddy. Is that clear?"

"No!" shouted Skye. "I don't like you. I want my daddy."

At the sound of a slap, Brooke hurried to the back patio.

Skye held a hand to her cheek, let out a cry, and screaming, ran to Brooke. "Mommy hit me!"

Brooke dropped the bucket and lifted Skye into her arms. “Shhh, shhh. I’m here.” She studied then kissed the red mark on Skye’s cheek. “There. The sting will go away. You’re going to be all right.”

Summer, Skye’s mother, marched over to Brooke and stood before her, hands on hips. “And who are you to interfere with what I’m doing with my child?”

“I heard the slap. That’s not acceptable,” said Brooke, steadying her voice. After smelling the alcohol on Summer’s breath, she studied her hazel eyes. “Are you on something?”

“That’s enough. Give me my daughter,” said Summer.

“No, Brooke! No! I don’t want to go with her,” said Skye, clinging more tightly to her.

“I’m going to stay with you. How about we walk over to Granny Liz’s house?” said Brooke, rubbing Skye’s back. “I think your father is working there.”

Skye buried her face in Brooke’s neck. “I don’t like Mommy.”

“I think Mommy is sick right now, which is why she’s acting this way. She’ll be better and then everything will be better too.” Brooke headed across the lawn toward Granny Liz’s house.

Summer ran ahead of her, and then stood in front of Brooke. “Stop! You don’t understand. I’m trying to get better.”

“But you’re not well,” said Brooke. “You smell like a brewery, and your eyes tell an even worse story.”

Summer pulled on Skye’s arm. “You come back to me right now, Skye Atkins.”

Brooke held on tight to Skye who’d wrapped her legs around her.

They all turned as Adam jogged over to them. “What’s going on?”

“Daddy! Daddy!” cried Skye holding out her arms to him.

"I'm afraid the situation is bad," said Brooke, holding onto Skye.

Adam's gaze swung to Summer and he narrowed his eyes. "I see. C'mon, Summer. Let's take care of getting you some help."

"I won't go with you, Adam. I promise to be better," she said firmly, turning her back on him and walking away.

"But you need help getting there," said Adam with more patience than Brooke would've been able to muster. He ran to catch up to her, leaving Brooke with Skye.

Brooke gently swayed in hopes of calming her charge. "It's Okay, sweetie. I've got you. Okay?

Skye nodded and burrowed closer.

When her breathing returned to normal, Brooke set Skye down on the grass and held out her hand. "While your parents work things out, why don't we wander down to our favorite shelling spot and see what shells have recently washed up. Shall we?"

Skye studied her. "Okay. I like you,"

"I like you too," said Brooke, giving her a hug and squeezing back tears.

They walked hand-in-hand to the sand and strolled beside the water.

Brooke laughed when Skye took off her sandals, dashed into the water as a wave drew back, and then raced out of the water as a wave chased her. As she continued to watch Skye play tag with the Gulf water, Brooke wondered what would've happened if she'd made a commitment to Adam. No doubt Summer would always be in the picture. Not a pleasant thought.

Brooke and Skye were shuffling through sand looking for shells when Adam appeared.

"Any luck?" he asked.

Brooke stood. "Skye found a lovely one, but we're still looking."

Skye held up a pink scallop shell. "See."

"Good job, Skye. Why don't you look for more while I talk to Brooke," Adam said.

Skye scampered away, eager to find more treasure.

"How is Summer?" she asked him. "She seemed pretty whacked out."

"Yes. When she agreed to try again to improve our relationship for Skye's sake, I didn't realize she's an addict. The only problem is, she isn't ready to deal with it, and I won't let her abuse Skye. I've asked Summer to leave until she's better." His expression grew even more grim. "I don't think that's going to happen."

"I'm sorry," said Brooke sincerely.

"I see how Skye is with you, and I wish you and I could've worked," said Adam. "But Dylan is a great guy. A good cousin."

Brooke sighed, not wanting to think about Dylan. "I hope everything will fall in line for you and Skye."

"Yeah, you're right. Though Summer is in the picture, Skye and I have to be happy."

"Are you still going to stay in Florida?" Brooke asked him.

"Oh, yes. I've got a great job as foreman of a construction company with an opportunity to buy into the business in time. Skye is happy here, and Mimi is ecstatic to have us. How about you? Are you staying in the area?"

"I haven't made any definite decision about that. A lot depends on what my grandparents decide to do with the Inn," she replied. "Things seem uncertain at the moment." She looked down and shuffled her toe in the sand.

"And Dylan?"

"I'm not sure if there's anything to mention."

"Is this about Tina and Dylan going to Naples together?" he asked.

Brooke shrugged, embarrassed to say anything.

"Tina has her eye on Dylan, that's for sure," said Adam. "What a piece of work."

"She's very determined," Brooke said. "I don't understand how she convinced Karin, the manager of the gallery in Santa Fe, that she and Dylan should work together to get a show in Naples."

"I've known women like her. She'll do anything to get what she wants one way or another," said Adam.

Brooke drew a deep breath and let out a long sigh.

Adam placed a hand on her shoulder. "You have nothing to worry about. Dylan is onto her."

"Thanks for your kind words. Is there anything I can do to help you with your situation?" Brooke asked.

"As a matter of fact, if you'd keep Skye busy here and then take her to your grandmother's pool for a swim, that will give me time to get Summer out of the house. If she won't go to rehab, as she's refusing to do, she'll have to find some other place to live. She said she has a friend in Miami who'll help her. But that woman is trouble with a capital T."

"I'm sorry it's come to this. Of course, Skye can be with me. I'll keep her here for a while."

"Okay, I'll drop off Skye's swimsuit in the kitchen at Gran's house. Summer can choose to say goodbye to Skye or not. Either way, I'll have a long talk with Skye after I drop Summer off to the place she chooses. I'm also going to call Skye's counselor and set up an appointment for Monday." Adam ran a hand through his dark hair.

Brooke gave him an impulsive hug. "Things will get better. I know it."

"Thanks. I was hoping this trial of getting together would

work for us as a family, but I realize that isn't going to happen."

Brooke stood aside, while Adam squatted beside Skye and talked quietly to her.

Looking out over the water, watching the sandpipers and sanderlings hurry along the sand at the water's edge, Brooke thought of the last weeks with Dylan and told herself things would be all right.

But later that evening, when she still hadn't heard from Dylan, she began to wonder.

CHAPTER FORTY-THREE

ELLIE

Ellie looked over the latest email from Liz and sighed. Life was continuing to unfold without her, and she was feeling as if she was missing everything. Yet, she and John were discovering such a beautiful world traveling together. She continued to read:

> **"You can imagine how Karen's happiness about Adam's move to Florida was threatened when he and Summer decided to try to work things out for another time. Summer hasn't changed a bit. Still the ego-centric shrew that she's always been. Spoiled, you know. Adam finally had to kick her out because of her addiction to drugs and alcohol today. Brooke has stepped in to help with Skye while Dylan and a friend are in Naples making arrangements for an art show. So, while Karen is happy to have more of her family around, there's been a lot to handle.**
>
> **"Brooke seems very happy with him. You wouldn't recognize your precious granddaughter, Ellie. Brooke's so alive, much more open than she's ever been. It's sweet to see that he brings out the best in her.**

"And your daughter, apparently, is having as wonderful a summer as Brooke. When I found out Jo was dating, I had to phone her. She's looking forward to coming to Florida in the fall for the family gathering. And she's bringing her new boyfriend, Chet. You must be thrilled, Ellie.

"Now we have to work on Livy to make sure this summer hasn't been wasted on her. Well, I suppose you're having a fabulous time. I can't get Sam to even travel to Miami for a day.

"Love to both you and John from your eyes and ears at Sanderling Cove."

Ellie got up from the table where she'd placed her laptop computer and walked outside to the balcony of the room they'd rented for a few days at a little inn outside Florence. She and John liked sightseeing for a couple of days in the city but really loved being in the countryside seeing life in a more natural way.

John looked up at her from reading his book. "How's life at Sanderling Cove?"

"Doing fine without us," Ellie said glumly and took a seat in a chair beside him.

He laughed softly. "Ellie, darling, that's what you wanted—time for our three granddaughters to find themselves and love this summer at Sanderling Cove."

"I know," said Ellie, straightening with resolve. She couldn't help the giggle that escaped her. "I think it's already working."

"Ah, that's my Ellie," said John. He patted his lap, and Ellie climbed onto it. This summer was working out well in many ways.

CHAPTER FORTY-FOUR

BROOKE

Brooke awoke on Sunday morning feeling unsettled. Dylan hadn't called her as she'd hoped, and she'd vowed not to break down and call him. So, things were at a standstill.

The wedding party in-house had planned a special brunch in the private dining room, and while Charlotte handled that, Brooke's job was to take care of the few hotel guests not part of that group.

One of the things she and her cousin had decided recently was to alert any guests making a reservation that special events were going on, but it shouldn't affect their regular service. It was a promise they all intended to keep, because as much as they liked the income from a wedding, the regular guests were the people who kept the Inn going day after day.

Forcing herself to push aside any worries about Dylan and Tina, Brooke dressed for the day and eagerly headed to the Inn. Reservations had grown with each passing week, and breakfast duty became more and more important. If a guest started the day right, it made for a good impression.

Livy was already at work with Billy Bob and the kitchen crew when she walked inside.

"Morning," Brooke said, grateful for everyone's hard work. Livy was excellent at running the kitchen and everyone seemed to get along. Even Billy Bob's normal gruffness softened around Livy.

Brooke automatically went to the sideboard in the dining room to make sure coffee was ready. Then she piled fresh muffins on a serving plate and placed it there, along with tubs of ice containing a variety of juices. Though a formal breakfast was served, guests could also pick up a snack and drinks to take back to their rooms until the breakfast they'd ordered was ready. By letting THEM choose the time for their breakfast, it kept the dining room from being overly crowded and also worked to keep service steady.

The first couple to enter the dining room for breakfast was an older couple who were repeat guests. Brooke spent a lot of time with them talking about Gran and John's travels.

"It all sounds lovely," the woman said. "May I leave a little note for Ellie. She and I spent quite a bit of time together when we last visited. She asked me then about travel in Europe. I'm glad to see they actually managed to get away."

"Of course," said Brooke. "After breakfast, come with me to the office and I'll get you settled there with a paper and pen, unless you want to send her an email. I can help you with that, too."

The woman gave her arm a friendly squeeze. "Thank you. I really appreciate it."

Brooke smiled. This was part of the business she really liked. Her mind spun with questions about the future. She wished she knew what it held.

When the breakfast rush was over, and the wedding brunch had ended, Brooke sat with her cousins in the office.

"I can't believe things went so well," said Charlotte. "It was such an easy group."

"Don't count on that happening every time," said Livy. "I have a feeling the next one won't be as easy."

"We have another wedding?" said Charlotte.

Livy made a face and nodded. "She's a cousin of SueEllen Sutton's. I tried to talk her out of coming here next winter. She's bound to be a big pain because she's as bad as SueEllen, and you all know how I feel about her."

"We do," said Brooke and Charlotte together. SueEllen and Livy had grown up next door to one another, and their mothers had been competing through them ever since. Livy was under pressure to find a man and get settled because SueEllen had married an ambitious lawyer and they had not one, but two grandbabies for SueEllen's mother to crow about.

"What's the bride's name?" Charlotte asked.

"MaryBeth Sutton. She's already telling her friends about the destination wedding she's planning. I can hear her now," moaned Livy.

"Well, let's concentrate on getting all the details of this one documented," said Charlotte. "We'll suggest certain meals at certain prices and make it that much easier to keep things under control."

"Right," said Brooke. "Let's work on package plans. We can adjust room rates and do other offers. When is she going to book rooms? I didn't see it listed on reservations yesterday morning."

"She wanted all the rooms at the Inn, but I told her we couldn't do that. Of the thirty-six rooms, she can have twenty-eight. We'll keep the eight rooms already sold together in one section so they don't feel overpowered by the group. Sound like a plan?"

"Yes," said Brooke. "We'll give the eight rooms the top floor of the main building, away from everyone else."

"The only thing is, MaryBeth is making The Sanderling Cove Inn sound as if it's The Beach House Hotel," sighed Livy. "As much as I love the Inn, The Beach House Hotel and our

Inn aren't the same at all. Apparently, MaryBeth tried to get into The Beach House Hotel, but they were booked for both rooms and their wedding venues."

"I hate when people put on airs," said Charlotte. "We have nothing to be ashamed of. The Sanderling Cove Inn is a lovely place, just not as upscale as The Beach House Hotel."

"Let's not worry about that now," said Brooke. "You said it wasn't until winter. We have some time before we need to be concerned."

"You're right. I'm happy to be here and not in Virginia where I'd have to hear all about MaryBeth's plans for a wedding for months," said Livy. "I'm tired of my mother's need to compare me to SueEllen. Mom's envious of SueEllen's mother because her daughter is already married with children."

Charlotte put an arm around Livy. "Don't you worry about a thing. We'll do the best job we can to make you, Gran, and John, and us happy. But are you sure this isn't just about MaryBeth's wedding?"

"The truth is, you and Brooke are settled, and I'm not. It does bother me. Not that I don't want the two of you happy. You know I do. It just makes me realize how much work I have to do on myself."

"What are you talking about?" Brooke said, giving Livy a worried look.

"Nothing. Just foolishness," Livy said. "Forget I said anything."

Brooke didn't speak, but she sometimes worried about Livy. Every once in a while, when she let her guard down, Livy seemed sad.

With a few free hours, Brooke decided to go see Skye. She

knew what an upsetting day she'd had yesterday and wanted to make sure she was all right.

When she arrived at Mimi's house, Skye was just getting up from "quiet time," a period set aside for reading or other quiet activities that Mimi had instituted.

"Brooke!" cried Skye upon seeing her.

Brooke hugged her. "What's up?"

"Mimi said I can paint. Want to paint with me?" Skye said.

"Sure." She looked at Mimi. "Watercolors?"

"Yes. We can set up in the kitchen. Skye got a new watercolor paint book with rip-out sheets which makes it easy for each of you to work on something of your own." Mimi smiled at her. "Thank you, Brooke. A certain someone is thrilled," she said, indicating Skye with a nod of her head.

"I'm glad to be here," Brooke said. "I still haven't heard from Dylan. I guess he's on his way back."

"Actually, he isn't," said Mimi. "I just talked to him, and he's decided to stay an extra day."

"With Tina?" Brooke asked, her pulse racing.

"Yes. I gather they did well at the gala last night and have some business to tend to," said Mimi.

"Oh, I see," said Brooke, feeling sick.

Mimi studied her. "Are you all right?"

"Absolutely," Brooke answered with false bravado. "I'm here with my best little friend and we're about to paint."

Mimi pressed her lips together but didn't say anything.

Later, when Dylan called her cell, Brooke was at the kitchen sink helping Skye wash her hands and couldn't answer. By the time her hands were dry and she picked up her cell, it was too late. She checked to see if he left a message, but he hadn't. Brooke frowned then forced a smile for Skye who was giving her a worried look.

"Okay, now that we've painted, are we ready to go to the

beach? I'll walk you down and then Mimi can watch you."

"Can you be my mommy? I don't like the other one," said Skye. "Daddy likes you too."

"Oh, sweetie, you know that isn't going to happen. But I can always be your very special friend. Right?"

"Right," Skye clapped a hand to her forehead. "Some days I don't know how I'll get through them."

Brooke held in a laugh. No doubt Skye had heard Mimi say those very words. Still, she understood Skye's disappointment. At the moment, she was disappointed herself by Dylan's lack of contact.

Reminding herself to be honest, she told herself she probably wouldn't mind the lack of communication if he wasn't with Tina.

Skye took hold of her hand and tugged. "C'mon, Brooke. Time for shells."

She followed Skye outside. The sand and Gulf water always made her feel better.

Later, as she was changing her clothes, Dylan called. Brooke let it ring twice, then picked it up.

"Hi, Brooke," said Dylan in a cheerful voice. "Just calling to check in." Music blared in the background.

"Hi, where are you?" Brooke asked.

"Tina and I are at a cool little bar. We decided to stay an extra night. It's been great."

"What's been great?" Brooke said, straining to hear what he was saying.

Tina's voice came on. "C'mon, Dyllie, you promised me a dance. Tell Brooke you can't talk now."

Dyllie? "How long have you been there, Dylan? It sounds like it's been a while."

"Yeah, we decided to celebrate. Henry is putting on a show for me next weekend. I want you to come."

"When are you coming home?" Brooke asked.

"Never," shouted Tina into the phone. "He and I are together again."

"Dylan, what's going on?" Brooke said. She heard of someone's blood going cold but she'd never felt it until now.

"I think someone's had way too much to drink," he said, sounding giddy himself.

"Call me when you can talk," she said, trying not to cry as she clicked off the call wondering what was really going on between Dylan and Tina.

She called Charlotte. "Would you mind if I didn't do social hour with the two of you tonight? I don't think I can do it after getting a call from Dylan and Tina."

"What's going on?"

"They're together at some bar. Dylan's decided to stay another night, and Tina said they're back together." Brooke's voice caught. "I don't know what to think."

"Look, Brooke, there's got to be a lot more to that story than you heard," said Charlotte. "Don't worry. Dylan isn't a jerk. He's not going to ditch you like this."

"The operative words here are ditch me," said Brooke. "I just need time alone to figure things out. I've been excited and deep in love, and I wanted him to feel the same way."

"He's shown you in many ways how he feels about you," Charlotte said.

"But to be fair, he hasn't told me he loves me." Brooke paced her room, wishing she could go to Naples. But that meant seeing him with Tina, and she could never do that. It would all become painfully clear.

She lay down on her bed and curled up.

The next morning, Brooke got up early, dressed, and quietly let herself out of the house. She needed her time on the beach. Being embraced by nature calmed her soul and lifted her spirits. After spending a restless night thinking of Dylan and Tina, she needed this.

She thought back to her early summer days at the cove. Then she might have been tempted to think of ways to lure Dylan back. But after a summer of growing strong and independent, she knew she wouldn't do that. Either he wanted to be with her, or he didn't. She still had things to learn about herself, to discover new ways to use her creativity. Most of all, she'd come to value herself.

Looking out at the waves rolling in with enthusiasm and pulling away again, watching the seagulls and terns swoop and swirl above her, Brooke felt at peace. Dylan would have to make his own decision, but she was moving forward.

She saw Adam emerge from Mimi's house and gave him a wave. Then she turned on her heel and walked to Gran's. She had an Inn to help run. That, she decided, was what she wanted to do. She went inside and prepared for the day.

Brooke was in the kitchen grabbing a cup of coffee when Livy walked in.

"You're up early," said Livy. "Everything all right?"

"Yes," Brooke said, feeling sure of her plan.

After changing for work, Brooke headed over to the Inn. She'd grown to love the place and was proud she was helping Gran and John. If things didn't work out for her grandparents to keep the Inn, she knew she could find other work. The fact that she didn't have to worry about her mother was a relief. Her life was her own now.

That afternoon, Brooke was in Dylan's art studio working

on a new design when he walked inside.

"There you are. I was looking for you at Gran's house," said Dylan.

"How did the trip go? At one point you said Henry was going to put on a show for you. Is that still happening?"

"Yes. You should've seen Tina handle some big spenders at the gala. They can't wait to see what some of us in the Santa Fe group can show them. I think I may have sold one of my paintings based on her description of it."

"That's nice," she said. "It's quite a partnership." Her earlier resolve to be strong weakened, but she remained quiet.

"Wait a minute. You don't think Tina and I ..." he let the sentence hang in the air.

"I know what she said, and you didn't tell me otherwise, so, of course, I don't know what to think," Brooke said calmly, though her fingers had clenched into fists.

He gaped at her. "You think Tina and I are together again?" He shook his head. "You should know that isn't true. But I'm not going to defend myself."

"And I'm not going to beg you to love me," she said. "Let me put the paints and brushes away, and I'll leave you to your space. Like you, I don't want to argue, and I need space of my own."

Trying not to cry, Brooke capped some paints and started to clean some brushes.

Dylan left the garage and entered the house, leaving her shaken. Fighting wouldn't solve anything, she knew, but he'd missed another chance to say "I love you."

CHAPTER FORTY-FIVE

LIVY

Livy was sitting outside the kitchen taking a break from preparing hors d'oeuvres for the social hour. With the wedding guests gone, things had quieted down. August was a busy month during the weekends, but Mondays and Tuesdays not as much.

She looked up as Dylan walked toward her. She waved, and he walked over and sat down on the kitchen steps beside her.

"What's up?" she asked him.

"I think I just messed up with Brooke," he said glumly and hung his head. "She thinks Tina and I are back together."

"And you're not?" Livy said, playing dumb.

"No." He straightened and frowned at her. "Why would you think that?"

"Oh, I don't know. Maybe because you and an old girlfriend travel together, stay an extra day, get a little drunk, and when you decide to call Brooke, she's with you. Not only was she with you, she tells Brooke you're back together?"

Dylan slapped a hand to his head. "Tina has this thing where she thinks I'm going to go back to her, but I'm not. I wouldn't do that to Brooke."

Livy placed a hand on his shoulder. "Well, my friend, as Desi Arnaz in the old television shows used to say, 'You got some 'splainin to do.' Did you tell that to Brooke?"

He lowered his head again and huffed out a breath. "No, I was angry. It seemed like she didn't trust me."

"Your relationship is new. Time to work on a few things. Get to it before it gets out of control."

Dylan jumped to his feet, leaned over and kissed Livy on the cheek. "Thanks."

Livy watched him head right for Gran's house pretty sure everything would be all right. Once more, she felt a weight fall on her shoulders and shrugged it off. It was much easier to tell someone else what to do than work on your own situation.

CHAPTER FORTY-SIX

BROOKE

Brooke was on the porch reading—escaping into a romance novel, actually—when Dylan arrived.

"Brooke, we need to talk," said Dylan, taking a seat in a rocking chair and pulling it around until they faced one another.

Dylan gave her a pleading look and took hold of her hand. "I know I've acted like a real jerk, and I swear I didn't know she told you we were back together again."

"Okay," said Brooke.

"Okay?" He drew back. "Is that all? What does that mean exactly?"

"I figure when you're really sincere about our relationship, you'll either let me know, or you won't. That has to be up to you, not me," said Brooke, thinking her low-key performance was worthy of an Oscar.

Dylan squeezed her hand. "Brooke, you know how much I care. I want you in my life. I understand you don't know whether the Inn will remain in your family, but I want you to be with me no matter what."

"Okay," she said, willing herself not to throw herself into his arms.

He stood and pulled her up against him. "Brooke, you're very special to me. I don't want you to break up with me. I love you. I want you to give me another chance. Will you promise to do that for me?"

With those three special words echoing inside her head, Brooke felt as if she could fly. "Yes," she exclaimed happily and watched his face soften. "Let's move on."

His lips met hers, and he told her in this special way how much he cared.

For the next few days, Brooke worked in the garage with Dylan. He planned on putting four of his paintings in the show in Naples. She helped prepare them for shipping in Dylan's truck and agreed to join him for the show on Friday. It helped to ease her mind that Tina had left her artwork with Henry but would not be at the opening at Gallery 535.

Before she left for Naples, Brooke indulged herself with a new black-linen dress that would show off her new turquoise jewelry. Livy trimmed her hair, and Charlotte painted turquoise nail polish on her toes.

"I have a feeling this show is going to be special for you," said Livy, giving her a bright smile.

"Me, too," said Charlotte. "You and Dylan make a great team. Maybe this will be the beginning of something wonderful."

"Even if I work at the Inn, I can still help Dylan with his Florida business," said Brooke, feeling hopeful about the future.

"That's what I'm talking about," Livy said, giving her a high five.

Brooke laughed. She loved the support they all gave each other.

When she arrived at the hotel in Naples where Dylan had booked a room, she quickly unpacked, freshened up, and walked over to the gallery to meet him.

Henry greeted her as she walked in. "Hi, Brooke. Welcome. Please wait by the door. Dylan wants to show you around."

Puzzled, Brooke did as he asked.

Dylan came from the back room, saw her, and hurried forward to take her in his arms. "You're here," said Dylan. "There's something I need you to see." He took her elbow and led her into a room displaying his paintings.

She glanced around and stopped in shock. "Wait." She hurried over to a side wall and stopped. "You've hung a painting of mine?" She studied the card with her name listed as the artist and gasped at the asking price of $1,000. Tears blurred her vision as she turned to face him. "This is the sweetest thing ever, but I'm not a real artist."

He studied her and said, "Why not? You might not have had a lot of training, but I admire what you've done, and I think others will too. I keep telling you that you have a certain eye for color and shape because I believe it."

"Thank you," Brooke said, unable to add words to the feelings that were racing inside her like kids playing tag.

Henry came over to them. "I was waiting to tell you, but your painting has already sold to a woman who appreciates exceptional art when she sees it."

Brooke clapped her hands to her face. "I can't believe it. It's like a fairytale."

"Enjoy the moment," Henry said. "I'll leave you two alone."

Dylan wrapped an arm around her. "I love you, Brooke. I have from the first time I saw you with that purple hair of yours, and I always will."

Brooke looked up at him. "Say that again? I never get tired of hearing the 'I love you' thing."

He laughed. "Greedy, are we? Well, I don't care who knows it, I love you, Brooke Weatherby, but ..."

"But?" she asked, her heart pounding.

"It's not enough." He reached into his pocket, got down on one knee, and held out a diamond ring. "Will you marry me?"

"Are you sure?" she said, then laughed.

"Never more sure."

"Yes, Dylan Hendrix, I will marry you. I love you."

"I know, and I love you," said Dylan, rising and sweeping her in his arms. "My family loves you too. This ring belonged to my grandmother. We all wanted you to have it because it's special to all of us. That's why I took you to Boise to meet them. I picked up the ring then."

"You had this planned a while ago?"

"Oh, yes, for weeks now," he said, lowering his lips to hers.

They'd shared many kisses but this one was different because she knew that he truly loved her, and they had a future together. She smiled remembering her early days at the cove, sitting on the beach looking out at the water, wondering what was in store for her.

She knew now that some sandy wishes do come true.

CHAPTER FORTY-SEVEN

ELLIE

Tears of joy sprang to Ellie's eyes as she read the latest news from Liz. Dylan and Brooke were engaged. This proved that she, Liz, Karen, Pat, and Sarah were right to bring their grandchildren together.

With the latest engagement, it meant that Livy, Eric, Kyle, and Austin were the ones they had yet to see settled. There was still time, but she hoped Livy would find someone who loved more than her cooking. Of her three granddaughters, Livy was most like her.

She gazed across the room at John. Their years together had been unconventional, but that hadn't stopped them from having a wonderful life together. Now that they were married, they wanted to share their love with everyone in the family.

When they returned from their summer travels, she hoped to see the entire family together. But who would be beside Livy? Ellie could hardly wait to find out.

"Everything all right?" John asked her.

"More than all right. Brooke and Dylan are engaged," she said, coming to stand beside him. "Two down and one to go. This trip is really working out as we'd planned."

"I'll take any trip with you anywhere when it makes you this happy," said John, pulling her onto his lap and hugging her tight.

Ellie cuddled up against him. Their adventure was turning out to be everything she'd wished for. Their love had grown stronger and two of their three granddaughters had found love of their own. She smiled. They still had time to make more of her own sandy wishes come true.

# # #

Thank you for reading *Sandy Wishes*. If you enjoyed this book, please help other readers discover it by leaving a review on your favorite site. It's such a nice thing to do.

For your additional reading enjoyment, please look for the other books in The Sanderling Cove Inn Series.

Waves of Hope is available in both e-book and print versions.

Salty Kisses – Will be released in 2023.

To stay in touch and to keep up with the latest news, here's a link to sign up for my periodic newsletter!

http://bit.ly/2OQsb7s

Enjoy an excerpt from my book, *Salty Kisses*, The Sanderling Cove Inn Series – Book 3, which will be released in 2023:

CHAPTER ONE

ELLIE

From her table on the plaza in a small town in Greece, Ellie Weatherby Rizzo looked out at the activity and sighed with pleasure. She and her husband, John, were fortunate to have this time to travel through Europe after working at The Sanderling Cove Inn on the Gulf Coast of Florida for years. They couldn't have taken this vacation without the help of their three granddaughters, Charlotte, Brooke, and Olivia, running the Inn together while they were away.

Ellie cherished the memory of their granddaughters' excitement at the opportunity to leave their old lives behind in order to accept her request for help. Little did they know that she and the four other grandmothers who lived at the cove had other plans in mind. Tired of seeing their beloved grandchildren's lives unsettled, they'd decided to bring all the cove kids together. What better way for their grandbabies to find suitable mates?

Charlotte and Brooke had already become engaged this summer. Charlotte to Liz's grandson Shane, and Brooke to Karen's grandson, Dylan. That left Livy still uncommitted.

Ellie had someone in mind for her, but planning can do only so much. Time would take care of the rest, she hoped. And then she and John could return to Florida and their inn. Whether the inn would stay in the family was another decision yet to be made.

"Ellie, you have a devilish smile on your face," said John.

"What scheme are you cooking up now?"

Her smile grew broader. "I was thinking how much I love you and our family."

He reached across the table and took hold of her hand. "Not as much as we love you."

She sighed happily. She and John were in their seventies, but age didn't matter when it came to love. This trip would be truly successful if Livy could find the man of her dreams.

CHAPTER TWO

LIVY

Olivia "Livy" Winters walked the shoreline of Sanderling Cove with troubled steps. Since coming to the cove to help her two cousins run their grandparents' inn, she'd tried to ignore her feelings, but different thoughts kept popping up in her mind like circling sharks about to attack. She couldn't continue. She had to find someone she could trust to help her. Her cousins, Charlotte and Brooke, would gladly support her, but she wasn't ready to share this with them. Not yet. They were happily engaged and thinking of bright futures with their fiancés. Livy didn't want to take any of that excitement away from this special time for them.

She looked down at her feet standing in the lacy foam of the Gulf water as one wave and then another reached her with salty kisses. Their soothing rhythm helped settle the turmoil roiling within her. Seagulls and terns whirled in the sky above her, their cries beckoning people to join them on this early August morning. In a few more weeks, Gran and John would return, and Livy would have to make some important decisions—career, housing, life.

Livy kicked at the water sending spray into the air, creating drops of water that resembled diamonds flying up to the sun. Nearby, the fronds of palm trees whispered in the wind as if they too had a secret to tell.

Following the trail of tiny footprints left behind by sandpipers, sanderlings, and other shore birds, Livy was startled when someone called her name. She turned to see Skye, Adam Atkins' four-year-old daughter running to her. Adam was Mimi's divorced grandson who was temporarily living with her at the cove.

Livy opened her arms, waited, and then swept Skye to her. She adored this sweet little girl who was curious about the world around her. "Hey, Skye. Are you looking for more shells today?"

Skye's blue eyes shone beneath the pink sun bonnet she wore. "I'm looking for pink shells. Mimi and I are making a wedding picture for Gran and Mr. John."

"A wedding picture? How lovely," said Livy, giving Skye another squeeze before setting her down and glancing at Adam walking their way.

"Hi, Livy. Not working the kitchen at the Inn today?" said Adam when he reached them.

"Not until later. Most of the breakfast group was off to an early start, so I could squeeze out some time for myself. I'm trying to do it more and more."

"We all need to do that," said Adam with a note of sadness to his voice.

They stood a moment and watched while Skye ran to catch a wave. "I'm sorry about what happened with your ex," Lily said to him. "I know you were hoping for Skye's sake that she'd changed."

"Thanks. That is the end of my trying to make any relationship work. I don't trust her anymore. Skye's happier when her mother isn't around. Moving forward, we'll just let nature take its course."

"A smart idea," Livy said. She liked Adam. A big affable man, he'd been a natural leader in the sports games the cove kids had played when they all were growing up. Now, after moving back to Florida, he'd bought an older house to fix-up while he started a new job as a supervisor with a local, well-respected construction company. This kept him busy as he began to set up his own business. His grandmother, Mimi, was delighted with his move and temporarily adding two people to her household.

"Happy shell hunting," Livy said. "I'm headed down the beach. See you later." It was such a relief to give herself permission to do her own thing. In the past, she'd ask if Skye needed help or continue talking to Adam out of politeness. She wasn't being rude, just allowing herself to make choices based on what she wanted.

As she continued walking, she considered her past. She'd had a pleasant childhood, but it had sometimes been marred by the competition between her and SueEllen Sutton, the girl next door. It was hard when your mother constantly compared you to someone else, and you came out lacking. The more her mother wanted her to be like SueEllen, embracing a southern feminine role, the more Livy fought against it. She could've married early like SueEllen—she'd had more than one man who wanted a serious relationship. But she never felt ready.

After graduating from culinary school, all she'd wanted was to run her own successful business. Too bad her business partner had been willing to throw away her dream and replace it with the goals her "boyfriend" was chasing.

Livy stopped walking and faced the water. Dating Wayne Chesterton had been the biggest mistake of all. A shiver raced through her. She didn't know if she'd ever get over what he'd put her through. She felt the sting of tears and couldn't prevent them from rolling down her cheeks. She needed to let it go. But how?

Moments later, she brought out a tissue from the pocket of her shorts and wiped her eyes, thankful no one was around.

As she headed back to the Inn, she heard footsteps pounding on the sand behind her and turned to see Austin Ensley jogging toward her. A smile spread across her face. He'd been her crush when she was a teenager, and though she tried to keep anyone from knowing, she still was attracted to him.

"Hey, Livy, just the person I want to see," he said, stopping beside her. He removed the white towel wrapped around his neck to wipe his face. His dimple appeared as he smiled at her. "I've been trying to set up a time to take you out to dinner as a thank you for standing by me throughout the memorial service for my mother. Knowing I could count on you helped me get through that difficult time. I really want to do this. How about this evening? I talked to Brooke and Charlie, and they said you don't have duties at the Inn tonight."

Realizing any attempt to sidestep the invitation would be rude, Livy did her best to smile. Being with him always made her nervous. She looked at his ripped body, his sandy-colored hair, and the way his blue-eyed gaze had settled on her and took a deep breath.

"Well?" he asked.

"That would be nice, Austin, but you know my intention was to support you, nothing more."

"And you did," he said. "Where would you like to go? We could try Gavin's at the Salty Key Inn, the Don Cesar Hotel, or any fancy place you want." He made it difficult to say no.

"How about we keep it simple?" Livy said. "How about The Crab Shack?"

His lips curved. "Should be fun. I'll pick you up at six thirty, if that's okay."

"Sure. Thanks, Austin." The melancholy that had gripped her earlier faded. Austin was an interesting man, and conversation would keep the evening going. She started to walk away.

He came up beside her and casually swung an arm around her shoulder. "Are you all right?"

She looked up at him in surprise.

He thumbed a tear from her face. "You can talk to me about anything, you know. We're friends. Remember?"

She nodded and looked away. "Thanks."

He released her. "See you later," he said, and jogged away, leaving her wondering about the way he'd made her feel.

When she returned to the Inn, Charlie met her in the kitchen with an impish grin. "You going out with Austin tonight?"

Livy's gaze rested on Charlie. She was striking with long auburn hair and green eyes that were now lit with mischief. "Austin said that you and Brooke told him I was free tonight. How could I say no?"

Brooke walked into the kitchen. "Say no to what?"

"To Austin," said Charlotte. "He's taking her out to dinner tonight."

"About time you two got together," said Brooke. Not as tall as Charlie, and with short hair dyed purple, Brooke was as attractive in her own way. "What fancy place is he taking you to?"

"No fancy place," said Livy. "I chose The Crab Shack."

Brooke laughed. "That's perfect."

Livy frowned and studied her. "Why? What are you two planning?"

"Nothing," said Charlie.

"It's just that he's been dating a woman named Aynsley Lynch, and she'd never be seen in The Crab Shack. Heaven forbid. Not posh enough for her." Brooke shook her finger. "I warned Austin that Aynsley was just after his money, and he seemed surprised."

"Wow, Brooke, I can't believe you said anything like that to him," said Livy.

Charlotte gave Brooke a pat on the back. "Our Brooke is speaking up these days. All that freedom from worrying about her mother is giving her wings."

"And a mouth," said Brooke, laughing. "It's true. After climbing out of the rut I was in before coming here, I feel as if I can speak up."

"Gran's asking us to come help out at the Inn for the summer has been a gift to all of us," said Charlotte. "We're each finding our own way."

"And love too," said Livy. "At least for you two."

"Aw, Livy, it'll happen for you," said Charlie.

"I'm not sure what I want," said Livy truthfully. "But as the summer is progressing, I'm thinking more and more about making a change and staying in Florida."

"Dylan and I are seriously thinking of splitting time between Florida and Santa Fe," said Brooke. "We haven't worked out the details yet, but we will."

"And you all know that after Gran and John return, I'll be moving to Miami to be with Shane," said Charlotte.

They looked at one another and smiled.

"We just might be able to do it," said Charlotte. "Run the Inn with Gran and John. Even if it's part-time or from a distance, each of us can help in our own way."

Livy wished she didn't feel so overwhelmed and adrift. Knowing where she wanted to live was a start, but there were still many other decisions she needed to make. But then, how could she make choices for the future until she'd dealt with the baggage of her past?

That evening, Livy waited with a mixture of anticipation

and dread for Austin to pick her up for dinner. Of all the men at the cove, he was the one she tried to avoid. He brought out conflicting feelings within her. He had her wanting things she wasn't ready for, and aroused feelings she couldn't deal with. Not yet.

His car pulled up to the back of Gran's house, and she went outside to greet him.

"Hi, Livy," he said, climbing out of the car. "You look great."

"Thanks," she said, happy she hadn't overdressed for the occasion. Her short denim skirt was comfortable. The light, frilly white top was another of her favorites. She had no intention of trying to compete with the women Austin had been seen with in the past.

Austin assisted her into his car and then took off down the coast to The Crab Shack, a favorite of locals and tourists alike. When they pulled into the crowded parking lot, Austin said, "I'm glad I made reservations. Look at the line waiting to get inside."

Livy liked the notion of the restaurant being crowded. It meant talk wouldn't be necessary to fill any quiet between them. She knew Austin might ask her again about her tears that morning and she didn't want to get into that discussion.

After she emerged from his car, Austin took her elbow and led her past the people waiting outside.

When Austin gave her his name, the hostess said brightly, "Right this way. I saved the spot you wanted." She led them to a corner table where they could get a view of the others in the crowded interior and gave them each a menu before she left.

Livy took a moment to glance around. It amused her to see adults wearing plastic bibs with a red lobster pictured on them. But they were needed if those people liked to dig into crabs the way she did. The room was filled with conversations as people enjoyed the casual atmosphere. Brown paper tablecloths were suitable along with the roll of paper towels atop each table.

"I know I'm going to order the crab special. I get it every time. How about you, Livy?" said Austin. "Should we order beer, or would you rather have a cocktail or wine to begin?"

"Beer sounds perfect with the crab," she said, putting down her menu. "Like you, I'm getting the crab special."

He smiled at her, bringing out that devilish dimple of his. "You sure make it easy." He signaled the waitress, and they placed their orders. After their beers came, he lifted his bottle. "Here's to a pleasant evening."

Smiling, Livy clinked her bottle against his. "Thanks."

They each took a sip of beer and then Austin set his down. "I meant what I said this morning. I'll never forget your offer to sit in the front of the audience facing me so I could focus on a friendly face while I spoke about my mother. It meant a lot to me."

"I was happy to do that for you," Livy said sincerely. "How are you doing with the aftermath of her death?"

Austin shrugged. "So-so. I'm talking to Shane's psychologist about my toxic relationship with my mother, and I'm trying to keep busy. As you know, I've been staying in Miami a lot, seeing old friends."

"Brooke told me you're dating Aynsley Lynch," Livy said.

"Yeah, Brooke doesn't like her. Told me flat out that Aynsley is interested only in my money." Austin chuckled. "She's not the shy woman she once was."

"She admits it," said Livy, joining in his laughter. "This summer has been great for all of us. It's a chance of a lifetime for this many cove kids to be able to spend time together."

"Two engagements have come of it," said Austin. "How about you? Any romance in your life?"

She shook her head. "I'm not looking for any. The more important thing for me at the moment is to try to make some decisions about my new career direction. After owning a bakery for several years, I've decided I want to do something different. Grace Hendrix wants me to supply some baked goods to her restaurant, Gills, in Clearwater. That's a definite possibility. I haven't mentioned it to Charlie and Brooke, but in the meantime, I'm thinking of offering cooking lessons at the Inn."

"You sure are a great cook," said Austin, giving her a look of approval.

Their meal came. They tied plastic bibs around their necks and dug into the plate of crab legs. The sweet tender crabmeat brought a murmur of pleasure from Livy.

Austin looked up at the sound and gave her a wink. "Tasty, huh?"

"Delicious," she said, dabbing at a bit of butter that dribbled past her lips. She didn't care. Getting messy was part of the fun of enjoying the meal.

Austin laughed, reached over, and swiped her chin with his napkin.

By the time, they'd finished their meals, their plates were mounded with soiled paper towels atop the empty crab shells.

"I can't remember a more relaxed meal," said Austin, wearing a grin.

Livy returned his smile. Despite her doubts about spending time with him, she'd enjoyed it. Maybe a little too much.

"Do you want to stop by the Pink Pelican on our way home? Sitting outside with a cold beer is tempting," said Austin.

"A great way to end the evening," agreed Livy.

After he paid, they left the restaurant and climbed into his car, an Audi 5 convertible. "Do you mind if I put the top down?" Austin asked. "If you don't want me to, I won't."

"It's fine with me. It's such a beautiful evening, and the wind will feel good. Nothing is going to help these curls of mine." Her curly locks were constantly in disarray.

He reached over and patted her strawberry-blond curls. "I like them."

They took off, and as she suspected, the salty air cooled her skin as they drove through the dark to the Pink Pelican.

About the Author

A *USA Today* Best Selling Author, Judith Keim is a hybrid author who both has a publisher and self-publishes. Ms. Keim writes heart-warming novels about women who face unexpected challenges, meet them with strength, and find love and happiness along the way. Her best-selling books are based, in part, on many of the places she's lived or visited and on the interesting people she's met, creating believable characters and realistic settings her many loyal readers love. Ms. Keim loves to hear from her readers and appreciates their enthusiasm for her stories.

Ms. Keim enjoyed her childhood and young-adult years in Elmira, New York, and now makes her home in Boise, Idaho, with her husband, Peter, and their two domineering dachshunds, Winston and Wally, and other members of her family.

While growing up, she was drawn to the idea of writing stories from a young age. Books were always present, being read, ready to go back to the library, or about to be discovered. All in her family shared information from the books in general conversation, giving them a wealth of knowledge and vivid imaginations.

"I hope you've enjoyed this book. If you have, please help other readers discover it by leaving a review on the site of your choice. And please check out my other books:

The Hartwell Women Series
The Beach House Hotel Series
The Fat Fridays Group
The Salty Key Inn Series
Seashell Cottage Books
The Chandler Hill Inn Series
The Desert Sage Inn Series
Soul Sisters at Cedar Mountain Lodge
The Sanderling Cove Inn Series
The Lilac Lake Inn Series

"ALL THE BOOKS ARE NOW AVAILABLE IN AUDIO on iTunes and other sites. So fun to have these characters come alive!"

Ms. Keim can be reached at **www.judithkeim.com**

And to like her author page on Facebook and keep up with the news, go to: **https://bit.ly/3acs5Qc**

To receive notices about new books, follow her on Book Bub: **http://bit.ly/2pZBDXq**

And here's a link to where you can sign up for her periodic newsletter! **http://bit.ly/2OQsb7s**

She is also on Twitter @judithkeim, LinkedIn, and Goodreads. Come say hello!

Acknowledgements

And, as always, I am eternally grateful to my team of editors, Peter Keim and Lynn Mapp, my book cover designer, Lou Harper, and my narrator for audio versions, Angela Dawe. They are the people who take what I've written and help turn it into the book I proudly present to you, my readers! I also wish to thank my coffee group of writers who listen and encourage me to keep on going. Thank you, Peggy, Lynn, Cate, Nikki Jean, Mel and Megan. And to you, my fabulous readers, I thank you for your continued support and encouragement. Without you, this book would not exist. You are the wind beneath my wings.

CPSIA information can be obtained
at www.ICGtesting.com
Printed in the USA
LVHW100727040223
738675LV00005B/314

9 781954 325432